Erotic Memoir Presents

Skyscraper Secrets:
Muriel & Sarah's 1950s Summer of Wonder

By Jennifer Dozier

Erotic Memoir
Imprint of Clocktower Books, San Diego

Skyscraper Secrets:
Muriel & Sarah's 1950s Summer of Wonder

This novel by Jennifer Dozier has been previously published by Clocktower Books, first as <u>Skyscraper Secrets</u>, and later as <u>Muriel & Sarah: Swimmers on a Fathomless Sea</u>. There have been some very slight revisions to the text. The current title is a blend of old and new concepts.

Erotic Memoir^{TM} is a publishing imprint of Clocktower Books^{TM}--world's first publisher online (1996) of true, full-length, proprietary (not public domain) digital novels for download.

Clocktower Books
www.clocktowerbooks.com/
P. O. Box 600973
Grantville Station
San Diego, California 92160-0973
Contact: editor@clocktowerbooks.com

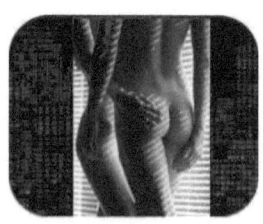

Contents

1. A Little Lunch Music 1953

We were both lonely, each in her own way, I realize now, but neither of us had any idea back then. We were innocent and laughed a lot and had fun, besides finding love and comfort in each other-- once in a lifetime, just those few weeks; nothing like it could ever happen again in either of our lives, and we would not have wanted anything better. It was a wonderful little summer, during a terrifying age (the 1950s), and the memory lingers like a sunset that won't grow dim, and a sun that never wants to set. Sometimes we felt like two swimmers, alone in a world of our own, swimming on a fathomless sea.

Nobody will ever know our names, or even the city among bland, puritan U.S. cities in which we lived--and it doesn't matter, because it's an everywoman kind of tale that really happened among the skyscrapers of anonymity. Here is our secret story.

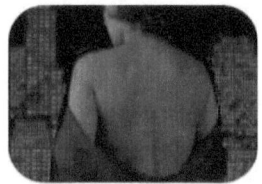

There was a woman, not too much older, and nice looking, who liked to give me something extra for lunch, or to buy an egg cream at the lunch counter in my office building, for me to come visit on my lunch break and spend time with her. This was during the 1950s, when I was 23 and working down the street from her as a secretary.

She didn't ask me to undress or do anything. All I had to do was lie face down on her couch, on my belly, while she touched me and talked to me. I listened well, or sometimes I dozed because I had been out all night having sex or dancing with my boyfriend Ronny; sometimes I would say something and we'd both have a laugh. It was all so new and daring, so warm and scary, that there were no labels for it--just it felt good to be like that.

I was casual and disinterested at first--just a pretty young gum- chewing office girl out for a lark, out to enjoy a tantalizing new adventure. Those were frightening times, and this was the blackest of forbidden pleasures if you really stopped to think of it, through the fog of denial. I was plenty scared, but the thrill got the better of my fears.

Though I was always plenty careful, my attitude was--if it felt good, and nobody got hurt, and the other person wasn't rough with me, and nobody ever found out, then why not? We were white, middle class, and innocent. Maybe we were crazy to be doing it and risk getting caught and ruined. We could have gone to prison or worse. Neither of us had any idea where our friendship was taking us.

In that day and age, people were afraid of their own shadow, of the Russians, of comic books, of sin, of atomic bombs, of the end times, and of demons and fifth columnists under every bedspread. Words like pregnant, sex, and orgasm were still dirty words nobody ever said out loud. It's not that I was a banner-waving commie slut--I was so naïve that I had no idea that I smiled too much and caused a lot of frowns and raised eyebrows. Never mind that those same prim and proper men and women stared after my plaid ass on the street. That and my smile, Muriel later told me, was what made her do something she had never done before, and flirt with me. She came to my office, right under everyone's noses, and seduced me like some boy flirting with a girl he must have in his car or at the hop. Nobody was ever the wiser, especially when she got Mr. Ferguson, my boss, to send me over with some files to be signed for a court case.

I started to like those secret, delicious summer lunches in her dark and quiet office. Outside, you saw blue skies; and big puffy white clouds slowly drifted by over those dainty old skyscrapers faced in red brick.

Muriel was one of the city's first women lawyers, struggling in a little office on the 20th floor of the Finncroft Tower, across the street from me in the middle of the block. The office where I worked for Mr. Ferguson, a CPA, was on the 18th floor. If you could have spun our building on its axis a little, Muriel and I could have waved to each other. But we couldn't even say hello if we passed each other on the street, not that it ever happened.

At first, Muriel just liked for me to lie on my belly on this couch by the window in her office. We'd both be fully dressed, where nobody could see us. She liked to touch my ass, to feel my butt cheeks through the light cotton skirts she wanted me to wear. She'd spend my whole lunch hour touching it, and resting her face against it.

"It's like a pillow," she whispered once as she lay with her cheek on my ass and patted one cheek or the other. "So warm and fragrant." She pushed it with a finger. "So tight and bouncy." We both laughed.

She couldn't get enough of staring at my behind, of having my rear end in her palms, and feeling my skin with the sensitive pads of her fingertips. She could run her fingers over me so slowly, so hungrily, that it was like being licked. Gradually, we got to be more intimate--but her fascination with my ass was always number one between us.

She once told me that she would marry my ass if it were possible, or marry me for my ass, if that were possible. Back in the 1950s, it wasn't.

"You're so lucky," she said. "So young and so perfect."

She was in love with my rear end. I was always pleased at how men and women stared at me on the street. As a young secretary, living alone in a gray matchbox apartment, it was about all I had in life--my clothes, youth, beauty, and a boyfriend named Ronny who didn't know a good thing when he had it. People stared after me--it didn't matter whether I was wearing a tight fall sheath, or a loose summer dress with the sun x-raying my walking shadows. I was a fresh young athletic fun sort of girl with a good figure and pretty face.

For an independent girl nobody could put on a leash, I enjoyed being a kept woman--my choice, a little part of our game, though we never spoke it, but we both understood our special juicy little secrets. Each time I went to see her, which was just about every day, Muriel gave me two dollars for lunch, plus a dollar for letting her touch me. We both knew it was just a little love present, not a bribe or a payment.

Because I could pretend she was paying me, in some crazy little corner of my heart I liked to think I was her girl, maybe even her whore. I knew in my hot little heart that she felt some sort of steamy kink about it and about me. I'm sure she saw me as her woman. She was on the skids with a fool named Leo, and she really didn't have anyone else in her life, in her heart, or between her legs. I think in our hearts we knew we'd go all the way, if that was even possible for two women. Like, who knew back then? Here I was, going steady with that two-timing Ronny, and I wouldn't think of paying attention to all the many boys and men who were always leering and winking at me or drooling after me. It never occurred to me that seeing Muriel made me a two-timer. Never occurred to me in my wildest dreams. There was no name and no concept for what I was doing.

All I knew is that it felt good, and got better all the time.

We just called my little gifts lunch money, with an extra dollar for an egg cream or any other little sweet I liked. It was payment for petting--there, I said it. In those days, you weren't allowed to say pregnant and other natural words, much less sex. We never really called it what it was--a free lunch and dessert or an egg cream--but really just three dollars for sex. I wasn't just her girl during that long, dreamy hour--I carried the seed of her around with me all day, and I was sure she thought of me the same way. Only I'm not sure she thought of me as her concubine or her slut--more like she felt this gnawing sense of being possessed by a power greater than herself--not me, but her addiction to sex with me, starting with the first little kisses and feeling up. I was an object of beauty too easily lost. I was her butterfly in a jar, and she dreaded the day she'd have to open the lid and let me fly away, though when that day came it was different than either of us might have expected.

In the fifties, your skirt was a fairly tight sheath--not too tight or revealing--above the knee, tighter at the knee, with a flare or extension down to middle or high mid-calf. It made a woman into a kind of spinning top on high heels for men to look at, and you can imagine how it made a splendid rear look divine--yet trapped in a corset to prevent impure thoughts. Corsets were the perfect solution for all evils--no jiggle in young flesh, no flop in older flesh. Of course because it was flesh-colored and so close to a woman's body, the corset itself became a sex thing to drool over. Men wanted to suck on those flesh-colored rubber holders with the hooks that dangled from your corset like a ring of pacifiers to hold up your sheers.

In an outfit like that, a woman on pumps or high heels could really rotate and strut. I was young and hungry--a pretty young woman with a fresh face and athletic figure, always reading up on the hottest fashion. Of course I spent every last dime on clothing and makeup, whatever I didn't pay for rent, so I was always flat broke but looked to any stranger like I was on top of the world. This had the added benefit, as I saw it, that I never had enough to eat, so my figure stayed lean and sharp. Don't get me wrong--I was never skinny. I would steal food where I could, and I knew all the cheapest eats around town, every 25 cent special from Chinese takeout to warmed-over French fries on Shady Alley uptown.

I once was walking down a crowded street at lunch time in midtown, with food smells all around driving me crazy. As I passed a sidewalk stand that sold coffee, sodas, and quick fried food, I saw a foreign businessman in a suit put his newly bought hamburger down on the stainless steel counter by the condiments to look for something in his briefcase. I reached through a crowd of asses and elbows, and stole his hamburger as I walked past. Like a ravenous animal, I stuffed it in my mouth with both hands. I downed it in gulps, like a dog, so in case they chased me I could eat it before they caught me, but nobody did.

Even when Ronny came in my mouth every night, that was like eggs--I was a big, athletic girl and I was starving like an animal on the street.

If there was a banquet or a party that I knew of, either in the office or around the building, or a wedding or a funeral, I'd make sure I got myself a big friggin' roast beef sandwich with cheddar, on a BLT foundation, and anything else I could get my pretty red fingernails into before I was politely seen to the door. A real red-letter day was if I managed to wheel and deal so that, to avoid me making a scene, they'd send me packing with a plate full of cake, melons, luncheon meats, and grapes, plus a bottle of beer hanging from each coat pocket--good reason to wear a coat and carry a large pocket book, even on a warm day.

Sometimes I thought if I didn't have my dignity I'd let strange men pay me a dollar for me to lift my skirt and let them look underneath. Or I might eat discarded hot dog ends on street corners while people waiting for a bus curled up their lips. There were limits on what I would do to eat and stay alive. The good thing of course is that if you are a beautiful young woman with half your wits about you, it's about as impossible to starve as it is for an apple to fall upward from a tree. Someone will always feed you, even some guy with beard shadow and an Al Capone hat in some dive full of beer, goons, and dim red lighting. Maybe Muriel figured right--she'd have me on a leash if she fed me so that I'd keep my silly nose out of all sorts of trouble. Also, I must say I don't think she was ever jealous of Ronny. She knew I needed a man in my life and a cock in my hole like any red-blooded, healthy young horse of a woman.

Like I said, I was young and life was intense. At that age, the world is still brand new, and anything is possible. You're open to everything, you don't really know anything, and you're just street wise enough to avoid the crocodiles and wolves all around. I was wise enough to recognize there was no harm with Muriel, only good. She was lonely, a widow with three kids at home, and I was her hot dog end. We were actually both pretty damn lonely, only I had no idea what that meant. On the good side, we both had our dignity, our nice looks, and our fine clothes, and we were always a class act together.

Muriel couldn't afford to pay me, but she did, and I was too hungry to say no. Maybe she lost a few pounds giving her lunch money to me, while I gained the pounds she lost. Our dark secret-- our breathless, shadowy game--brought us both many little pleasures and surprises.

Muriel liked to look at me as I lay face down. She'd raise my skirt to various lengths, especially the loose summer dresses.

This one X-Ray dress especially, as I called it, which blew around me like a white sail when I walked down the street--young boys would follow me at an angle to the sun. They'd check on the sidewalk to see which way the shadows were falling. Then they'd run around me and ahead of me, if necessary, and sit brimming with anticipation on a low wall or a stoop, waiting for me. Their eyes were like nuclear x-ray machines, hard as marbles, as they stared through my dress and watched as the sun caught my skin inside and reflected it out to them in its naked glory.

More than one boy would fall over backward, landing on his head on the lawn behind him while his high-waters and pointy shoes waved toward the clouds above. I knew that, aside from my white panties--and my girdles and those rubber diddlers holding up my stockings, they got a good look of my strong, smooth thighs. I might as well have been walking down the street in my birthday suit, except for my panties and bra, and of course my saucer and my purse and gloves. I knew (well, let's admit it, I was vain and proud, and enjoyed the theater thoroughly) that they could see my Irish-Mediterranean caramel legs and my flat belly with that shadowy navel. I could have charged them a buck a feel to put a fingertip in my innie--meaning my navel, not my fur patch or my exhaust. Young and crazy as I was, it was good that Muriel took me under her wing and gave me something solid to chew on. I mean, not just a manner of speech or a literal something, but both. I learned a lot, and grew up a bit, as I spent time with her in her office.

I'd lie on her couch and doze. Frankly when you are 23 it is boring as hell to be felt up for 45 minutes while lying on your face being totally still, almost afraid to breathe. Then you hear the other person breathing faster, and you start breathing kind of raspy yourself.

Or I'd think about Ronny last night or the dance this evening, while Muriel cuddled my ass. She'd arrange the hem line across the backs of my knees, so she could nuzzle and kiss them. It tickled on the sensitive skin there, and I'd squirm. She'd snort a funny little laugh, and slap a palm down firmly to give my cheek a squeeze and a wiggle. Sometimes she'd put her lips on the back of my smooth young thigh and blow--a kazoo sound that made me laugh out loud. Or she'd pull my hem up higher across my unblemished thighs, or higher yet so the fuller line of my unspoiled young thighs spread before her.

The higher she moved my hem, the harder she'd breathe. Pretty soon, I was breathing hard too. It took me a while before I cared for anything more than a couch to snooze on while getting paid to do nothing but look pretty. I didn't even have to wiggle my ass--she did it for me.

I was young and kind of hard, because I didn't know anything. I hadn't been hurt enough in life. I'd been raised good, and even though I had sex with a prick like Ronny, I was naïve and sweet and brash. I could cry over a squished bug.

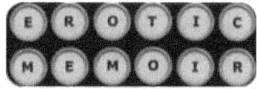

One day, when I was wearing my X-Ray dress, she got carried away. Until then, she'd been content to touch me with my clothes on, and I kept my hands to myself.

That particular day was very warm. She had the window open, the blinds all the way up, and the little fan working over time swinging left and right.

She was sitting in a chair near the middle of the office, which was a cluttered space. Almost anywhere you put a chair, you could lean one elbow on something--a cabinet, a stack of files, a pile of boxes. So I didn't think anything of it when I walked in and put my things on her desk--my gloves, my purse, my hat. While the area around the open window was vivid with light, the rest of the office was marooned in shadows like a shipwreck.

"Take your shoes off," she said in a simple, unassuming tone. "It's hot today, huh?" That lecher, I didn't know what she really meant. I was still a kid, and it went over my head, though I have no regrets. I'm happy for everything she said and we did. She'd maneuvered me to stand between her and the window. What is it they say about men? She was undressing me with her eyeballs. She was x-raying me with the blast of sunlight through the window and across my naked limbs under that sheer dress.

What was she thinking? *You have pink legs. How your thighs bulge and make my mouth water--hard in the right places, soft in all the right spots. Your pink waist is like an hour glass. Your delicate hip bones are like china. You are woman-wide and girl-soft. Those are the bubblegum-pink panties I bought you at Schaumberg's. Did you paint your toenails and fingernails with that rouge glow I bought you? Are you spritzing that expensive cologne I gave you on your pussy fur? Do you get a little damp when I look at you, or are you oblivious?*

"Yeah, it's hot," I said as I leaned down. I had planned to take them off anyway, in preparation for my lay on the sofa. As I bent over to put my shoes together, beads of sweat fell from my forehead to the floor. The floor was made of plain, worn oak boards about three inches wide. In several spots, worn carpet rectangles with faded Oriental designs lay over the floor, pinned by boxes or other weights. The floor before me, where my sweat fell, was as bare as my feet. What a show I must have given her as I bent over.

"How about adjusting the blinds?" she said. I could hardly see her over there in the gloom. She sat in the semidarkness, wearing a loose black skirt and a white, sleeveless blouse that showed off her full breasts. Her hair was a mess of large ringlets and curls the color of golden-brown topaz. She had her hands folded together on the chair between her legs, pressing down her black skirt, with her knees parted like a man. Like she was praying to lick my strong thighs, my soft cheeks, my red toenails, my spritzed and fragrant furry muff.

Obediently--she was paying me, after all--I walked to the window. Since the blinds were all the way up, there was only one way for them to come, which was down. I reached up to grab the strings, which someone had thrown up on to the valence.

"Stop."

I froze. "Did I do something wrong?"

"No. I just want to see you like you are right now."

"Can I put my arms down?"

"Put your hands on your head."

Puzzled, I clasped my fingers together over my rakishly cut, dark brown soup bowl hair (nearly black and glossy like on Italian or Corsican girls, with dark-ruddy Irish undertones like wild blood or a melancholy song). I stood like a ballerina, with one foot flat and the other on its toes.

"Turn slowly. Arch your back a little."

I did as she said, doing leisurely little yoga twists, arches, and bows with my arms up in a pretzel. It felt good on my spine, and my ribs thanked me.

"Stand with your legs apart."

Barefoot, I walked my feet apart. My long legs made an upside down V. Then I had my *a-hah!* moment. "You're watching the sun shine through my dress."

"I am adoring you. Please don't stop."

"I won't. I like it when you look at me."

"Me too."

"It makes me feel special."

"You are special."

I felt warm inside. I wanted to tell her to touch me if she wanted, but I was afraid. Maybe it was a missed opportunity. Or maybe she wasn't ready. I didn't care. If it happened, so what. She wasn't a dirty old man. Nor was she a dirty old lady. She was a fox, like my brothers used to say about some of the women in Capri pants and colorful beach shirts or bathing suits--older than my brothers, much younger than my father--who would come in for car repairs in their convertibles, with the rag top down, on hot summer days. What made little boys interested in a grown woman striding by being x-rayed by the sun? What made young mechanics like my brothers drool over full-bodied woman old enough to be their aunts, even if they are dressed for the beach? What made a woman like Muriel lust after a girl who was like a photo copy of herself almost half a lifetime earlier?

She didn't touch me, or even ask to touch. Instead, she kept her hands folded together and gazed at me with those garage mechanic eyes.

I asked her: "Would you do this for me some day?"

"Maybe."

"I would like to look at you."

"If you buy me lunch."

"I'll give you two dollars for lunch, and an extra dollar to buy an egg cream and a candy bar."

"You don't think I'm too old for such a thing?"

I vehemently shook my head. "I think you are very interesting."

She laughed. "What?"

"You make me feel good all over. That's all I care about. Yes, you are still a very nice looker."

"That's so sweet of you. I will carry the glow with me all day" She rose and smoothed her black dress down over her long legs. With each hand, she gave her pussy a little rub through the dress, because her slot was probably extra crinkled and damp just then. It's like Ronny's ball sack sticking to one leg on a hot day. Her lips probably stuck together from all that looking. "Let's sit together a little bit."

We walked to the couch and I lay down with my rear end in the air as usual.

Muriel sat beside me, as she always did. I could feel her thigh against my thigh, in opposite directions. We could feel each other's hip bones rotating under tender flesh as we moved, touching one another.

With a fully open palm, she made circles slowly rotating over my ovals. "Where did you ever get these beautiful cheeks?"

I sighed and prepared to doze off. Then I felt my dress being lifted. It was a light dress, and she had a light touch. I only knew because I felt cool air moving over my butt cheeks. It was the first time she touched me under my dress. She lifted my loose white x-ray dress and dropped it in folds onto the small of my back. My rear was naked in the air except for a fine pair of silk panties she had bought me. They were robin's egg blue, with perky little cream-colored bows over my hip bones. I was wide awake now. If it were Ronny, he would have been kneeling between my legs, holding his cock in one hand and tearing my panties to one side without even bothering to check if I was wet enough so he could ram the head up my vagina--I would certainly have been, as I was for Muriel.

A woman's touch is so much slower, unless she's in a hormone frenzy. Muriel's fingers lightly played right and left over the elastics along the bottoms of my panties. Her fingertips were as delightful as watercolor brushes, the way they painted me.

She played with my soft, quivering cheeks for about five minutes.

I could feel her finger pushing my panty-crotch aside, and touching the soft, sweaty folds of skin between my thighs, between my two holes. "Hmmm, your thick, curly fur comes right up to the edge of your back slot."

I thought she was going to continue, getting sexier. I was ready. Next thing I know, she lifts one panty half and exposes the pink melon-slice of one of my cheek bottoms. She puts her lips on my quivering tight butt slice, and blows a loud kazoo noise that fills the room--so hard it almost hurt.

I was so startled that I shrieked and farted at the same time.

I don't think she noticed. She sat back and pulled my dress back down. "Sarah, one day soon I'm going to simply eat you up like a gingerbread doll."

She rose and walked away, saying in an overwhelmed tone: "If I don't stop now, you'll never get out of here this afternoon. I've got to get my head out from under your dress or I won't be prepared for court."

"It's time for me to go back," I said feeling kind of frustrated. How could I tell her she was killing me with her teasing? I was a little thick. "If you start something you should finish it."

She stood by her desk, almost holding my purse as if to give it to me and hurry me out of her life for the day. "What do you mean, darling?"

"Never mind." I put my shoes on, stumbling a little, as I went to get my things.

When I got to her and the desk, she put her arms out and captured me around the waist. She pulled me close to her. I gave no resistance, but looked away so she couldn't kiss me.

"Can I have a little kiss?"

I looked out the window, not at her.

"Miss Pouty. I had no idea--."

"Never mind," I said. "I come here to let you pet me. You pay me for it. That's all."

She reached deep into one of the side pockets of her skirt and pulled out my three dollars. "I'll give you an extra quarter today if you'll kiss me." She handed me the money, which was hot from having been in her skirt next to her sex.

I gave her a peck on one soft cheek.

Why is it that, as you start to love someone, you see her for the first time? Not only did Muriel have those wild ringlets of honey hair that always came loose when she pulled her otherwise straight hair back in combs? She must have been a knockout when she was my age. She was still really hot. She had this healthy, plain English kind of face, kind of narrow and high, with wide lips and a straight nose. She had fun brown eyes under even caramel eyebrows. Her high, intelligent forehead was a little narrow, and tapered toward the temples. She had little crows' feet around her mouth and eyes, but her cheeks were still smooth. The slight furrows across her forehead were less from age than from a lot of worries. She'd say I made her smile, so the wrinkles went away up into her hair. She had nice even jaws that made her look handsome and her long pale neck strong, so that her soft lips and eyes were even prettier.

Smelling her powder and perfume, and seeing the light in her eyes, I got a little soft in the knees. "You don't have to give me a quarter. Just kiss me on the mouth."

"I'll give you a quarter's worth of a kiss, and then some." She pulled me close by my shoulder blades and put one hand on the back of my neck. She pulled lightly--more of a signal or a command, not a real pull--and I knew I should yield to her. I put my head back so my face tilted upward, and she embraced me so that her face descended on mine. It was like that famous picture of the sailor kissing the nurse after the war. She held me, and I was her girl. I liked that a lot. It felt nicer than being Ronny's girl.

Muriel's lips snuggled hot and wet on my lips. I stuck my tongue up into her mouth. Her tongue descended on mine and dominated it. She mastered me with her mouth, breathing heat and spit and sex into my open and hungry mouth. My tongue let her. My tongue fondled her tongue--invited it into my mouth, yielded the way I yielded on her couch.

While she kissed me, she swung me slightly around so that my head rested between on one breast, with her arm on that side like a life preserver around my head, like the sailor and the nurse. Muriel was my sailor, and she could hold me all she wanted. I had my eyes closed. Her tongue in my mouth occupied all my senses. At the same time, I could feel her free hand roving over the curves of my waist and my hips, down my thigh. Her hand roved strong as a man's down my belly, down between my legs where she pulled my x-ray dress up in a bunch with her fist while her knuckles rode up and down on my clit, and instinct made me start riding on her hand. Her hand slid back up in a cottony rustle and palmed my small titties one by one, with my soft puffy nipples.

I pushed her away. I gasped: "Let's not get all worked up again." Towering over her by two inches, I put my arms around her neck so I had her head in my embrace, and I tilted her face back and kissed it. I just wanted her not to feel like I jilted her or something. I wanted to leave her with a warm kiss. I longed for her do more to me. She sighed as she let go. I took my three dollars and strode out the door. I felt her eyes on me.

Sometimes things were still like the first week, when she was overcome by desire, stopped flirting and seducing me, and took me to the couch holding both my hands.

"Honey, I don't know if you'll ever speak to me again," she said on our third time together in her office. Until now we had tea and talked a lot. We came close to touching a few times, and I got the idea she wanted to kiss me. It was weird, sure, a woman and all, but I took things as they came. "Would you sit on the couch with me?"

"Sure," I said.

Fingers entwined, we sat side by side. I got the idea she wasn't letting go of my paws.

"Are you okay?" she asked full of concern, scared at what she was doing. She had no idea--I could have gone to the police or something.

I nodded brightly. The world didn't have to be complicated. Things that felt nice didn't have to be bad.

Holding my hands in hers--tightly, urgently--she shook my hands and looked into my eyes. "Ever since I first saw you, I wanted to be with you. Is that wrong?"

I shook my head.

"Are you mad at me?"

I shook my head.

"Are you scared? Disgusted?"

I shook my head.

She stared at me, never letting go of my hands in her fists.

I said: "If you want to kiss me, you can."

She didn't need convincing. She leaned forward with her eyes closed, and brought her lips to mine. Our first little kisses were dry and awkward. She was trembling. I wasn't.

I put my arms around her and pulled her close. "You won't have to be scared. I wouldn't be here if I didn't want to be."

She hugged me back. "I won't hurt you. I just want to be close to you."

"You want to touch me?"

She pressed her cheek against my chest and nodded. Her arms were like cables around me. I reached up and unclenched her hands from me. I lifted each hand to my lips and kissed it lightly. Neither of us had any idea what came next. There was no plan, no play book. I knew I was safe with her. What could she possibly do to me? Kiss me? Look through my dress? She'd already done that, with hungry eyeballs, and no harm done. "If it makes you happy, it's okay with me."

"You don't have to do anything. Just having you with me is so nice."

"Okay."

She guided me to show me what she wanted. It took some wrong turns and little misdirections, but she got me to lie down facing away from her, with my belly on the couch. The first day, and the next, she just massaged the small of my back. I thought we were going to trade back massages. She kneaded my flesh, pressed on my spine one vertebra at a time, palmed my shoulder blades. I sighed happily and said "That's nice."

"You feel nice."

"Keep doing that, Muriel."

"Let me know if you get sore or stiff or something."

"Oh no, you can do that all day."

Like a boy, daring to see how far he can go--toward the end of our hour, the second day--her hand stole down my spine and touched my ass. "That feels nice," I said, trying to encourage her.

A minute later, she had both hands on my cheeks and was massaging them. I could see out of the corner of my eye that she was red, and breathing hard. If we were a boy, she'd have an almost painful boner right about then. It was so much like being with a man, except gentler and nicer in its own way. She was so sweet. I couldn't tell her, for fear that she'd faint from shock, how every evening in his car, Ronny pounded away with his cock up my back door. I was terrified of getting pregnant. He wasn't coming up the front way--not even close. I was sure I had invented a new form of sex.

I was still the girl here, just like with Ronny. That's how I liked it. I didn't know if that her my boy or my man. She was almost always my woman. Other times, we were both the woman. Or sometimes she was my girl. I liked it most when I was her girl. It was a lot of fun, like trying on each other's clothes from a closet of surprises.

I wasn't allowed to look while I lay on her couch, so I'd rest my face on folded arms and relax while she felt me up. Muriel wouldn't say anything, but I would hear her breathing.

"You are a work of art," she told me that first week. She touched my waist and ass like an art collector. You'd think I was a sculpture.

"Who's Art?" I asked brightly, lying face down on my forearms, and we both laughed. I was 23 and just a secretary. Muriel was 37 and one of the city's first women lawyers. She was educated, and I was still in night school learning steno. She knew about art and cinema. She said penis and I said dick. She said *tomahto* and I said *damaydah*. She ate *hors d'oeuvres*, while I blew bubble gum. We came to like each other a lot, even though we had next to nothing in common--except a soft touch for each other.

Like I told her one day: "Love me--I'm easy." I had just come over at noon. Before I could peel off my gloves, or set my hat and purse aside, she embraced me in a lover's squeeze.

She was so worried that I would think she was queer. They didn't call it that in those days. That was a term for men. Nobody knew what to call women, and we weren't that type of woman in any case.

I could tell she liked me so much her heart was going to burst. As I set my gum aside, sticking it to the edge of the desk where I could grab it on my way out, "Like I tell Ronny. You can do anything you want with me, as long as you're not rough."

She was having a kitten day. She moaned faintly and pressed her cheek against my breast, which wasn't saying much because I was flat as an ironing board despite the perfect womanly hourglass figure, and the ass from paradise that I rented to her for a dollar a day plus lunch.

I hugged her tightly and gave her a little rock. "If it feels good, and nobody gets hurt, and nobody finds out about it, what's the harm?"

Yes, she paid me. I wanted the money, I liked the way she felt me up, and I enjoyed the feeling of being paid for it, like I was being kept. That's a laugh, because I was always the most independent-minded broad you'd ever meet, but this was my choice. And she was really sweet. I almost expected she'd soon offer me a little more, maybe to look up my dress or get her hand up into the wet stuff, but it turned out differently than either of us expected, and better.

She'd feast on me with her eyes and her hands while I lay there with my chin resting on folded arms. Her breaths were slow and shallow at first, as if she were sleeping or reading her law books. She'd lay her hands on my ass cheeks, or on the delicious cotton skirt that barely concealed them and my panties. She'd move her hands out in both directions so she was holding my whole butt between her palms. I could feel the heat of her hands, the heat of her breathing, the heat in her desire as she'd sigh over me, give me a little shake to make it jiggle or to seat the smooth, firm young skin better in her fingers. She'd lightly run her fingers up my skirt and down the crack of my ass.

After about a week of my visiting every day, she began to feel safe. I wasn't surprised. I figured she'd have been really weird if she didn't get bolder. She'd touch herself under her elegant skirts and dresses--I'd hear a faint rustling of fingers in silk--and she would start breathing the way a boy does when he's petting a girl in his car. Or how the girl sounded, or was that me?

No matter where her one hand roved, she always kept the other hand firmly on my behind. I wasn't allowed to look, but I could hear her breathe harder. That made me breathe a little harder too but it was kind of odd. She made the sound a girl made when a guy was petting her up. I wasn't allowed to do anything but lie there and listen. It was very restful. I needed the money and the sleep, and besides it was nice getting felt up.

* * * *

I was seeing my boyfriend Ronny nearly every evening. We'd sit in the back seat of his car by the lake with the windows steamed up. It was so quiet around us that, even with the doors locked and the windows cracked just a hair, you could hear ducks splashing out on the lake. After a while, I would hear myself starting to breathe heavy--in, out, in, out--like a machine, as Ronny's fingers got into my pussy where it was wet. He'd slip his fingers there while he petted me. He'd have his tongue stuck between his teeth, and his eyes closed. He'd breathe harder too, and we'd go in rhythm together. He'd make me cum, and then take out his cock for me to look at and pet like it was a little hamster. I liked stroking his balls too, which were soft as mouse ears. When I was hot for it, I'd put my mouth on his cock, wide open so my cheeks looked sunken in. I'd lick him and suck him until he started to paw the air around him. I'd take as much as I could into my mouth. He'd hold my temples, with my long hair dangling down on his cock, while he started to convulse with his orgasm.

* * * *

Those sounds Ronnie and I made with our breathing--that's how Muriel sounded as she felt me up. We'd spend almost my whole lunch hour together like that, while she worked herself up. She stopped being shy, and let out these little moans when she wanted me so. At first, she just felt me all that time and breathed hard. After a while, we both relaxed and got our nerve back, and she loosened up. She'd kiss my cotton panty ass cheeks. She'd nuzzle them with her mouth and nose. She was really in love with my ass. It was kind of nice, and it made me hot too.

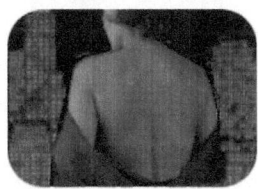

Each day as my lunch hour approached, I looked forward to going down the elevator in my skyscraper. I'd cross the street, and ride up to the 20th floor of her skyscraper, the Finncroft Tower. She had a small, cluttered law office with one window overlooking the street below. If I leaned out the window, assuming the screen was out, I could look left toward the intersection and there was the Century Building. I could almost see Mr. Ferguson's accounting office on the 18th floor of, where I worked as a secretary and receptionist along with three other women.

At first, I just lay on Muriel's couch and rested. Muriel was very gentle. For a lawyer, she had fingers like an artist. She soaked up the softness and smoothness of my young skin. Her palms would slide on that cotton, with the fine silk panties underneath, so that she would cup the curvature of my butt cheeks. Sometimes it tickled, and I'd almost laugh--then again, her palms felt warm, and I began to enjoy it. I began to tingle downstairs. I'd lie with one hand under my Venus mound, feeling it because my skirt and panties were so thin, and I'd make sure my long finger lay right over the hood. My little lady would feel pressure as I lay there, especially if I thrust out a little with my Venus mound. I'm not sure Muriel even noticed that I was enjoying myself more and more. When I stopped in the hall ladies' room to pee afterward, I'd notice that my bud was still tingling under the hood. My father and both brothers owned a garage, so it wasn't so weird for me to talk about cars, or know how boys think. Truth is, I was afraid of one thing. I was afraid I'd enjoy it to a point where I'd pee on her couch, soak my dress, and have to go home to change. It never came to that.

I might also have been far more afraid that I'd like it too much, but I never thought that far ahead. If I liked it too much, would that be the hunger that dared not speak its name? My brothers and my father had a stack of those worn, torn magazines in the toilet at the garage--all these stories about raging GIs with Tommy guns, and terrified women holding their knuckles to their teeth while crazed men in Nazi helmets stood over them, and women in short skirts and Nazi armbands whipped the 'girls'. I'd get in there if I must, squat, pee without fully sitting down, and get out as fast as possible.

In her office, Muriel would murmur to me, or to my ass: "You are such a pretty girl, an easy girl, a kind girl." She'd splash her hands all over it and kiss it so it shook. "What makes me love you so?" Did she mean me or my ass? I didn't complain, ever, and came to enjoy Muriel's attentions. It was a massage, in a way, and she paid me. Sometimes I dozed off, after I'd been out all night with Ronny. It all developed so slowly that I wonder how I had the patience for it as a young woman. I worked all day, went to school in the evenings, and went out dancing with my boyfriend most nights. On my lunch hours, I'd carry on a secret life of forbidden lust. We only needed prison bars and armbands; torn skirts that were shorter than anyone ever wore; bruised cheeks; knuckles on our teeth; and scared eyes.

The view in Muriel's office--specifically, on her couch--was through Venetian blinds, always of the sky--sometimes bright blue and sunny, other times gray and rainy. At first I was a bit stiff and unsure when I would come across the street from the Century Building, where I worked as a secretary for the accountant Ferguson. My path took me through the chrome and glass diner on the first floor of the Century Building, and the boutique in front with its green-edged plate glass windows. I'd walk down the side street a few hundred feet, then cross diagonally to the middle building, called Finncroft Tower, where Muriel had her law office. Almost no women practiced law in those days. I knew she was struggling, but she held her own. I never asked her for anything. The three bucks was from her heart, and I took it to my heart. I don't remember that we ever talked about it. She'd either leave it on the corner of the desk for me, between my gloves, to put in my purse; or she'd press it into my palms while she gave me a kiss so-long on the lips when I had to hurry back to work.

Muriel was specific in her instructions. She told me not to wear girdles, but thin clothing so her fingertips were practically touching my bare skin. It was all okay with me. When you are 23, the world is still mysterious and people always surprise you. I'd lie on my belly in my cotton dress, with little or nothing on underneath. In those days, a good girl wore a girdle you pulled up like a second skin--it left squish marks. You pinned your silk or nylon hose to it with these obscene skin-colored rubber hooks. The best part was escaping from your girdle in the privacy of rented efficiency every evening, and not wearing it at all on weekends. The idea was to not let your flesh quiver sinfully for others to see, in our puritan society. Heaven forbid, men might look but women would stare, even glare. For older women it was to stop their wattle from flapping, but on younger girls it was a way to suppress our sex pure out and simple. All that did was make the hungry hungrier, and the horny hornier. Our souls were frail vessels of corruption into which the proverbial gin-soaked preacher could pour out poison, while licking his lips and playing pocket billiards with himself. Like sheep, people went along with it.

My lady friend insisted that I wear only sheer panties. She'd give me ones she liked, as gifts, in beautiful packets from Shaumberg's. It was fun to receive presents and even more fun to wear things that pleased her. I was always surprised and delighted. It was kind of like dressing for a man, except a woman's eye chooses little nothings so much better.

Muriel was a real looker for her age. She had a lively, pretty face. She was a shapely woman, ample breasted, whose body had borne three children. Her kids lived at home in the care of a gray-haired, live-in matron in her 60s. One of those bustling tisk-tisk types that acted stern but then spoiled them silly. Muriel kept herself well. She would be a catch for the right man. When she reached out to me, she was on the skids with Mr. Wrong--but of whom whatever, we need say no more. The prick's name was Leo, and he didn't appreciate what he had in her...any more than stupid Ronny knew a good thing when he had it. Like that thing we had to memorize for school, from Thoreau: "Lots of men live lives of quiet desperation." Now we know why, and I'm sure Ronny was doomed to it in memory of letting a girl like me get away. Another word for quiet desperation is regret.

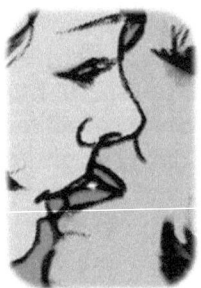

2. Hot Steamy Cleavage

I soon relaxed and enjoyed my hour on the couch. I'd smile and snooze and listen to her breathing while she felt me up. I wasn't allowed to face her, or look, but I could see enough from the corner of one eye. She was so sweet, that expression on her face, like she heard angels singing or something.

Sometimes she would lean close and kiss my neck above the collar, and under my ears, which tickled and made me laugh. I could feel the heat in her cleavage and smell her expensive perfume when she leaned close to me. It was a scent ever so subtle, but comforting and sweet. It was a honey sort of scent. Her smell mixed with her body heat between her tits. When I say tits I mean I had titties but this lady had two handfuls. She wore a hardy white brassiere under her blouse, that must have cost a pretty penny, but she'd need it in court with those old mustache rats to avoid their hard eyes. She'd bend over me to whisper in my ear. I wasn't allowed to look, but I could nod my head or whisper back. Sometimes she'd kiss me in the ear, making it wet.

Like she'd say: "I like your cotton dress today."

"Mmm, nice." What could I say to that?

"How smooth your skin feels. I like it when you wear panties and cotton." Her fingers were almost like pens, writing on my skin the words she was saying. We had a machine like that at Ferguson's office, a signature machine, to fake his name on documents when he wasn't in. "I could touch you like this all day long."

"I wouldn't mind."

Truth was, the only way a young woman like me could lie still for an hour was because I was so cotton-pickin' tired from the night before with Ronny. A lot of times I'd doze, or fall fast asleep. I wonder if I snored a few times. She just loved touching that ass of mine, and gradually I noticed she'd be touching herself at the same time. At first I would say "mm" a lot. When I wasn't afraid of her anymore, or embarrassed, I would actually say something back: "I like it when you do that."

She always responded, usually with a sharp breath or a little moan. "You are a very pretty young woman." She was 37 and quite pretty for her age. "You're so young and smooth." I didn't say Muriel or Miss or Missus or anything. We still had a long way to go.

"I'm glad you think so." Her hands grasped me tighter, showing her pleasure. "Do you think I'm pretty?"

"I think you're pretty." I knew she wanted to hear me say the whole thing out, every syllable, not just yes. She was paying me, for one thing, though it was just lunch money and a little tip. Plus she trusted me--I could have ruined her. But to ruin her would have meant ruining me. She had nothing to worry about. I was the one who was worried at first, but I relaxed after a little while. Every day I would visit her on my lunch hour. Every day I would lie face down on her couch and relax. I didn't have to do anything, just let her feel me up. Truth is, Ronny felt me up too, but he was impatient. He was always rushing to a destination. Muriel was all about the journey.

One time, she asked me those words she liked my answer to. "Tell me I'm pretty. Am I pretty?"

I answered: "I would like one thing."

"What is it, honey?" Maybe she thought I'd ask for a dollar more.

"I'd like you to wear a little makeup."

"Ohhhh." Her whole life must have fleeted before her at that moment. How she was letting herself go, and she needed to stay feeling young.

"You work so much," I said, terrified that I might offend her. I was lying face down, talking into the couch between my crossed wrists. "I think you forget about other things."

For that, she bunched my cheeks in her palms, and kissed me long just where the Y was under my skirt I back, through my panties. I could feel her breath hot down my crotch, even with the hair and cotton.

From then on, every day she'd apply a little makeup just before I came across to see her. She'd make herself pretty for me.

She'd show me magazines and catalogs, and ask me which lipstick or which eye shadow I thought she'd look good in.

One of those moments just happened to be the first time I kissed her, not on the mouth but over her eyes and on her nose. She had me look at makeup models in some magazine, and I framed her face in my hands to look at it. We were face to face, and her eyes looked so trusting. For a moment, she looked younger than me. I kissed her on each eye, and on the tip of her cute nose. He had a small, curved nose like maybe there was a little bit of Jew or Spanish in her. But her skin was pale as pearl. There was nothing you could do with that except play sports, have sex, get flushed, and like it. I did get her to powder her cheeks a bit. I liked having a pretty woman fuss over me. I now know, looking back, that I was a brave young girl all alone in the city, making up with brashness for the empty apartment and Ronny's rough attentions. Muriel added something warm and wonderful to my life, which it took me a long time to appreciate. So we two were good for each other. At the time, I didn't really see past that snooze, the dollar, and my lunch-- usually a grill cheese sandwich and an egg cream or a vanilla milkshake in the diner in the Century Building, as I was usually rushing and ten minutes late on my way back to work. Did you ever hear the expression 'the good old days'? I'd always ask for a pickle on the side, and the gray-haired man behind the counter would put it on a lettuce leaf that he carefully tore for me with his hands. Sometimes he'd throw in a large, juicy tomato slice with the pickle, or a few chips if they had them handy.

I'd lie there on Muriel's office couch, snoozing so the leather steamed up under my wrists. I even drooled once or twice when I was really knocked out. I could feel Muriel's hands sliding around on my ass, enjoying the tight feel of my loose globes and the tight muscles connecting my thighs to my waist.

Sometimes, she'd bend close and kiss the backs of my knees just below where she raised the hem of my skirt. Sometimes she would press her cheek against my calf, and murmur to herself. At times, the couch quivered faintly when she stroked herself, fingers going in deep and wet. There was a different little rhythm, still always delicate, when she'd fan her lady with fast fingers in a blur.

I caught a lot, things like that, from the corner of either eye. At first I was a little scared, then curious, and finally interested. On a good day, I wished she'd go a little further. If she looked up my skirt in back, why didn't she touch me up there? It was getting so I'd be worked up, and I wished she would scratch my itch. But a woman can't say that to another woman. In time, it got so I would touch myself silently to show her, and she'd get the idea real quick.

I never did have to ask her why. We were on the same wavelength, even though we didn't really know each other. I had an hour for lunch, with about twenty minutes' grace because Mr. Ferguson, my boss at the accounting firm, often stayed out late with other men over steak and martinis. When he came back on days like that, he'd lock his door and I swear he probably snoozed in his office with his feet up on his desk. You could smell beef and booze and smoke on him when he walked through the office with extra-long steps that didn't quite go in a straight line, all dark red around his neck. We girls would pretend he wasn't lit up like a Christmas tree.

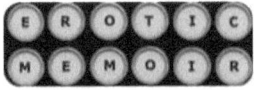

Mr. Ferguson never asked about my time. I almost always stayed an hour or two late in the evenings, or came in early, so punching the old brown wall clock with that yellowish card-stock time slip was more of a formality. Maybe people were more trusting in those days, and we got along better--though everyone knew their place, and the differences were cut and dried. I'll say one thing--Mr. Ferguson always managed to hire some kind of hawk for an office manager, like Old Witch Harriet, the Bosom Bomber, who could stare daggers.

But nobody had the slightest idea what I did when I'd hurry out of the office with my handbag and my hat, little fishnet dangling over my eyes like a movie star, all by myself. I told the other girls I was taking steno lessons uptown if they asked me to lunch with them.

I'd wait until I got to Muriel's building before touching up my lipstick and mascara in the first floor ladies' john. Hell, I was a kept woman, which got my little imagination going--Muriel always gave me a dollar for our sex together, and two dollars cash extra to buy lunch on my way back. She would have slipped me a fin if she could, but I knew she was just making it in her little hole in the wall up there. It gave her pleasure to pay me, and I enjoyed taking the money. An extra five bucks a week, plus free lunches, was nothing for a single girl totally on her own to sneeze at back in those days.

I'm 5'7", just on the tall side for a girl. I was slender, with a bit narrow hips for a woman. That doesn't mean they weren't curvy or feminine. I had been athletic all my life, playing softball and swimming in high school. Like a boy with lipstick, someone once told me, but she was some jealous old twat in the hat department at Schaumberg's. If that was true, I would have been a gorgeous boy with blue eyes and a sweet face, and a wide, crooked, naughty smile. I was self-conscious about myself. What woman isn't. Was I soft enough? Was I feminine? It was like when I was pubescent and spent all that time in my bedroom at home, on a chair with my legs up, looking all that pussy hair--when my ass had not yet filled in, but was just starting to not look like a boy's.

I could feel Muriel, measuring with her hands how my thighs were tight and bulged in a low, smooth curve with a flow of muscles under soft female flesh.

At 23, I still had pretty much the same strong thighs I had while running track in high school. I'd played field hockey, got clobbered a few times, and could smack the other girl with my wooden racket as good as I got. I still had all my teeth, which is less than I could say for a few other dames around town who played against us.

We were prissies from a middle class, private high school, with nice uniforms, and we always ranked in at least the top ten for field hockey, a game they never even heard of down at Public Number One. I'll never regret all that running, because it gave me the wind and the power that set the tone for the rest of my life.

Muriel sometimes liked me to wear my old school uniform, which--go figure--makes adolescent girls look as lickable as lollypops. If figure everyone in the world sells with sex, so why should parochial schools be any different? Of course we girls always thought we looked stupid in those outfits. Pity the Catholic school girls, who had nuns for their bombers on top of it all. We had old prefect ladies. Same thing.

With my long legs, I did okay on the quarter mile in track, but my frame was always more filled in, so I couldn't pump out sprints like those spidery girls with tiny bodies and long, thin legs. Muriel said she liked me because I had a little meat on those long bones.

We're all self-conscious about something, starting with our looks and our weight. I always had a thing about having tiny boobs. One day, I would have children, give quarts of milk, and fill out. My tits would never to return to being hints on my chest, with puffy nipples so pale and pink they stuck out a little, but you couldn't say where boob skin turned into nipple skin. My long frame would never again be as thin as back then--but there is a time for everything.

I had no regrets about anything.

All that happened so long ago, working for Mr. Ferguson at the Century Building on those lazy summer days; and visiting Muriel in the skyscraper down the street, with its thousand little rectangular windows looking out over the world and its secrets.

A person could just imagine--or not--what all went on behind those many little shadowy windows.

3. Finger Licking

"You're probably wondering if I have seduced other girls like you," Muriel said one afternoon as we sat side by side on wooden office chairs, facing out the window. We were using wooden spoons to scoop vanilla ice cream from paper cups. A vendor in a white paper hat sold them from a cart going down the halls on each floor. She wore a little blue and eye liner, and some shiny new pink lipstick that really made her look young. Funny thing is that her legs were just short enough so she could cross them at the ankles and swing them, whereas with my legs I just sort of sprawled in my chair beside her.

"Is that what it was? You seduced me?"

"I should have asked if you thought I had other friends like you."

"I don't want to ask questions," I said. "I'd be afraid to spoil things." What if she had ten other dumb girls like me on the hook for different hours of the day?

"You are the first and only one," she said. "I don't know what came over me. I saw you and just melted inside."

I believed her. "You saw my ass." I felt relieved.

"Yes. I saw your figure. The rest of you is lovely too--the short dark hair, the Irish face, the saucy smile, the bright blue eyes full of mischief, long solid legs."

"And flat as a board." I licked my spoon.

"Good things come in little packages. I've been so busy loving your behind that I haven't gotten to your sweet little puffies yet. If you were a horse, you'd have legs like a mare."

"You like little titties?"

"Yours, yes; otherwise, I never thought about it. I've always liked men, and I'm not about to start chasing women or girls. It's just you I wanted, for reasons I will never be able to explain. There will never be another you for me."

"I used to look at girls sometimes."

"We all do, honey. It's competition more than attraction. Sometimes we see each other as we think men do, just to think how they see us through men's eyes so we can look better for them."

"Lots of men look at me on the street," I said. "Women too. I think mostly the women are jealous--although I get real hungry looks from some women. Talk about the hard stare. It's not just men. I think these women are unhappy with their husbands, and need a little strange meat."

"And the men who look at you?" She licked her spoon, with melted vanilla oozing in the corners of her mouth.

I leaned forward on impulse, and licked the sweet corners of her lips.

"Mmm" she said, liking it.

"Vanilla and spit," I said. "Yum. The men--the other day, one in a car almost rear ended a car in front of him from turning his head to look at me. The women and the men both. They have *fuck* written in their eyes."

"They're desperate, both the men and the women."

I laughed.

"What were you wearing?" she asked, licking her wooden spoon.

"When he nearly rear-ended someone? Let's see--my tight gray sheath that comes down just below my knees." I struggled to remember. "Navy pumps, sheer nylons, my silk blouse with the ruffle down the front, my black gloves, navy purse, and my white saucer with the navy trim all around and the little net over my eyes."

"I'll bet you were a knock-out. Lipstick?"

"Red. Fruity. I was feeling fruity that day."

"You make me feel fruity every day. Fruity and Nutty."

"Tutti-frutti."

We both laughed.

Muriel reassured herself: "I know you like seeing me."

"I wouldn't be here if I didn't like it."

We talked like girlfriends, all matter of fact and girly. We felt like we'd been friends for a long time. That vanilla was so sweet and pure, it was part of that early summer or late spring day. For the first time in years, I had a little money building up in my savings account. I was having a good time, and I was enjoying that little secret of ours.

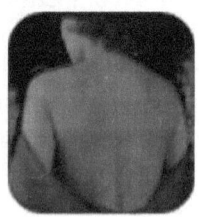

Sometimes I'd come over in this outfit put together from my old high school uniform. I looked like a parochial school girl in it-- pleated gray skirt to just below the knee, white blouse, little navy blazer with rounded corners and cute little narrow lapel, red butterfly bowtie, white socks with tiny flowers around the edges up to my knees, and black loafers. I'd wear one of my saucers and nets, and gloves, and carry a smart purse so I'd still look like that jazzy woman on the street.

Wearing that outfit, in Muriel's office when we were alone and private together with our secrets, I'd sit on the chair so she could look at me. I'd sit with my butt down and my knees up, with my heels digging into the edge of the chair. I'd let Muriel gaze at my white undies and long thighs.

My smooth young skin was a warm, very light *café au lait* hue. I'm part Irish, part Mediterranean--we're not sure if that's Italian or Corsican. I let her see how the skin grew darker and earthier in the direction of my Y in front. Under the thick, curly honey bush, I have a brownish-reddish crotch with chocolate lines down the edges of my pussy lips. You'd think someone drew eyeliner down my labia. I'm shocking pink inside.

I liked that little touch of being owned, as part of our little pal-games. Sometimes our lunch trysts were more like pajama parties. I'd bring ice cream from the Century Diner, and she'd call out for pizza or sukiyaki. The delivery boy always brought a couple of cold bottles of very creamy, sweet sarsaparilla or root beer, which we sucked loudly through straws.

I'd always been straight forward and uncomplicated, which is not the same as simple. What I mean is, I was always very independent. I'd see the way to go, and not much could stop me. Young ladies weren't supposed to do this or that, which made me all the more eager to try it.

With Muriel, I felt safe. It was fun, kind of gooshey-sweet, to let other parts of my nature come out and play. Like opening a garden door that's otherwise always closed. I liked having her be the only woman who could look at my thighs in that certain way, full of longing and desire--my undies, the bulge of my Venus mound, the promise of what lay under that clean white cotton. She liked that fluffy white cotton with my school outfits, which looked a bit like those cloth sanitary napkins of long ago.

If she was intrigued by the strong blonde curls peeking out on either side of my panties, she didn't say. I was saving that surprise up for later, if it ever came to that. I wasn't going to push it.

Being easy going, I was prepared to let her do what she wanted. I'd go along with anything, as long as she went easy on me and I liked it, or at least could sleep through it. Like her pawing my backside. Honestly, people make too much out of little things.

I was very self-conscious about three things: my tiny boobs, my loose pink vaginal tunnel, and my curly, honey-colored pelt. I was to learn that my worries were about nothing.

The pelt made my lovers hot. It was almost gross--a pretty chick with caveman fur. Ronny, and Muriel got hot over it.

The loose tunny--nothing to do about that. It should be a wet, numb fuck for a guy without a super huge dong, but it was fun too. It was great for someone to kiss and suck. I often held it open for Ronny, pinching my labia. He had a long tongue, and he liked to see how far in he could stretch it. I'd help by having him hold my lips open, so I could pull on his head with both my hands and squish his hot little face in there. Makes for beard burn inside you.

Cunt skin is about the same as the skin in our mouths. I had a theory that you could walk down the street and look in women's mouths--the color of their lips inside was probably the same as the color of their pussy tunnel. So you could sit and talk with some woman of your choice--I liked doing it--and look inside her mouth while she talked, and pretend you were looking into her vagina. It was true of Muriel. The color of her pussy lane and her lips were both the same creamy light brown sugar with pink undertones. Same thing goes for a woman's nipples. If she had a nice pink mouth inside (the tongue doesn't count), then you could bet she had a nice pink pussy and pink nipples. I tested all this by crawling around on Muriel, while I had her lie naked on the couch. I examined all her holes minutely. She let me, and seemed to really enjoy it. We giggled a lot, too. She came up with her own theory that a woman's eyelids are the same as her labia, but we only had our two cases to explore, so it wasn't a scientific survey endorsed by the American Association of Labia and Nipples, unfortunately, AALN for short. They have a lot of clout in Washington, mostly in hotel rooms where Congressmen stay.

Why did I have such a flat chest and small tits? Muriel thought that it was due to being athletic and making too many androgens, which probably also had to do with my firm personality--not sure which was the chicken, and which was the egg.

The cool thing about having tiny tits was that men--and women--couldn't leave them alone. Muriel was like that, when we got that far. Aside from my ass, she was always at my nipples with her mouth. It didn't matter what kind of nipple they were--little cherry pits on some girls, or puffy marshmallows like mine. People couldn't keep their mouths and fingers off them. And it tickled so.

So there we sat, on a summer's day, licking our wooden spoons and scooping ice cream from paper cups in her office. I liked the way sunshine warmed up the bricks all around. There was a plain wood-framed screen, and two horizontal steel bars, overlooking the city canyons all around. Most of it was built in the 1890s, with another burst in the 1910s, so it was nice to sit up on the 20th floor like in a time machine, and wonder if another girl long ago went to visit her older woman friend, get free ice cream, and have her cup licked.

Or to wonder if, a hundred years after our time, two women would sit in this very spot with their vanilla ice creams, each licking their spoons and each other's cups.

"I don't mind telling you." Muriel polished her wooden spoon the way she eventually licked me, with visible, languid pleasure, one long, self-indulgent lick at a time. "You are a book I've never read before."

"What ever do you mean, Muriel?" Sometimes, being older and wiser and smarter, she intimidated me so. If she embarrassed me, she never made me feel bad. There was no boo-boo she couldn't kiss and cuddle and make better. I always left her office moist between the legs. Was it love? A crush? Or just lunch? I was young and had the virtue of taking things as they came, without looking too deeply as long as nobody got hurt, nobody else knew, and it felt good.

"I mean, Sarah, I used to sit in high school on those long spring afternoons, on those hard benches made of wood and steel, surrounded by all those bosomy girls and muscular boys, and just ooze. With forty boys and girls jammed into a hot classroom, or sitting together on a wall outside after lunch, you could smell the sweat and the juices, just flowing into the prime of their lives. We were all slightly drunk on hormones. The air was filled with birds and bees. It's a wonder we didn't all just have an orgy, but nobody would think of such a thing." She looked at me in shock. "My god, you were still an infant when I was already a young bitch getting sweatered by the top cock on the football team."

I could picture her. "You must have been a knock-out. You're still beautiful." She blushed. I continued: "When I'm 37, if I'm as sexy as you are, I'll be a lucky woman."

"I got my boobs sucked a lot," Muriel said. "I was still a virgin at your age, but I was the hickey queen around town. " She waved her wooden spoon and laughed at the thought. "We were all so straight-laced, dull, and unimaginative." I laughed at a picture of them, and nearly choked on a wad of icy vanilla. Creamy stuff ran from the corners of our mouths as we collected ourselves and wiped our lips with the same single rumpled paper napkin from the Century Diner in my office building down the street. She said: "Sometimes I would rub my thighs together on my fist, when nobody was looking, to try and make it go away. I hadn't learned about scratching the itch yet. Do you masturbate when you are alone?"

I shook my head. "That's what boys do." I did, actually, but women in those days did not admit anything to anyone about anything, including ourselves, not even to their best friend if their life depended on it.

She chortled around her spoon, tonguing it while tilting her head this way and that. "You do it, but call it something different. That's what we do, isn't it? You've read that Kinsey Report?"

"I've heard of it. I wouldn't know where to find it." That was a lie.

"It's a report about what men and women do--sometimes women with women, or men with men. Women do touch themselves down there."

"They won't allow it at our library." That was a lie. We had it in a back room in our local library under lock and key. It was just that Adolfine Hitlerette, the puritanical librarian, who commuted on a broomstick every day, only wanted middle aged white men or sexless old bag-shaped matrons to see it--and only if she could count to ten and then slam the book shut on their noses.

"I know, honey, so you ask for special permission to go into the stacks. Apply for permission to research medicine or psychology. That's where you'll find it. When nobody is looking, sit and read. Just know one thing--when they asked women if they play with themselves, I'm sure eighty percent of them lied and said no."

"And the other twenty percent?"

"Admitted they satisfy themselves, but gave a phony name and address."

"Is that what you call it? Masturbating?" I thought: *Is that what I secretly do when Ronny isn't around to make me feel hot and breathless?*

"It's Latin," Muriel said. "It means turbulent hand movement."

We each suddenly, on a whim, held up a fist and shook it, as if we were a man masturbating his dong. We shrieked with laughter.

But I understood the truth. I pictured myself plunging four fingers into my wet hole in the dark at night, hearing my ragged breathing echo among the bare walls of my little efficiency while neon and city lights dimly shuttled on the walls around me. I pictured myself holding my lips open on one side with one hand, with my index finger gingerly pulling back the hood. Or, being sensitive there, I would push the hood down, while my other hand rapidly fanned my little pearl.

"I admit it, Muriel. I do it when I'm alone, and I did try to look it up in the library, but some old witch wouldn't let me." I remembered those dark stacks and their secrets, and the prim library police with her thin lips and wire frame eyeglasses spying on me from the next row of shelves--before she rushed in and stared at me and slapped books around to make it impossible for me to read any more.

"So," Muriel continued our earlier train, "you are the only girl I ever made a move on. I was so careful. You could ruin me if you talk. I'll never do this with anyone else again."

"I promise I'll never tell." I put my hand on her thigh. It was the first time I ever really touched her on my own. We were both fully dressed. She wore a brown wool outfit and apricot blouse that day. I think I had my school uniform on for her, this time with the robin's egg blue silk undies she bought me at Shaumberg's.

"I know you won't, sweetheart. I was so careful. Okay, I was scared as all hell. My heart was pounding in my throat when I first asked them to send you over with those documents, that first day."

"You knew you were going to put the make on me?"

A variety of expressions flickered over her face, including confusion and guilt, before she brightened. "Yes, I suppose you could call it that. To be honest, I just wanted to linger in the same room with you. I never imagined anything more. I was terrified. My heart was beating so hard it hurt my chest."

"How did you ever overcome your fear?" If I were looking for a young woman to feel up, how would I do that in a world full of men and their greedy eyes and hot horny paws? And women who made sure we all followed the rules and had no impure thoughts--or any thoughts at all, for that matter. Could she go to prison for doing what she did? Probably yes. Be humiliated in court, a leper in the newspapers, an outcast people avoided on the street? Be known in hushed tones as a 'forsaken woman', like in that Scarlet Letter book we were supposed to read in school and I read the trot notes instead. All I really wanted was for Ronnie to fuck the living daylights out of me in his car without getting myself knocked up and both of us ruined. That was bad enough. But those unspeakable desires in fallen women--not just adulteresses or temptresses, but actually the damned, women who sought each other in the dark corners of prisons, the way it was shown in the magazines at the garage.

I added: "I can't imagine how scared you must have been, but you got it right on the first try."

"I figured it out," Muriel said. She rubbed her spoon down her lips. The whole room smelled of sunshine and vanilla, so much so that a bee flew in through the breezy window, from out of a blue sky, and hovered over the slowly melting mound of scooped ice cream in her paper cup that Muriel held before her bosom. "I watched how young office boys flirted with young secretaries. I looked at how the secretaries reacted. If they shut the guy out, that was one thing. If they were angry or busy or whatever, that was another thing. But if they were interested, they'd play with a lock of their hair, or touch their blouse button, and bat their eyes a bit, or look down. You know..."

"I know," I said. I'd done all those things myself on occasion. "I wonder if I did that when you were honey-talking me."

"When I first stepped into your office there at old Fergie's, I walked up to you without a thought on my mind. I just needed those documents. I didn't have to do anything. Our eyes met, and I almost peed my skirt right there. You looked up and got flustered."

"I don't remember any of that," I said.

"You have people flirting with you all day long. I stood there like a stammering school girl. You touched your hair and a button on your blouse, and looked down. Your cheeks were pink."

"I'm always shy when spoken to," I said. As forward as I was, I think I always felt a little guilty, like what trouble am I getting into now.

"You had no idea, but you were just a little peach ripe for plucking."

"You dirty old lady."

"You loved it. You just needed a little guidance. Like I had any idea what I was doing."

I said: "I used to look at the girls too in school."

"Boys and girls, or just girls?"

We both put our bare feet up on the window sill. We could have wiggled our toes to wave at passing airplanes. We could hear planes droning around, but they stayed far away from the buildings.

"Both." We were being so candid. I had not even thought about these things myself in years. Here I was, 23 and long out of school. It wasn't the same in my secretarial classes. Some people were older. Some were married. Nothing could be like high school again. And I'd met Ronny, who worked as a surveyor. He was a tall, brown-haired boy with a brash attitude but a tender heart. He was the kind of boy who'd play around, but settle down and do the right thing. He'd marry a girl if he got her in that certain way that couldn't be spoken out loud by decent people in gray coats and tall gray hats, with muskets and turkeys. I was just total rebellion yet, even at 23. Ronny looked very sexy in his leather pants and heavy white shirt and helmet, so my mind didn't need to chase stray thoughts and flirt.

"We were on the same wavelength," Muriel said, "so the rest came naturally. It was still scary all the way, but I'm no longer afraid."

"Me neither."

"You were scared too?"

"Mm-hm." I nodded. "I wasn't scared of you, though, but of getting caught somehow. I always get caught. I'm always in trouble."

"You didn't fight it," she said gratefully.

"I'm pretty easy all around. I'll go along with just about anything, if it feels good and there's no harm, and nobody needs to know."

"And you like an egg cream."

"You make me feel kept."

"I pay you for your prettiness."

"I'm all yours for one hour a day."

She rubbed my neck gently with her forefinger, the way you petted a cockatiel. "I like that."

She squinted at me, and I squinted back in the sunlight. I said: "I like it when you keep me."

"You're sweet. Seriously, it's not like getting a tattoo. You can back out any time, and it'll be like it never happened."

"I know," I said. We talked about our friendship so much because it was so new and scary. "I'm here because I want to be with you."

We sat together looking out the window for a long time, with our feet up, saying little--with our fingers entwined as we held hands, swinging them a little as they dangled between our chairs. The empty cups lay by our chairs, and the licked spoons were all spent.

4. Gone To Lunch, Back Soon

Some days, she would start at my feet and work her way up, ever so languidly.

She'd begin by slipping my shoes off. Then she'd slowly peel my long nylons off my thighs, my calves, my ankles, my feet. She'd kiss my knees, and then suck my toes.

Other times, I could feel my silk stockings get damp as she slowly licked them. Muriel had a big tongue, and she was very thorough. I guess as a lawyer you have to be. She would raise my foot up, bending my leg at the knee, and hold my foot in both hands as she licked the bottom of my heel, and the long arch of my instep, and the ball of the foot.

On other days when she really took her time, she'd first kiss and lick my bottom as I lay face down. She'd get my silks or nylon bottom warm and wet, like I'd peed my pants. When she finally peeled the stockings off, one leg at a time, she'd hang them on one of our two chairs by the window to blow dry in the breeze.

I was like on a time clock or something. I was getting paid to lie still, be quiet, and not fidget too much unless it was to move a body part closer to her mouth or fingers to make it easier for her. At first it was like almost an annoyance, from a very curious woman. If I thought she was crazy or dangerous, I would have sensed it from the start. I would have shied from her like I avoided a whole lot of men and women who stepped before my desk at work and said strange things to me with weird grins. I trusted her completely, so much that I'd fall asleep while she touched me.

Muriel would lift one of my feet, usually the one closer to her, and suck gently on my toes. It felt kind of nice, like getting licked by a dog or something. I could feel her big tongue sliding between my toes, like a polishing cloth, very thoroughly, not missing a spot. She took her time on the bottoms of my feet, and on my toes. She liked my heels, too, a whole lot, but didn't waste much time on the tops of my feet.

She didn't show much interest in the tops of my feet. She'd lick the high arches a bit, down to where the toes fan out. She'd nip at the tops my toes again, with puckered kisses, before turning to my ankles, and then my calves. She'd lick my ankle bones, and the depression behind each, but my calves were the next hot stop.

I could tell--she enjoyed my calves almost as much as my buttocks. I had long limbs, and strong muscles from running and ball sports. Not to mention swimming. The same way she'd hold my ass with both hands, and lay her cheek against it like on a warm, soft pillow, she'd hold my lower legs and snuggle her cheek against my long calves. She'd lick them a long time, and kiss them many times.

All the while, I'd be half asleep with my face in the hollow formed by my arms over the dark leather upholstery. My mind would wander...how many asses had sat right there where my mouth was? I'd secretly make slow *mwah-mwah* kissing motions with my mouth, like a goldfish looking out of its tank. I was pretending to kiss someone's ass, or maybe a man's balls. I was always partial to men's balls because they are so soft, and it is a man's most vulnerable spot after his ego first and his heart second. A mean girl can really do a number on a guy. Of course, a guy with a mean streak would be a pretty good match for her. I never had such a streak--I was always kind of easy and cuddly and would smile with anyone. Then again, I could be a red-card terror with a stick at women's field hockey, with my big hands and muscular legs, so I was nobody to mess around with if you got serious about being an asshole. Growing up with two rowdy older brothers teaches a girl to play goalie most of her life. Shoot it to me, but don't get your face near my stick.

Anyway, while the clock ticked slowly away, and Muriel sucked on my leg, I'd make *mwah-mwah* mouths and pretend I was sucking some man's cock that had sat there. Of course he had to be really handsome and hot. Wow, just thinking about it, I would have done *mwah-mwah* to his crack as well if he asked me. He'd just have to do *mwah-mwah* to my crack first, though.

I thought all these funny and sometimes serious thoughts, wondering what is reality, what is the universe made of, why are we here, and why do dogs have brown lips. I had never thought of myself as one of those women of unspeakable yearning or anything--although I was often as interested in seeing the girls in the shower room in high school as watching the boys running track or practicing football. I figure most women like to look and compare. I was in a few sports, and did okay, nothing to write home about, but it firmed up my body while I was still young. As I got into my twenties, I walked a lot, and played some tennis. I always have enjoyed swimming, so I was quite tight. Good calves, long legs, strong, but with all the right soft spots a girl ought to have. Just the damn tiny tits, loose hole, and jungle fur. Actually, about the loose hole, Ronny and I figured out that if I squeezed my legs together with his machine in-between, and he had his knees outside pressing my thighs together, it made for a rip-roaring fuck in the park. We'd come together, shouting and shaking each other, and tonguing up a storm.

Meanwhile, Muriel would be holding my calves, massaging them with her fingers and thumbs, and bending low to kiss them. I'd see her from the corner of my eye, holding her crotch with one hand, and licking me as if I were an ice cream cone.

It took a while before she invited me to play.

She would loosen her bra and open her blouse a few buttons, while I sat beside her silently watching. Then I'd lie on my back so I could see everything. She would lean closer and pull my toes into her cleavage. I could feel the warmth and heaviness of her breasts. I wondered what color her nipples were, and stared into her mouth. I hoped I would find out in due time. I was working myself up to doing a little sucking of my own. If it worked wonders for her, why not try it myself?

It was all just so nice. And dangerous, in that shady room, with the lights off and the Venetian blinds drawn but just open enough to let in some slats of half-light. What if someone came in and found us? Could they call the police? People were terribly uptight in those days. They were really scared, I think. Wives undressed in dark closets and then snuck guiltily to their husband on the bed for some of that forbidden carnal knowing. They were scared to have impure thoughts and go to hell. Maybe someone around them could pick up on their thoughts by some weird brain radar and tell all the neighbors. It was like thought control in those black and white science fiction movies, with the mad scientist in a white coat, the girl wearing next to nothing and looking scared, and the good guy chained down with a kind of shiny salad bowl on his head with wires twirling out of it with shiny ping-pong balls dangling in all directions-- like Houdini on meatballs. How did he escape from there, save her, defeat evil, and make the world safe for the next issue? Buy your next issue of Gruesome Gals hot off the news stand every Tuesday. *Blah blah blah...*

In reality, nothing was going to happen. I could see that. I could grab my hat, my gloves, and my purse, walk out of Muriel's office, and totally deny everything. But how silly. We were totally safe. Nobody could get in. Muriel always locked and bolted the door. There was a sign outside that said *Gone To Lunch--Back At--*

and then one of those little comic clock images with two red plastic pointers (a minute hand, an hour hand) you could set to the time of return. Muriel's always said 1:30. You had to figure it meant 1:30 p.m., unless someone was nuts or a zombie and came back after midnight. Best not to be there when they came, so nothing lost.

Sometimes messenger boys and other people would come rushing up the stairs and down the wooden hallway floor outside. Muriel and I would be terrified. We'd freeze as we were, with Muriel's hands on my ass or up my skirt, or my tongue in her ear. I could feel my heart pounding in my throat. I could practically hear the blood beating in Muriel's throat--I could see her arteries leaping in the shadow of her dainty collar. It was always a false alarm. The person might leave a package or write a note and then they'd rush away as fast as they came. Sometimes we heard men's shoes, other times women's heels. Once it was a woman sobbing. Another time it was a man sobbing and thrashing his fists softly against the wall outside. Muriel was a lawyer, after all.

Sometimes, Muriel would sit on a chair beside the couch. Other times she'd sit on the edge of the couch so I could feel the firmness of her thigh through her skirt. If she was close like that, she could lean over and lay her cheek against my cheek, her face against the cotton covering my buttock. I showered for her every morning. She'd say: "You smell nice."

"You're smelling my backside."

"Yes. I smell soap. It's a nice smell. Don't tell me--you don't dab perfume on--."

"No. What ever are you talking about?" I had to laugh, muffled as my mouth lay in my folded-together palms. "Let me think...I take my shower, towel myself dry, rush around eating and drinking and starting makeup all at the same time. I'm always looking for my watch or my bracelet or my purse. I spray one shot of Night that you bought me, on my chest, and maybe I wipe my hands on my rear. That's what you smell."

She leaned close and murmured: "There is Night in your slot." I could feel her nose softly traveling across my rear, and then down the crack to where my skirt spread out over my thighs in a taut sheet. She was not yet exploring further. That would come soon. "Yes, that's what you do." She took my hand, bunching the fingers, and raised it to smell. "I smell all sorts of office things. Ink, rubber bands, paper. You are a busy girl. The perfume must have worn away from these busy fingers, but I can still smell it where you wiped them on your bare behind in the morning."

She was the kind of woman who was more likely to say 'breast' or 'behind,' where I'm just as apt to say 'tits' or 'ass.' She held my fingers to her mouth, bending low, and kissed them all over. She didn't tongue them the way she did my toes. She sniffed them and pecked kisses at them, little moist kisses as if she were putting my fingers on a bus to school. At the same time, she ran her hand up the inside of my thigh, and touched my panties at the crack. She fingered my pussy lips with a thumb and forefinger as she finished kissing my hand.

I wanted to ask her to come spend a night some time, but I never did, to my regret. We could have slept together and made love all night. We could have showered together and sponged each other's spines and asses and pussies. We could have had so much more. Maybe it was best that, like in the saying, good things come in small packages.

I'd be afraid Ronny would barge in, or the neighbors would talk. She had her kids to go home to. She was afraid to take me home for fear they would find us together. In the end, no pun there, we just kept it to our usual hour of bliss.

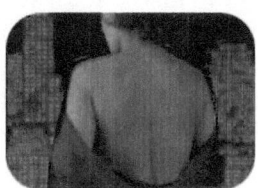

She was imaginative too. One day, she had me wear that school uniform and sit on the chair the way she liked me to. I was fully dressed, including my navy pumps, nylons, white panties, pleated skirt, white blouse, red bowtie, and blue blazer. I sat the way she wanted me to. Holding my arms behind me and around the back rest of the chair for stability, I had my feet on the seat, with my knees spread apart so she could see really good. We'd struggle together while she peeled my panties and stockings down so they lay around my ass provocatively, still around my ankles. My legs were bare for her to see. My long Mediterranean-Irish limbs were spread before her, framed by the pleated skirt.

She would sit in the chair facing me, fully dressed, with one hand up her skirt and one hand down her blouse, diddling herself slowly while she drank me in with her hungry gaze.

I liked it. "You want me to do anything?"

"No, honey. Just sit for me and look so ravishing."

In silence, I'd watch her play with herself until she got good and hot. The humidity in my jungle was also hot and high, when I touched to see. Sometimes I'd fan my pearl and we'd come together, watching each other.

Other times, I would crawl to her on my knees and suck her little lady while playing with myself. She'd lie down suddenly, graceful and quiet as a falling leaf, so her face was under me and she could watch my fingers and hear my pussy crackling with wetness.

Or she'd fall on me like a ravenous bitch in heat. She'd tongue fuck my cunt while she ripped her hand in and out of her hole so it sounded like a dog drinking, so wet was she and so fast did hand go in and out.

Sometimes she'd go real slow on me. She'd sit opposite me, while I sat showing her my school panties. She'd touch my thighs lightly under the pleated skirt, with her fingertips, which tickled and made me giggle. She'd have this serious, starved look, and cock her head to one side the way a jeweler does, looking at an emerald. Or she'd lean close and kiss my legs. Half the time, she'd get directly on the floor, on her knees, do not pass Go, and would use a finger to touch my panties. Her other hand would still be either kneading her boobs, or playing with her little lady. The finger touching me would lightly push in the significant bulge made by my thick curly bush contained in those clean white panties. Then she'd hook her fingertip around one edge, and move it to one side so she could see the curly blonde hair shining in the light from the window.

"Do you wipe it after you pee?"

"Yes," I said. "Sometimes I forget to hold myself open, and then I have to mop my pussy hair dry."

She murmured something that got choked in her throat because it made her so hot. Her fingertip would do circles in my curls. When she touched my lips underneath, it excited me. This was actually how she started becoming more intimate with me. It was one thing for her to make love to my fully clothed ass on her couch, which was usually how we started. She might run a probing hand up my thigh, and match the edge of her hand to my crack. It got to be more complicated and exciting for both of us as our barriers went down, and we dared to imagine new ways of satisfying each other.

During one of these school things on the chair--not the couch-- was the first time I felt her tongue inside me.

She pulled my white panties aside to reveal all that hair. "There is a pink squiggle in there," she said.

"I hope it's not moving," I blurted.

We laughed.

"It's just--pretty." She took her other hand out of her blouse. I glimpsed a bloated nipple the color of chocolate, all puckered and looking like it wanted those fingers to come back and knead it some more. There went our lips-nipple-twat theory, sort of, until she showed me that her eyelids along the edges were the same color-- like natural eyeliner.

She put the tips of her index fingers on my lips. First she had to clear the bush aside. I squirmed and made a little squeak when I felt her warm fingers on there. I brought my hands forward and reached down there in a kind of involuntary motion. I had big hands for a girl, but they were light and feminine anyway, with square neat fingertips my mother used to say were made for sewing or tasting puddings. I was proud I could hold a basketball with them like any boy my age.

Or such hands were for parting your lips so your lover can put her tongue inside you. I held myself open while Muriel got her mouth into my hole and licked me. I make a lot of cunt snot when I am sexed up. She did some snurfling and swallowing.

"Do I taste good?" I asked.

"Forbidden fruit--I'm in paradise."

I held my pink hole open while she gorged herself on my juice, and licked herself silly on my wet snot hole inside there. She put one hand back down her blouse to keep those two prune babies happy. Her other hand went downstairs, and I imagine she had four fingers up her snatch, pumping away, because she got all excited. I could hear her cunt snot like a milkshake mixer. I pulled my underpants off and stepped out of that tangle of stocking around my ankle. Still holding myself open, I stood over here, like a man holding his dick to take a pee, only I was holding my loose hole open while she drank from it and choked and cried with longing. She started tremoring all up and down with her orgasms. I pinned her head between my thighs while her tongue ravaged me inside. I was shaking too, as I felt those warm electric waves starting to travel outward from my pussy. My lover had a wonderful tongue. I closed my eyes and had to brace myself on the desk to keep from falling over. I pictured the tide coming in at a warm, sunny beach, one long sheet after another of quietly foamy water sliding hypnotically over sand and stones and shells and broken bits of driftwood.

I raised my face to heaven and rolled my eyes as I felt the waves and rings spreading, the way a rock drops in a pond and ripples shoot out in all directions. My thighs started twitching and fluttering. My stomach was in knots. I lowered myself deeper, holding my cunt lips open, and my hood back, so that she could find my little lady with her tongue.

She was fingering her little lady at the same time, so we came together. I heard myself, as if I were listening to some stranger, let out these hoarse breaths almost like yelps, one after the other, and I could hear Muriel crying while she drank at my crotch. I could hear her moaning as the pleasure on her clitoris became unbearable. Together, we collapsed toward the couch.

I lay on my back, with my lower half hanging off and my naked ass in the air under that pleated skirt. Muriel had her hands on the ovals of my butt cheeks, cupping them to never let go, while she burrowed her face into my pussy. How wet and open I was for her! I could feel her tongue, mopping in circles in there, and then coming out loaded with cunt goo like jelly, which her tongue then carried down an inch and pushed into the pucker of my asshole. I heard her spit like a vulgar dock worker, and use her tongue to push that into my asshole as well. I had another orgasm or two while she finger-fucked my asshole, licked my lady, and fanned herself to a few more crashing breakers.

We sailed those waves together, and lay exhausted in each other's arms, all smiles from ear to ear, as we snuggled together and clasped all our fingers entwined with each other. Her shorter, heavier thigh lay jammed between my longer, muscular thighs. I pressed my pussy down on her firm thigh, the way a man rides on a saddle, but was too numb to feel anything other than wet, and too exhausted to start a new round.

I had to go to work soon after that, feeling as if I had run for miles. I stopped in the ladies' room in the Century Building, thinking about how I'd go after sex with Ronny, but this was funny--all I got was a pee out of it. All afternoon, my cunt and asshole kept dripping that stuff Muriel had been swallowing and spitting. I was tempted to call her and ask if she was dehydrated, for laughs, but we had a firm pact never to call or see each other except in her office on my lunch hour. I'd sit on a wad of toilet tissue all afternoon, rather than leave a big wet stain on my cloth-topped office chair.

One time, while we sat side by side on the couch in her office, she did something that was so Muriel. She took my hand--my large basket ball player girl hand--and put it down her blouse. She pulled up her blouse, and undid the strap in back so her brassiere hung loosely from her boobs. She pushed my hand down and said: "Squeeze them. Play with me."

I did, and enjoyed it. I took each pruny hard erect nipple between my thumb and forefinger, and gently twisted. "Am I hurting you?"

She nodded, rolled her eyes up, and closed her lids. "Suck them."

So I held her boobs and sucked her nipples. She pulled my hand out, just as I got going good and her nipple swelled in my mouth. She put my hand against her cheek. She kissed the inside of my palm.

"Why?"

"I wanted to feel how you feel me, and then feel the hand that felt me."

I touched the tip of her nose in acknowledgement. I reached for her tits again, but she stopped me.

"Later." She rose and turned her rear end to me. She had a nice enough ass--a little wider than mine, and quite firm. "Put your hand up there."

I reached up her skirt. I worked my hand up her firm thigh, diddled her ass cheeks with my fingertips to enjoy their roundness and firmness. I palmed one ass cheek, like it was a ball. "I can see why you like doing it," I said. "You have a nice ass. It feels good."

"Put a finger in me."

I reached up with the other hand, while I laid my cheek against her rear the way she did to me. With one hand, I pulled her panties down a little, so I could stick my other index finger up there in to the ready wet and waiting wetness of her cunt.

"Now the other hole."

All wet from her pussy, I ran my fingertip backward over her crotch until I came to the pucker. I stopped, enjoying its softness on my fingertip.

"Push it in," she said tensely.

I kept lightly wiggling the tip in that soft skin. I licked my finger tip to get lots of the mouth snot on it that came when I was horny. I rubbed it until it felt coated with jelly.

"Go on, Love." She reached behind with both hands, found my hand, and pushed my finger in. Her asshole was tight around my finger. We stood like that for a good two or three minutes. There is almost no way to be more intimate with another human being than to have your finger up her asshole while you are both still dressed and close together. She had her eyes closed, enjoying it. I was thinking about her nipples--I was beginning to get horny for her, to really suck on her.

She pulled my finger out, my hand away, and brought that hand to her face. There, she pressed it against her cheek with both hands and kissed it repeatedly. "I wanted to feel the hand that was up my skirt. Only because it's your hand, and I love it so."

To prove my love, I let her put that hand in her mouth to suck on it, while I put my other hand back up her skirt and put a finger back up her asshole. I liked doing that. I pulled her down toward me, so that she sat facing me on my lap while I sat on the sofa, with my one hand in her mouth and the other hand up her skirt and a finger up her asshole. She let me. She liked it. So did I.

It was my turn to order her. With both my hands occupied, I said: "I want you to open your blouse and give me a tit to suck, right now."

Obediently, she unbuttoned herself. Her bra was already loose. She took one heavy boob in both hands and twisted herself toward me. She gave me her tit to suck. I strained my hungry mouth toward that squished plum between her cruel fingers. She forced it toward me, and I took it in my mouth. My lips melted around it, and my eyelids fluttered as I sucked. I drooled on them and sucked my own spit as if she were giving me milk.

"Suck me, baby. Go on, suck me good. Don't stop, darling baby." She licked my hand, which had been up her skirt and had poked her holes. She sucked on my finger that had been in her asshole the way I sucked on her tit.

"Is any of you left on my finger?" I asked amid mouthfuls of suck.

"Mmm," she murmured. Keeping one hand on her tit to force it into my mouth, she took my hand with her free hand, and guided it down. Her skirt had ridden totally up, exposing full, smooth thighs. Holding my hand like a paintbrush, she rubbed it against her wetly melting cunt until it was slick with her desire. Then she lifted it back to her mouth and resumed devouring the juice on my hand.

Still sucking that rich breast, I took my finger away and wiggled it in her asshole. I liked the feel of it and the cheeks on either side. I spread my other fingers, so they found her pussy hole and got wet and warm with her total surrender. Soon, we were both trembling and shaking. She held my hand to her mouth with both of her hands as we clung to each other and came, again and again, in rough waves.

All through that summer, I'd cross the street looking like one of a million pretty young girls going to lunch, with my hat and my purse, my stylish dress and my heels. Men and women would look at me, follow me with their eyes, each with their dark reasons.

In a summer dress with pretty straps and my shoulders bare, or a tight autumn business suit, drooling after the moving shadows of my long legs and tight ass, you'd never guess what kind of furry, bushy saddle I was riding on--what lay beneath my taut, near-athletic frame with its soft, darkish pink curves and rounded edges.

I had every kind of sex imaginable with my boyfriend Ronny, except the real thing. He could do anything with me that he liked, except vaginal intercourse. I enjoyed everything he did, as long as he didn't get rough. I was terrified of getting pregnant and being ruined. That made it easy to fib and say I was saving myself for Mr. Right.

Maybe I carried an extra glow. Maybe I looked like a secret agent or Mata Hari, with dangerous secrets to hide. I'd disappear into the dark corridors of the Finncroft Tower, stop in the ladies' room--for a pee and a powder--a touch-up on my lips and eyes, maybe a dab of powder on my neck and cheeks--and hurry up in the elevator to meet my girl.

That's how I began to think of Muriel, though she was older and wiser and more experienced. Usually, she'd be sitting on the couch when I came in. She'd waiting for me with her palms down on the leather on either side, as if foretasting the touch of my skin.

I liked seeing her desirous, radiant face before she even said hello. She knew I liked it, and didn't say anything. She knew just how to give me that look that made me rush to her with both hands open to take her face in my hands and kiss her hello. It takes two to tango, and I'm sure she read all sorts of messages in my look as well. We didn't need to say much by way of hello or goodbye. That's how it is between lovers.

5. Rainy Afternoon, with Tears & Touching

One day I came over, to find she was sobbing.

It was a rainy, dreary day. Gray clouds moved slowly across the window. Wind rattled water against the glass. The Venetian blinds were half open, but the slats were closed tightly, so the room was partially gloomy, partially in a silver light like a gelatin print.

Muriel sat in the big plush leather chair behind her big desk, and held a hankie over her eyes. "I can't today," she said. "Take your lunch money and go." She nodded her chin at my $3.00 lying in three crisp new bills on the front corner of her desk.

That's what we called it. A dollar for sex and two dollars for lunch--we called it lunch money. Nothing wrong with that. It was my lunch time, after all. It wasn't like whore money, although I wouldn't have minded. It would have been like playing pirates or dolls together. Just a game. I was going to talk with her about that some time. It was really like I was a kid, and she was giving me this cute little allowance, as if I were shoveling snow or mowing her lawn or raking leaves in the fall. For a dollar and lunch, I was a kept woman. That was nice.

"Maybe I can stay and keep you company. What's that matter?" I took off my hat and set my purse aside.

"Men are such bastards."

"Leo?"

She nodded.

"He dumped you?"

"I found out he's been seeing someone else. I dumped him last night."

I laughed. "But honey, you've been seeing me."

She blurted a laugh through her tears. "I see you for love, not for sex."

"Aw that's sweet." I sat on the arm rest of her chair, put my arm around her, and kissed her head. Her hair looked curly that day. She smelled of Chanel No. 19. "If this is cheating, the men in our lives can only benefit."

"Makes us far more sexy."

"Leo's the loser." How little did I realize I was about to get a taste of the same medicine.

"You're so easy to love," she said. "Not like love-love, you know, get married have babies kind of love. Just easy loving on a spring afternoon."

"Just a little girlie crush," I said. I'd been thinking about it, and about her, and what we were doing together. There were no guide books, not even specifics about what not to do, which surely would have listed every little thing we did during our daily tryst. I was good at putting things out of my mind in little boxes here and there, but I did think of her sometimes when I was alone at night in my little apartment downtown, just checking to see if my little lady button was still hard from her, for her. If it wasn't, it got hard when I thought of her.

I was usually so tired that I'd drift into a deep sleep with one finger next to my little lady, with the hood pulled back just a teeny bit. I'd try to see if it was wet, and it always got wet the minute I touched it. Did that mean it was already wet, or did I make it wet by touching it? I'd sneak my fingertip close and pounce. Sure enough, it was wet under the hood. I'd run my middle finger around the inside rim of my pussy, and hear a tiny, liquid sound, but then Ronny says I have a loose cunt. Men don't like that in a girl--makes for a numb fuck. Ronny admitted it made him hot because he thought I'd been shoving things in there to make it so loose. We both knew there was never a dick in there. I didn't use bottles or bananas on myself like some girls did, so that's just how I was made.

Back then, it was all new still, and I wondered if Muriel would be interested in touching me sometime--more than endlessly fondling my ass with my clothes on. That was before the chair thing with the school uniform. What would she think about my pelt or my loose twat? I'd look at her small, not quite pudgy hand, and I'd wonder if she would squeeze her fingertips together to make a point, and fuck me with her hand like that. It would feel nice to have her inside me, and no worries about getting knocked up.

As we sat on chairs, half facing each other and the window, she pulled me onto her lap so I straddled her with my long legs and gawky body. She squeezed me to her with both arms. I was bigger than her, but light for my young thin frame. She nestled her soggy face against my chest. "Thank you, Sarah."

I held her head in one arm and didn't know what to say. I pressed her against the flat of my chest and wondered if she'd prefer someone with a full bosom. What a silly thought.

"Can we just lie together?" she asked.

"Of course."

We lay together on that same old plush couch, facing each other, each with one arm folded under her cheek. We looked at each other. The window was half open, and it was raining audibly outside. Her office was on the 25th floor of a tall brick and concrete building with gargoyles and enamel flowers. The window sills were brick, with a little moss on them, and fine cracks in the mortar. Sometimes, a bug would crawl around, and I marveled at how it could live so far from the ground. Under the window, inside the office, a ribbed steam element produced too much heat, which smelled rubbery in the damp air, and escaped out the half-open raiser.

Muriel rested one hand on my waist. "Thank you, Sarah."

We cuddled together. "This is what I need. To hold you like a teddy bear. I hope I don't cry again."

"You can." I wiped a tear from beneath her eye with my fingertips.

"I'll give you an extra dollar for an egg cream," she said in a low voice. She held my ass and rocked me. I straddled her lap and clung to her.

"I don't need an egg cream. I enjoy being with you like this." I did, honestly. Nothing serious. It as a good way to spend lunch, and fun, getting felt up and getting a little lunch money or allowance for it. Muriel was so interesting and nice, besides. Getting an extra egg cream made me feel like a kept woman. It was all such a little midsummer afternoon's dream, these short interludes between Mr. Ferguson and his sexless dictations, his bad breath, his dandruff, his droning voice, his cadaver fingers even though he was only about 45, his fussy hard work and attention to all those painfully boring debits and credits and details. He'd been to college long ago, before the war, during the Depression. I wonder if once, long ago, he'd dreamed of playing a ukulele on some South Pacific beach while hula dancers swayed before the surf. Probably never did. Married to a woman like that fascist librarian, had six kids (how? By osmosis?) and belonged to a stamp collecting club. How fun. How not. How so very, very not.

As Muriel and I lay together, facing each other, Muriel pulled me close with her free arm. She pressed my cheek to her bosom. A palm that loved to fondle my cheeks rested against my other cheek, so warm that I scrunched my lips to one side to kiss it. "Thank you, sweetheart." She added: "The Leos and Ronnys of the world come and go. This is special. Just you and me, and nobody in the world knows."

"It's none of their damn business," I agreed.

We lay together, listening to each other breathing.

"You had tuna," I said into her cleavage.

She quaked with laughter. "I ran out to your building for a sandwich at ten. I cried so much last night that I got up late and didn't have time to boil my egg."

"You eat a boiled egg?" I asked to make conversation. Her breasts were right there, warming me like heating elements, and reminded me of big eggs. I was having a good day, feeling rested (because Ronny was out of town for a few days), but my thoughts were getting scrambled.

"Every morning, sweetie, with toast and coffee." She hugged me with both arms. "Oh my good girl." She let out the longest sigh I have ever heard--pure contentment.

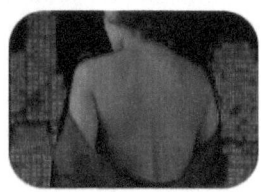

I watched goose bumps blossom all across those spheres at the touch of my nostril breath. I must have been breathing fast and hard. She felt it, because I heard her moan softly deep down. We were both still partially dressed. She snuggled toward me, by instinct more than conscious thought. I put my free hand over her waist and felt her firm, broad curve with my palm. I closed my eyes and let the feeling wash all over me, how lucky I was and how nice it felt that she was sharing herself with me and letting me do this with her.

I imagined that if I were to get my hand up her skirt, would find that her slit was as damp as mine. I wondered if she had a dainty little cunt like I wished I did, with little curly golden hairs if you had to have any hairs at all. I reflected sometimes that women had pussy hair, which is so unlike our dainty nature, to remind us we are still animals.

She wiggled a little closer, making my palm feel welcome around her buttock. I felt her skin, hot, under the wool. I felt her undies, which were as sheer and sexy as the ones she bought for me to wear. I felt the first orgasm rising in me as my abdomen and thighs began to faintly tremble and twitch. I felt a kind of sick, terrified joy rising up my throat. My heart pounded in my chest.

"Want to see them?" she whispered.

"Yes," I choked.

"I'll let you kiss them." She sat up, and removed her blouse. She turned her small, smooth back to me, and I undid her bra. For once, I could almost see that librarian with the dagger eyes peering at me through the book shelf, pursing those horrid lips. What if someone found out? What if it was all over the newspapers tomorrow? My fingers shook with fear more than desire, and with cold. My hands were so cold. I was trembling all over. It was my first experience with a woman. It was all new and so overwhelming, despite how level headed and clear sighted I usually am. This wasn't me dozing while someone touched me distantly-- this was me doing stuff while the other person waited and let me.

Muriel unfolded a fresh, fluffy blanket that she'd kept folded on a chair nearby. She draped it over her nude upper torso, so that she looked like a shadowy stranger in a tent. "Come, baby," she said, "warm up with me." Like a wing, she spread that blanket over both of us. I huddled under it, balling my fists under my chin, and lay motionless in the darkness while the air around me grew almost too hot to breathe. I could smell the fibers in the blanket, the leather in the couch, but most of all the faint essence between her breasts. She must dab a single spray of fragrance down her cleavage, before rushing out the door each morning. I became aware of her breath coming and going, rasping. She was hot for me. She had her arm over me, while her other arm was pinned beneath her.

I pushed the blanket away just enough to gain some light and fresh air. In so doing, I became aware of her pale fullness and the ripeness of those huge nipples. It was all there for me. Muriel was letting me touch her and have her. I could do anything I wanted. I could hear her breathing hard.

It was the first time I ever touched her intimately. Instinctively, I leaned close, ready to stop if she didn't let me. She waited until I had arranged myself. I snuggled closer with my legs entwined with hers. It was an electric feeling to be so close, so tight, thigh on thigh. I began kissing the tight, smooth surfaces of her boobs. Her blouse was buttoned right up to the cleavage, and her bra was formidable underneath, but her fullness swelled toward me. I undid the top two buttons. My fingers were trembling so much she had to help me. Her fingers were short, smooth, almost pudgy, and reddish in the fold joints. I hungrily licked the warm, faintly wrinkled red crotch between her tits. I could see that a man would want to fuck a woman in there, although I didn't have the bazongas to get it done on myself. I frustrated Ronny in so many ways, but I made up for it in others. He could do anything he wanted with me, as long as he didn't get rough, and as long as he didn't knock me up. Honestly, I didn't know if I could say I was a virgin or not. I couldn't say if I masturbated or not. I did what felt good, and didn't over-think things like so many people do. As long as it felt good, and nobody got hurt, and nobody found out, it was okay by me. Being young meant enjoying it while you could. Being with Muriel eased my mind because I could see that a woman with the right frame of mind could stay young for a long time.

I was 23 and Muriel was 37, a fourteen year difference. If she'd been knocked up at a very early age, she could be my mother. A creepy thought. My mother at that time was in her fifties. I'd been an afterthought. Muriel was old enough to be a young aunt who was teaching me things I needed to know. She was old enough to be wet and loose and experienced in that hothouse way, but young enough to be still so pretty and full of orchid energy. Her cleavage was a bit ruddy, as if worn from who knows what lovers and orgasms and ecstasies over the years, not to mention feeding three hungry mouths. Her kids were still very young, but past the breast milk phase.

"Did you ever suckle two babies at once?" I asked from below.

Her face hovered over me, and her hands stroked my hair. "You mean one on each side?"

I nodded.

"I don't think so. That's for women with twins. Each one usually weans before the next one comes along."

"You always had plenty of milk for them?"

"Hm-mm. That's one thing we were never short on at our house, was milk. I was built to have babies."

"Do you miss having a mouth on your nipple?"

"Sometimes."

"Is it sexy?"

"Yes." She pushed my head toward her. "Honey, shut up and suck."

I held each boob in my hands and gently but firmly sucked on her. She closed her eyes and began to moan.

"I'm onna gum," she cried in a feeble little voice.

"I'll help you," I said in-between mouthfuls of taut, pitty nipple.

She moaned again in a tiny, overcome tone. She pulled her blouse open for me and lay back with her arm dangling, letting me have my way with her big naked boobs. I played with them, sucked on them, rubbed them, lifted them. While I was sucking on one, I would lift the other to her mouth. She would suck on herself, while sliding her middle finger of one hand in and out of her panties. I could smell the heat and the cunt juice on her as her body began to quake. I laid my palm on her mother-belly, to feel the rich womb that now was my plaything.

"Take me," she whispered. "Suck me. May me 'ome."

"I want to come with you," I said. I wanted to soak up her essence, her mama-ness. That was me, the loose cunt who wanted to fuck Ronny night and day but was terrified of getting knocked up. With Muriel, something in me began to change. Maybe I was just growing up finally. I began to think more seriously on the wonders that her body held. I loved her so much. I admired who she was, and what she had to teach me. I was so grateful that she let me touch her and do anything I wanted with her.

"I'm yours, sweetheart. Take me and touch me anywhere you want." She spoke in a faint whisper, as much to herself as to me, with her eyes closed as her head lay back beside mine. "Play with me."

It is almost scary when you are so intimate with another woman, and you ask something, and she knows what you want before you say it.

I was already sucking on her nipples, but I said: "Let me suck on you. I can't get enough." I pushed or pulled somehow, gently.

Without a further word or prod from me, she rolled over on top of me. Her knees were spread apart with my waist between her thighs. Her calves rested firmly with my thighs between them. Her chest was bare, and her big tits hung over me. Her nipples stuck out at me from brown pools. Her boobs were pendulous, swaying heavily while I hung from each by my mouth. I held them in my palms, but they were bigger. She reached up and held which ever tit I was sucking, to bring the nipple closer to my mouth. She forced her tit on me and into me. She'd look as her nipple went into my mouth, and then roll her eyes up in ecstasy. From her closed eyes and pale, hypnotized look, I could see she was starting to orgasm thinking about my mouth on her nipples and my hand up her cunt. Lying on my back, I was able to make a pointy hand with my fingers together, and push the point up into her wet hole.

She started to rock her ass violently up and down, so that the couch creaked, to impale herself and fuck herself on my fingers. We came together in a chorus of wails. She spasmed on my thrashing body until she threw herself down on one side of me. I kept sucking on her, and she still pushed and held her big heavy tit up with one hand so that the nipple stayed in my mouth.

We fell asleep together like that.

When I woke up, in her arms, the clock said 1:30. I would have been in trouble except Mr. Ferguson was at his weekly client meeting, and Harriet was out at the dentist for a major filling. It was a slow day, and the other girls were goofing off as well, but I wouldn't be missed.

Muriel was snoring softly, and I enjoyed her weight partially on me. Her blouse was open, and her pale tit and huge nipple still lay there on my chest. I gazed at it, and thought about sucking it, but drifted back to sleep.

About two, we woke up and lay together French kissing and petting in a languorous way. She rose up over me again. "That was so nice."

"I like it when you dangle over me."

"I like when you suck them." She pushed first one, then the other to my mouth.

"I wish I had bigger titties."

"You will, baby. When you get milk, yours won't be perky little buttons any more. Then you'll miss them."

"Did you have small boobs when you were young?"

She nodded. "They were perky, and they stood straight out. The sag only came with the milk."

"I like milk," I said. I caressed each of her big dry tits with their generous but exhausted nipples. I kissed them over and over again, and she closed her eyes with pleasure. I spit on them to make them wet. She spit in her palm and rubbed her nipples with her mouth goo. "They get sensitive," she said. "If we do this a lot, I'll have to dip them in those egg creams you like so much."

"I like when you give them just to me."

"You can have them as often and as long as they give you joy."

We were saying things we both knew already. We repeated things we had already said. The joy was in talking sex with each other. It was nice to hear the other speaking intimately and say things she would never say to another person except a woman lover. Just the sound of our voices made each of us hot for the other.

It was time for me to leave. I kissed her quickly and rose. As I straightened my clothes, she sat up and touched my thighs. The blanket fell away. Her breasts were large and slightly flattened, with protruding nipples that had suckled three children, and pleased how many adult mouths with their generosity? Her tits were full, ample, motherly. Her nipples were like engorged prunes--erect, ready to give endless satisfaction, and receive endless sex. She held one, like a mouse, in both hands, and had me kiss its nipple. It was better than any chocolate drop in the windows at the Century Diner or gift shop. I reached over and lifted the other one. She helped me with her hands, and I kissed its hard, pruny nipple too. I sucked on it gently, the way you make the most of a sucker to make it last, while getting its taste into every bud in your mouth.

"You make me feel so much better," she said. It was the first time she ever looked needy. "I'll see you tomorrow?"

I nodded, grabbed my purse and hat, and ran out the door. She locked it from inside, half naked. I wouldn't miss tomorrow for anything in the world.

And so the days floated by, one by one, like clouds in the sky.

6. Radiator Joy--Radiant Forever

I think it was that day, or the day after, that we sat on the floor under the window, laughing and giggling like silly school girls. I had brought along two root beers from the Century Diner, which we sat there sipping from tall paper cups through striped straws.

It was one of those rare days when the light, bright sunshine of morning never seemed to quite lose its haze. The faces of skyscrapers, faced in brick or tile or marble-smooth concrete, still glowed with a soft lemony light like early morning. Their green copper and tin roofs hung around us like blankets being dried. It was a day when you were aware of trees lining the avenues, and birds soaring from one green park to the next. It wasn't a day you felt much like working--like a shot of spring fever in young and carefree bones.

There was a metal radiator of steel pipes under the window, which the building super's boys came and painted silver every fall as they got the heaters ready for winter. To do that, they had to take the heating element off with a spanner wrench to get the back with their silver paint. At that moment in question, the workmen had taken the radiator off and painted it. It looked all new and fresh and smelled like enamel. It had dried, and was ready to be put back on. It leaned against the grayish wall nearby.

Muriel giggled as she took me by the hand and led me to her desk. We were like going to get in trouble with the principal at grade school or something. She showed me a fat, stubby pencil and smiled with a conspiracy face, while making scrunchy shoulders. Together, we tiptoed back to the window and plopped down.

The blank wall had a sort of grayish, warmish-custard look. The workmen, who had gone to lunch, had brushed the dust off it, but painting it with a fresh coat of latex wasn't on the budget that year. Muriel drew a big heart on the wall in #2 pencil, repeating and overwriting the lines so the heart was good and black. This was under the window, where the radiator would cover it up. She handed me the pencil, and I made a big arrow through the heart. I drew it slowly and carefully while holding the tip of my tongue between my teeth. I drew a straight line coming in at an angle, with six lines on top for feathers, and a pointy thing coming out the bottom of the heart for an arrowhead. I handed back the pencil.

"Perfect," Muriel said. "They'll probably paint over it a year or two from now at the same time when they take the radiator off to paint it again. But you know what--whatever we write here today will be under the paint for a thousand years. Layer after layer of paint, year after year, decade after decade. We'll still be there--or however long it is before they knock the Finncroft Tower down and build some new futuristic thing in its place. We'll never know."

"Now why would anyone do that?" I wondered. Such a dainty, perfect building with old 1800s touches like a Gothic front portal and leaded glass coach lights. At one time there were two doormen in fancy uniforms, but that went out during the Depression.

"Want to be on top or bottom?" she asked.

"How do we make love?"

"Is that what we do?"

"Oh yes." I cocked my head to one side and thought about it. I really didn't want to seem pushy. I really wanted my girl to be on top. "You always give me the lunch money," I said diplomatically.

"But you make me so happy."

I thought about it. I knew what I wanted her to do. I was just hunting in my poor brain for the right way to tell her to go ahead and do it. "I'm always on the bottom, and your cheek is on your pillow."

"That's my favorite way to have you," she said. While she held the pencil in her left hand, her right hand reached out and give my arm a squeeze. "I will always remember us like that."

"So you be on top," I said. "My rear will be your pillow forever.

"And I will enjoy you that way forever." She transferred the pencil to her writing hand. In big, bold printy block letters, she wrote inside the heart, above the arrow, *Muriel*.

She handed me the pencil.

I positioned myself to do it right, because I was going to lie on her couch for a thousand years, and I wanted her to be comfortable. Carefully, in the same size dark block print letters, I wrote *Sarah* under the arrow, inside the heart. I contemplated our work. "Won't the workmen notice it? If they know you are Muriel, and they saw me coming in as they left..."

She shook her head. "Help me."

Together, we lifted the dried, freshly silvery radiator back onto its floor pipe, onto the two mounting brackets like little bicycle racks that it sat on. I grew up around a garage, and Muriel was a plumber's daughter before they got rich and she went Ivy League. We took turns with that heavy old spanner. We cranked those long, threaded bolts in. Muriel and I carried paint, brush, drop cloth, spanner, and tool box to the little foyer between her office and the outer door. When the men returned from lunch, laughing noisily and smelling of onions, farts, and beer, they saw the radiator, thought they'd already finished it, excused themselves, and closed the door as they tromped away never to be seen again.

Muriel was raised Protestant in the Midwest and was taught that only her sect knew the right path et cetera. Meanwhile, I was raised in a traditional Catholic home, fish on Fridays, confession on Saturdays, Mass every Sunday morning, and Catholic grammar school. With three kids, we were a small family. I didn't get accepted for St. Mark High (also known as High Marks) because my test scores were a little south of brilliant, but my parents sacrificed and sent me to a private school without crucifixes on every wall. I still hung out with a lot of my old girl friends from St. Mary's Grammar School, got into the usual beer chugging and singing contests--"In heaven there is no beer, that's why we drink it here, chug-a-lug, chug-a-lug..." and all the typical trouble--but not preggers. I was scared to death of getting knocked up, which is why I invented anal sex for myself starting in 12th grade. A certain Eddie got to stick his pickle in my rear end while I stuffed my fist up my twat to avoid sin. All my hand needed was bunny ears--no sooner it got scared, it dove into my hole.

Muriel was, in her own way, an adventurer and a rebel, and went to law school. Also, she defied the men in gray hats and ladies with white bonnets, and married an Irish-American cop named Joe Gallagher. She could never go home again. Anyway, the big city was more her cup of tea. She took to the city like a fish takes to water, even though it was a tough time for her. If Joe Gallagher hadn't died, things would have been easier. Certainly, for the three kids. I never met them, but she had photos of them all over her office.

By the time I came along, she said: "I was always jealous of the Catholic kids in the part of town where they lived, where I was never allowed to go. They always had such big families and stuck together, even when they were piling on and beating the crap out of each other. They had all these signs and symbols and rituals...well, need I go on...but you know what? I loved seeing the girls in their plaid skirts. They always wore their dresses an inch shorter than anyone else, even in my private school."

"I went to private school, but not Catholic," I told her as we muttered softly to each other on her couch over milk shakes. "Who cares about any of that?" We'd look into each other's eyes while sipping--eager to sip from each other's eyes. We always had so much to share and tell each other.

I would eventually take my position lying face down, with my arms crossed, while Muriel fondled my cheeks. She said my rear was poetry in motion when I walked. When I lay down for her, it spread a little and became a broad ass that she couldn't get enough of--smooth, honey-colored, soft as down, and beautifully curvy.

"I know, honey, but the point is, they were these pale, freckled girls and boys with round faces, the Irish, or blond Polish, or else they were these exotic brown sorts of children who horrified my folks."

"And I'm both."

"You are. The girls had long wavy beautiful black hair, and dark eyes. I couldn't look at their skin enough--a color sometimes as dark as forest honey, like wild gypsies. And those stick legs and knobby knees, the color of caramel or honey, with white socks and black loafers. I wanted to be like them so much. I'd stand in a store window up the block, while my mother shopped, and watch them as they played hopscotch or skip rope. They were like a tribe, with the older girls in charge and the younger girls safe, and those rough boys sweating and cursing at football nearby. They all had huge families. All I had was two sisters who my parents must have bought through a catalog from Montgomery Ward--we had nothing to say to each other. We were such a bland and ordinary family." She pulled up my dress and rubbed her hand lovingly up and down my leg. "You have a little of both."

"I'm Irish-Mediterranean," I said. "I wish I knew if it was Italian or Corsican, but it was one of the two."

"No wonder I am in love with you."

"You're just in love with my ass," I teased.

"Your rear end, in polite society."

I wiggled it for her, and she melted. She laid her face on my soft, broad honey-colored ass, and held it between her arms. "My pillow," she mooned with fluttering, crazy eyes and smile--a girl with a crush. "When I lie here like this on you, and close my eyes, it's like drifting off to sleep and having the warmest, safest, gushiest dreams."

I gave it another little wiggle, and felt the weight of her head. I reached back and gave her curly head a rub. It was so nice to know her face was right there at my most intimate spot. It might just be an old garage for Ronny to park his rod, but I couldn't think of a more perfect person to lie on it. I wanted her to have my rear end-- all hers to play with. "I want you to enjoy it."

She palmed one cheek and, without lifting her head, said in a quavering voice: "It's so warm. It gets hot when we lie here together. Makes my cheeks flush. You like when I rest my cheek on it?"

I got goose bumps and shivers all over as she gave my cheek a squeeze with her palm, right through the thin material. She snuggled her face back down on my cheek.

I whispered: "I do like it so very much."

7. Dear Rear Derriere Surprise

Muriel was two inches shorter than my 5'7", and of medium build. She was pretty, with a jazzy face, wide mouth with red lipstick, clever dark blue eyes, and long wavy brown hair. Her hair got curly on humid days--big, loose curls that stuck out like bicycle hoops in all directions and bounced when she moved her head.

A beautiful woman changes constantly, like a sunny, cloudy sky. I couldn't get enough of looking at her to capture all her many tiny moods and expressions. With age comes character. I had a long way to go, that was clear when I looked in the mirror that leaned against one wall in her office. A woman gains patina and maturity. At 37, she was still young, but I was only 23. I sometimes felt privileged to have an older woman in love with me as if we were equals. It made me older and made her younger.

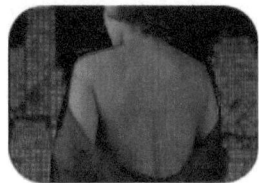

We would lie belly to belly, chest to chest, just holding each other and looking into each other's eyes. Sometimes we'd doze off. Or I'd doze off and then open my eyes to find her looking at me. Looking into her eyes was like looking into a cool, dark forest on a warm summer day, like when my brothers and I would go hiking back home.

"You let me be young," she said one day while brushing my eyebrows with her fingertip.

"I learn a lot from you," I said. "Are you combing my eyebrows?"

She murmured: "I am grooming you, like the monkeys do in the zoo."

"I've seen that," I said. "When they like each other."

"We are all just monkeys anyway."

"Speak for yourself, Bongo."

She liked to wear creamy blouses with gathered sleeves and pleated fronts done all pretty in pearl or satin buttons. Sometimes it was a collar blouse with a flouncy dark blue bowish tie floppy thing. Other times it was a lacy white collar dotted with tiny, colorful flowers. Her skirts were always tight sheaths, either dark brown or deep forest green or navy blue with matching half-heels, and always honey or navy nylons. She had a bit of a varicose problem on her legs. She either didn't mention it, or else sometimes made more of a fuss about it than she needed to. Her legs were as pale as the rest of her, which made her self-conscious of the bluish and reddish lightning strikes on her thighs and calves.

Forever, it seems, she liked for me to lie on my stomach while she touched my ass.

"You have the most perfect behind I have ever seen," she'd say. Like a happy sailboat, she'd navigate her hands inside the bay of my waist, out over the sharp point of my hips, and down the long shore of my thighs to my knees. She'd do this several times, and maybe stop to knead my strong calves a bit, or lift a foot to kiss its instep or spend slow minutes sucking my toes. She always ended up back where she started, admiring my rear.

She liked palming my rear end, for long minutes at a time. I could feel the heat in her hands, and hear her breath going in and out in short, ragged piston strokes of desire as she stared at my ass. I couldn't see her, unless I turned my head and looked out of the corner of my eye. But she'd make a little fluttering motion over my face with her hand. She'd press my head gently, firmly, to turn my gaze away. She didn't want me to look at her, because I think she was shy.

What woman in those days wasn't reserved, whether she was just shy or had something to hide. We were all furtive, like prisoners in the yard together, or in our cells. Prison books about women were big at the time. My father and brothers had a stack in the bathrooms. Those rags were torn and rumpled. I'm sure they were handled a lot. I knew what those men did in there with those magazines. I bet a lot of women read them, too. Women were starved for heat--something more than polyester and platitudes. Those crude, stupid stories told fantasies about what women did together in the shadows, under those bars, when no man or librarian could see them. It wasn't anything like what women did, but it was a rough, lush, erotic jungle owned by men. A brave woman (me) could sit and read, and imagine what it was like to bite her knuckles like that while a gorilla in a Nazi helmet drove up in a Kraut jeep while the U.S. hero blazed away with his Tommy gun. I figured out pretty soon that it was really a wild sex orgy. Take all the guns away, and put dicks in their place. In our world, it was forbidden to say Sex or Breast or Pregnant. Imagine saying Lactate. That would drive the puritans into a rage. So they had to hide the dicks and pussies and tits (barely!) and pretend it was a shooting match. Hell, the boys didn't go in that toilet to check their ammo--they went to shake their spermo.

I never went in there unless it was absolutely necessary, but when I did, I would sit and read. What do you call a pretty girl reading men's magazines in a gas station toilet? Interested--and amused.

Muriel would hold me every day, staring at my behind, touching it with wonder and delight. Soon, she became bolder and started lifting my hem to look underneath. Or she would feel up there. I could imagine: dim pink spheres, shadowy curves crossing at a Y. She'd swoon and moon.

I never wore flesh-colored girdles and those awful rubber obscene dangling hooks again in my life. I wondered if Muriel had an old cardboard box in her cellar somewhere, full of girdles gathering dust. I'm sure they made Gallagher hot to look at them. Discarding them was part of her mourning. From that, she was reborn, like, new and free.

When Muriel played with me, I was not permitted to turn around, or look up, or touch her. I could close my eyes while I felt her hands on my butt, softly gripping my soft ovals with so much desire than sometimes I could feel her fingers tremble and knew before she did when she was going to come.

She said very little at first. I can remember what she said. "Are you okay, Sarah?" and I would nod so she wouldn't worry. I was there because I was enjoying myself.

Her voice was soft, like honey, and a little mooney--she was in love, and afraid I would push her away. A clock ticked in her office, as if underwater--hard little spidery clicks of fine machinery, measuring the passage of time--pleasant time, sexy time, snicking wetly as if the jewels in its works were coated with our separate cunt juices. At first she was very tense and scared. After the first week, she loosened up and breathed hard. Then she rubbed herself and had an orgasm. I was already secretly fisting my little lady as I lay face down. I would start trembling all over myself. Between Ronny in the car most evenings, and what I did alone in my bed in the apartment, I wasn't exactly a virgin--but I had no idea.

When I was small, before my father ordered a Wringer, my mother would do laundry by hand in the basement. She would plunge a shirt or skirt into warm soapy water to wash it, rinse the soap off under a brass faucet, and then squeeze the item dry on a stone shelf so the water ran like a twirling waterfall down over the edge and into the second sink. My mother would move her upper torso backward and forward in slow rhythm as her strong arms and knotted hands manhandled a skirt or shirt. Muriel manhandled my ass slowly and gently in the same sort of motions. I'd be in a trance, smiling at the thought that Muriel was laundering me.

"You still okay, Sarah?"

"Yes."

It was so still and shadowy in that office with the lights off and the shades partially drawn. She was a lady lawyer with a limited practice in paternity cases. For her time, she was a strong and advanced woman. It never occurred to me to do more than secretarial school and hope for a good steno job until Mr. Right came along. Then I'd be in the basement with a Wringer all my own, the way everything was supposed to be.

"You don't mind?" She massaged my thighs from behind and above.

"It feels nice." I didn't orgasm at first. I was busy sleeping, for one thing. It was so pleasant to feel her massaging my thighs and butt while I floated in a delirious twilight. The Venetian blinds would sway back and forth, and bang against the window frame in little rattles and slaps. Sometimes my eyes would track a black old fly that kept buzzing in the same circles from window sill to mahogany desk to book case full of fat law books with gilded titles and back to the window again.

"You're not just saying that?"

I sighed with pleasure. "I wouldn't if it weren't true." It was restful, because sometimes I was so worn out from last night's partying that I just needed to sleep. I'd been out until 3:00 a.m. dancing with my throb Ronny, and woke with a slight hangover. Her hands and fingers felt nice as I lay with my eyes closed.

If I seem to repeat myself sometimes, it's because I put this all together from little notes. I work late at night, alone, at the kitchen table with the usual condiments and napkins before me along a blank wall full of memories, under a single yellowish light that just brightens the space on the table between my arms, and makes my face shine softly.

Please forgive my grammar sometimes. I can't let some high school English teacher proof this, for obvious reasons. I sent a copy off to some editing agency in New York, and they charged me a good amount for a manuscript that maybe nobody will ever read. I had two years of secretarial college, and I know a little about proof reading.

When I write, I use a dictionary to look up words--a little paperback I use for crossword puzzles or Scrabble when the kids come over. I try to keep it so I don't sound over my head. I write as much as I can remember on lined letter pads, like for letters I mail to friends. But this information is Top Secret. If you are reading this--well, more on that later.

She picked me because she said I had a beautiful ass. The world was full of pretty young secretaries on a lovely summer day. Our heads were as empty as the blue sky, and about as full of clouds. Don't get me wrong. I was studying for a certificate in secretarial arts, which involved taking two semesters of a foreign language and a good deal of general sciences.

You never knew where you were going to make your career, unless you got lucky and found Mr. Right. It was all so wonderful and cut and dried from there. You must be perky and poised and serious. You must be ready to work anywhere--a fish cannery, a telephone company, a machine screw company, a factory for bombers or bonbons--whatever.

Yeah, it still was far from a law degree at Harvard, but I had to buy a dictionary and learn the secrets of steno. I could also type while chewing gum--75 correct words per minute. With my wide hands and long fingers with square little tips, I was a natural.

I always had blue ink stains on my fingers--like at school, because we used fountain pen--sort of a badge of combat like Ronny's Korea ribbons (U.S. Army). I didn't know how many chews per minute while typing. I tried counting for fun a few times, on a bet with the other girls--we did have a good time at Mr. Ferguson's sometimes--but I couldn't keep count by myself.

Marcie, the mail room clerk, once elbowed me. "Hey Sparkie."

That's what they called me because Mr. Ferguson once said I light up a room. That was after he came back from lunch, lit like a Christmas tree. Earlier that morning, because I came in late and hung over and made mistakes, all the more because he got me flustered and made me cry, he was yelling he was going to fire me. Then he felt bad and brought me a candy bar from the gift shop downstairs (after lunch and three martinis).

Marcie was a red-head with freckles. She was wearing her pale mauve and yellow dress with the overlapping blocks of purple. She popped her bubble gum. "Ten chews a minute, Sparkie. I counted when you weren't looking. That's one chew every nine keystrokes, I think."

"Wow, I'm fast."

"No, you're steady--like a washing machine."

"I'm just talented and you're jealous."

"Yeah?" She rifled through the stack of envelopes stretching from her hip to her chin, from her hand to her shoulder all on one bare, freckled arm. Her tongue was orange, like her hair. The hair was natural. The tongue was from bug juice. She kept a little jar in her desk, and mixed a tall glass from the cooler every day. She said it had minerals and made her lose weight. *Yeah, I said one day, about one dram a week. You'll lose a pound a year for the rest of your life.* I always went to Marcie for a glass of orange bug juice when I had a hangover, plus two aspirin.

"How's the hangover? How's Ronny treatin' ya?"

I wrinkled up one half of my upper lip. "Don't ask."

Marcie breezed through the mail slots, sorting and distributing. "I tell ya, Sparkie, the world is fulla swell guys. Dump him and find Mr. Right."

"Easy to say. You know that, Marcie. How's Freddy treatin' ya?"

Freddy was her plug. What a bum. He'd borrow her meager millions and blow them at the track. Poor kid. He'd smack her around too, after a few drinks. Poor Marcie. What a good kid. More than once, she'd come in with a bruise or two. When I said Freddy she wrinkled her lip. "Don't ask." She swished off to deliver mail elsewhere, looking cute in that happy dress.

The office was a rolling storm of clattering typewriters, men with plans in their eyes, gals chewing gum and worried about the men and kids in their lives, and Mr. Ferguson belching as he came in from lunch. It was a dark, foreboding world, but it was simpler in many ways.

For example, penicillin had just been invented, but most people didn't really know that VD, which was common, was no longer a horrifying sentence of insanity and death. No wonder everyone was afraid of sex.

Our lives were scary, but natural. You just followed the rules blindly, and hoped for a Wringer in your basement, and a ride in your man's hot rod.

We didn't have central air or white lights, which made a building seem like an artificial underwater reef.

You just opened a window to let in sunshine and fresh air.

8. Why Muriel Seduced Sarah

I relished my freedom and enjoyed the adventure. Why did Muriel pick me, I asked her after about a week, when we broke the ice and started talking, before we started touching. She still pretended to give me little back rubs or massages, and I was starting to wish she'd do a little more. Thinking about it later, I saw how I wanted her too, but didn't realize it for the first week or two. Who ever thought of such a thing? It was enough to make you stop and think, and give that bubblegum a loud pop.

"So many pretty girls. But my heart knew, before my head knew, that it had to be you."

"So you were looking for someone? A girl?"

"No, honey. It never even occurred to me until my eyes met those sparklers of yours."

"I don't remember."

"I know. That's part of what makes you so cute."

"What was I doing?"

"Oh, I don't know. You were--."

"See?"

"I do remember the one important thing about the moment."

"Oh?"

"Yes, I came over to Ferguson's shop to deliver some files on a case. I was busy and not paying much attention. There I am, holding this stack of papers and looking around. Someone points to you and says *Leave them with her*."

"I must have been filling in for Louise. She was the receptionist. She got married and left in the Spring."

"Yes, so I walked toward you and said Excuse me. That's all it took. You were smiling at some banter with another girl and a copy boy. You were chewing gum and typing."

"Figures."

"I said *ahem* and you looked up. That's all it took. The sunlight sparkled for a second in those bright blue eyes, and that smile of yours...I nearly dropped my papers. My heart went plunk."

"I was probably hung over."

"You didn't notice. I know. For the first time in my life, I had something more than just a silly school girl crush on another woman."

"You knew right then and there?"

"Yep."

"Like falling for a member of the opposite persuasion?"

"Yep. If I didn't have you, I was going to die."

"That sounds serious."

"It was. Is."

"I feel that way about you. Do you like men, Muriel?"

"I am a widow."

"Oh my god. I'm so sorry."

"No problem, sweetie. Life must go on. I have a man on the side, yes. Leo. We've been on the outs since we met."

My idea of the unknown Leo was that it was natural for a woman to have a man in her life, like it was for a dog to have a bone, or a door to have a handle. I never even thought of him as competition, any more than the thought of Ronny ever entered my mind as I talked pals and gals with Muriel. There wasn't any connection. "Leo is not Mr. Right?"

She shook her head and smiled secretively, as if she knew something Leo didn't. "I have not met Mr. Right again, if there is such a man for me. I'm a pretty independent gal, and he'd have to tolerate a lot."

"This would be 'again'?"

She nodded. "I was married to a nice man for fourteen years. A police detective named Joe Gallagher. We had three children. Two girls and a boy. Then he was killed in a car crash during a hot pursuit, and I've been a widow for five years now. A widow with three growing kids hustling for a buck in a profession where men don't give you an inch or a break."

"Makes me feel kind of safe doing steno."

"You keep doing steno," Muriel said. "Nobody takes me seriously when I show up to argue a case. But I win some. I do some commercial law, like the case with Ferguson, but my bread and butter is divorces. I put my gal on the stand, she starts bawling, and I recite all the ways her prick has been beating her, two-timing her, comes home drunk..." She got worked up and had to stop talking.

We were quiet for a minute or two. I thought about her and Gallagher. "You were young when you started."

"Oh yes, my Joey and I, we were in each other's pants even in high school. We never told anyone, or he would have gone to jail. He was a senior 18 years old, and I was just 15, not quite 16 and legal." She laughed. "I still tell everyone I was a virgin until we got married. I was 18 and pregnant. Joey was a gentleman. He always did the right thing." Her eyes got wet.

I touched her eyelid, and looked at the salty drop on my squarish pink fingertip. "I'm still a virgin, sort of."

"Darling." She brushed a little perfumed hankie over her eyes, and kissed my forehead. "How sweet."

"I think so. I am saving myself, sort of. But--."

"Butt?" She ran her palm over my buttocks.

I nodded.

"You mean--?" Her eyes widened with shock. I mean, gen-yoo-wyne *I've seen a ghost* kind of shock with wide eyes and pale cheeks and open mouth.

"He does me in the ass, yes."

She sucked in her breath sharply. "Why didn't you tell me?" She moaned softly and squirmed, holding the hand of her pinned arm between her legs. "I love touching your tush. Now that I know..." Her eyes were large, looking at me. Her mouth failed words. "Oh my god."

"What? Who cares?" I suddenly felt like the one more mature and experienced. "Have you ever had a man take you from the rear?" I knew she hadn't, and was just rubbing it in, not to hurt her feelings. Maybe to get both of us to loosen up a bit more. Here we were, two forsaken women in a dark prison of the love that dares not say its name. You had to live near a garage to understand all that. Or maybe I read about it in Ann Landers. She was always more open than all that fear and ignorance we lived in. She'd talk about how girls did get a crush on each other, and it usually passes without fuss, which made me a little sad, like it was just silly and didn't mean anything.

Muriel was just recovering from her shock. "I've done everything within the bounds of decency, but never thought of that. Did you like it?"

I kissed each of her pale breasts. "Yes. He's pretty tame, really. We use a lot of lubrication." I laughed. "My dad owns a garage, so I know all about lubrication and oil. You can get filled with air and screwed down tight, all in fifteen minutes while you wait."

"And then you get taken for a spin," Muriel added. "Is he gentle? You mean this is going on now?"

I said, almost like pleading my case for anal intercourse: "I'm just terrified I'll get pregnant. It just seems so common sense.

Ronny would stick it in my front in a heart beat, but I pull away in a panic when he even gets close." I must have looked like a sheep. "I stick my hand--."

"Does it hurt?" Her eyes looked dreamy. She wasn't listening. Her words sounded numb.

"I make sure he puts his finger in with a lot of jelly first. He rubs it around. Then he does two fingers. With his other hand he fingers my clit up front. I squirm a lot and tell him to take it easy."

"Front or back?" She looked so shocked. Nobody ever spoke of such things. It was unimaginable. I thought I'd invented fire or something.

"Both. He starts sliding three fingers in my asshole, very gently, while he rubs me in front." I laughed. "I'm so jellied up by then I can hardly feel a thing. It's the front that's more sensitive. I like him to use one fingertip and draw rings around my butt hole. When he's hot for me, he starts drooling. He must gin up a teaspoon of spit, he's just all so hot for me. He wets his fingertip every minute or so and keeps rubbing around my little lady, pushing the hood back, massaging it on one side until it gets nice and big against his finger."

She nuzzled her lips against my ear. Her breath was hot and moist. "If I were a man, and if I were your boyfriend, I'd put my penis in your pretty rear end too." She held my head in both her hands. "If I could ever think of such a thing."

"I'd let you," I told her. "Poke me in the rear and keep it in there."

"I'd stick it right in there and spoon with you."

"You'd like that," I teased.

"I bet you like it too."

I did but I wouldn't admit it.

"What does it feel like when Ronny does it to you?"

I blurted out: "It's divine."

"Tell me, baby." She rubbed her hands over me softly.

"Not much to tell. It feels full, the way you want it to feel." I'm not too good at describing the indescribable. Ronny's hot rod slid in and out, spreading my sphincter apart. A million nerve endings tingled like birds singing on a telephone wire.

"Does it hurt?"

"Only a little. It's a nice hurt though, if you do it right. If you let a man be rough, you'll get ripped and bleed."

"Do you wish it was up your front?"

"Sure. All the time, but I've gotten to like the rear door stuff. I can play with myself while he does it, or he plays with me. Like I said, he can stick anything in my holes, as long as he doesn't get rough or hurt me. He likes that." I confided in her: "I had a boyfriend named Eddy, years ago. His father owned a drugstore, and he could steal anything he wanted, like rubbers. We did it a few times up front with rubbers, and it was okay."

"They can leak or tear," Muriel said.

"I know. I read about that in Ann Landers. After that, I was scared to death. One time, Eddy forgot the rubbers. We were petting hot and heavy, and he wanted to stick it in be so badly. I wanted him too, but it was just impossible. So I turned my virgin ass cheeks to him, and said to go easy. He was kind of disgusted at first, but when he saw how much tighter I am back there--my front is pretty loose, especially when I'm all wet--he started liking it."

"How old were you?"

"I was fifteen. We were in Catechism class." I laughed at the memory. "We called it cat-jizm. His family moved away, and I never saw him again. I bet he remembers me, or at least my butt hole."

Muriel pawed my ass cheeks while we talked. I could see she was hot for me, with what we were discussing. "I'd like to watch a man fuck you," she said. "I would die from jealousy, but I'd be in heaven already, so who cares. I could still touch your tushy while he was making jelly up front."

"I've never been with two people," I said. "I mean, at once or separately, unless we count you here and Ronny there."

"So you have been fucked here." She didn't use words like that a lot. Now she grabbed my front slot the way you picked up a pack of cigarettes. Not that I smoked. She almost crushed my lips with her fist. "Here?"

"A couple of times with Eddy, before I got wise. Last time, I was scared to death, and douched all night. I was a nervous wreck. Eddy felt terrible because he didn't get it. He thought he did something bad to me. What do any of us know when you aren't allowed to talk or even read about the really important things in life?" It was the age when police still raided homo bars like it was a giant drug bust in combat gear that made headlines and ruined lives, drove men to suicide. They'd report their names and addresses in the newspapers to be extra stupid and cruel. The police also used spies to infiltrate Planned Parenthood clinics. They'd break down their doors and raid them--just for counseling women or giving out pamphlets with life or death information. Why did people think this was normal? I always rebelled when people were cruel to each other.

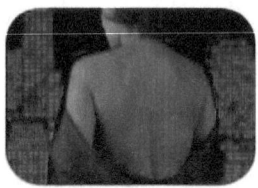

"Do you look forward to having pussy sex when you're married?"

"Ten times a day, only--."

"Only what, darling?"

"When will I ever meet Mr. Right?"

"Oh honey, every girl asks herself that."

"I'm already 23, and not a sign of him."

"That's because you are spending your time with me."

"No," I said, "with that stupid Ronny."

"A nice man will come along. You just have to be patient."

"They can be pretty mean. Eddy liked my other end, but he or Ronny would never marry a girl like me. You don't marry a girl who likes sex."

Muriel made a wistful face. "So that's your theory of marriage?"

I probably looked in the dumps. I remember looking down at my hands because I couldn't meet her eyes. Maybe because I knew in my heart I didn't really believe what I was saying. I was just discouraged. "A man marries a woman who doesn't approve of sex, so the neighbors will approve and she doesn't cheat on him. Then he goes out and finds someone like me who's easy and likes to mess around. It's the oldest story in the book."

Muriel stroked my hair slowly. "Maybe I can show you what it's like when a person loves you a whole lot, and enjoys kissing and making love with you. That's what it's called. Love."

"Wow." I was amazed. "You still believe in love?" I did too, suddenly, again. I thought about my faults--my fur, my loose, my tiny... "Like, Eddie, the boy in high school, he liked me on the other end. It wasn't just me because I was afraid to get knocked up. He said I have a loose pussy. He said fucking me was like fucking an elephant--big, loose, and wet. We were friends, but he admitted I started disgusting him. He thought, you know, I was disgusting even though he couldn't get enough and he came every time. Wasn't that sick?"

"Why did you even let him after he said something like that?"

"Because that's what I figured people would say if they knew."

"So you were disgusted about yourself?"

"Well, yes and no. I don't get disgusted with myself so easily. No, I'm a little sensitive about certain things. I've told you the three things. But I'm not going to let anyone make me feel bad about myself. I guess that's why I ignored him and we kept on going with what we did."

"And Ronny?"

"He will never marry a girl like me. He's crazy about my body, and he's okay to talk to, but he admitted it not too long ago. He wants to marry a solid gal, is how he put it. We were having one of those intense, silent sessions in the front of the car instead of banging away in the back. He finally came out and said it."

"Yes?"

"He wasn't ready to get married, but when he does, it will be a gal he can respect."

"I'll bet you cried."

"I did." It was a painful memory. I almost cried again, so humiliated and bad did I feel about myself. "He could do anything he liked, and look what I get in return. Disrespect."

She pulled me close and hugged me. "Oh, poor honey."

"You were married to a nice man?"

"Oh yes. My Joey. I waited all my life for him. We had our good years together, and three wonderful kids. Just our luck it had to end early."

I reached up and stroked her cheek. "Poor darling."

She looked far away as she rocked me, like I was one of her kids. "Joey...I'll always remember him as a young man, smiling as he comes up the driveway with a cigarette dangling from his mouth, and such a jaunty smile, and a bottle of good scotch under one arm for us to celebrate when the kids were asleep. There was always something to celebrate."

"That's the Irish in us," I said as I reached up with one fingertip and caught the tear that rolled down her cheek.

She shrugged off her feelings and dove down on me, making a big kazoo noise on my neck that left a hickey. We shrieked with laughter and held each other.

"I broke up with him a few weeks later when he left town with his folks. He could be really cruel without meaning to be. But he got me going on butt fucking. It's called bumming."

There were simply no words or concepts for two women having a little crush and petting, like with a certain two women from the 1890s I'll talk about shortly. Nobody could imagine this about women. And what was the harm? We couldn't make each other pregnant. The pilgrims and prudes running our world didn't pay much attention to women unless it had something to do with men's money or property. Then they started shrieking and waving their bibles. That's when the lynch mobs and ropes came out. Other than that, Muriel and me, we had the time of our lives in that comfy little office of hers--be it ever so humble, it was home. It was our very own secret garden, just for the two of us.

Muriel and I often lay together on her couch. We talked and talked about everything--silly things, man stuff, woman things, sexy things.

All that talk was enough to make a girl cream. But she wasn't ready to go further at that point yet. I could see that she wanted to see my bud, but wasn't ready to tell me. It was okay. We were taking our time. It was a first for each of us. I think we each knew in our hearts it would be the only time for each of us. We didn't care about anything. We lived for the moment that summer.

I did once gather my courage to sneak into the back room in the library, where they have the medical books. That old crawfish of a librarian, who smelled of sulfur from hell, she eyeballed me through those mean little glasses--*what is a young lady doing in there?*

I had to sneak a good peek in a medical book to see a picture of the inside of a cunt, to understand how it's set up. Honest, that's how ignorant I was. But what a good cause to learn it for. I was going to look at the Kinsey Report also, but that old bitch came in and stood near me, banging books around much too loudly, to make me leave. What possesses people?

I practically ran out of there, she made me feel so dirty--but she was the deviant, not me. If she woke up one day and found her cunt had disappeared, she wouldn't know what she was missing. She'd pee through her other end and not know the difference. Or if her tits turned into fuzzy dice. She still wouldn't play with them. It would serve her right.

But I digress, as Mr. Ferguson said when he was dictating and started thinking about all the footnotes in his quarterly statements and P&L reports. Or when Mrs. Ferguson called to remind him about some horrid dull party they must go to on Saturday evening. When she called, we girls could hear her voice coming out of the phone all the way down the hall.

I was trying to imagine what would happen if Muriel pulled my skirt up and my panties down and started playing with my ass for real. What was she thinking about this startling idea that I let Ronny butter up my asshole, stretch it with his fingers, and then slide his enormous cock in? It felt good to me, and I know Ronny would rock away like a piston on my nice round cheeks until he came. When Ronnie came, he was loud. I would cry out with him, because his voice got me all horny and excited, even more so than feeling that huge salami inside of me with its head like a Japanese carp. The thought of it turned me on. I felt empty or hungry, and he filled me up. With him inside me, I'd feel helpless, as if I were sitting on a pole and blowing in the wind. He'd grip my ass--not gently like Muriel, but slap his palms down hard--and slam his hard abdomen against my soft behind. We did it in his car in the park, most evenings, with the windows all fogged up and the air smelling like crotch sweat and cunt juice and cock dribble. "Ronny," I would wail, "get inside me, baby."

"Oh..." he would moan or growl, or whatever you call what comes out of a man's mouth, when he has his cock in a woman's hole and goes out of his mind with pleasure.

I often begged: "Push, Ronny. Jam it in me. Ram it up there. Come on, rock me. Harder." I'd hop up and down with my rear end on his cock to make him go harder and faster.

He used to tell me my voice made him hot when I was half out of my mind and begging. It was nice feeling my tight asshole around him, but my words were what made him go soft in the head and start trembling all over as he jerked and squirted inside me.

That's what we are here for, the way I feel when I'm heading into ecstasy--holes to put cocks in. The wetter the better. "Give it to me, Ronny. I want it up my ass good. Go on. Spread me."

He said he felt so good there between my cheeks. I thought he would never leave me because of that. No other girl would let him do that, that I knew of anyway. I'll bet, years later, he would think of me as the girl that he let get away. Honestly, I was never one of those girls who'd hang around and be bitter, and say men are assholes. I was easy, I guess, although I'd been with maybe two other boys besides Ronny, if you counted Eddy. I was easy going. I could see how men would be assholes. It's like this. There's these two cheeks, that are side by side, touching each other, but they will never be of one mind. The left cheek thinks a girl is nice to be with, easy to talk to, and a real slut in the back seat. The left cheek likes that. The other cheek wants to marry a virgin. Go figger.

I wonder if that nurse he knocked up and was forced to marry even let him see her asshole. A lot of women in those days dressed or undressed in a dark closet so their husbands couldn't see them naked. It was all in Ann Landers, which I read every day along with the funnies and a glance down the sports page and the lingerie ads. What a fool Ronny was. But we were so young and had no idea of anything.

"Get in there, Ronny, between my cheeks. Find it. Spread them apart. Open me."

He'd grunt and groan, doing me. I would wait for the goo to drip down, all that hot jelly and ass sweat not to mention the juice making my pussy hole wet with all the excitement. I would put my hand down there and get my palm wet and slippery with goo. I called it cunt snot. I would rub myself until my little lady throbbed. Too bad women can't ejaculate. My little lady would have loved to squirt all over his face.

Sometimes Ronny would just fall apart as he came, and goosh into my asshole in big squirts while his body shook and spazzed. Other times, he'd pull out just before he came. I could turn my head and get my mouth on it, just in time to get half his cock snot in my mouth and half across my cheeks. One time, I got flying jizm in my eyes and was almost blind while I swallowed in big gulps, but I was too crazy with sex to care--I busily fucked myself with four fingers bunched together--my hand cupped like a pointy scoop. With my other hand I'd hold his cock or grab his balls or stick a finger up his asshole (with all that lube around us, it went in easy).

When I fucked my open hole with my hand, I could hear my own wet slapping sounds. It made sucking sounds like a plunger, so hungry and loose and wet was my hole, gaping for more.

Yeah, I was the fun girl boys like Eddy and Ronny would never marry. One time we were both so drunk that we tried to have sex, but we couldn't so we just lay there in the back seat laughing. He had his pants down around his ankles and his dong hanging limp over the edge of the car seat. I pointed at it and couldn't stop laughing. He looked down at himself and thought it was hilarious. I had my skirt hiked up and my knees pointing away from each other. After seeing his dong like that, a big limp snail hanging in a curve, I stuck my fingers in and did myself. Not that I could feel sexy in that condition, but I was wet as ever. I'd be wet all evening, from the minute Ronny picked me up in his car to when we went to the diner. We were in the back seat, laughing, and I tried to do myself. My hand was like a blur, and the car filled with this noise like *ahhh-bladd-ibble-dibladdle   bladd-ibble-dibladdle   bladd-ibble-dibladdle.*

It was hilarious, like when you twiddled the side of your finger rapidly up and down over your lips, same sound. *Twaddle-di-twaddle-di-twattle-di-twattle-di-twattle-di-twat.*

We didn't have sex that evening, for obvious reasons. We crawled out of the back doors, me one way, him the other, and lay in the grass puking. We must have laid there for a half hour, passed out in our barf, me with my ass in the breeze and my skirt up my back, Ronny with his pants around his ankles and his dick limp like a fish.

Good thing nobody saw us. Good thing a cop didn't pinch us, or a bunch of high school kids…I was horrified later, to think about the disgrace or worse, but we were sooo lucky. We were so wasted we could have died from alcohol poisoning. Back in the car, we sat passed out like two greenish ghosts, until he could find the keys and drive me home. The keys were in the ignition, once he could find the dashboard.

I didn't miss work, though I should have. I didn't have too bad of a hangover because I got it all out of me. Ronny was sick and missed two days of work. I was still feeling half blind and sea-sick at my typewriter the next day. Try typing when the keys keep getting blurry and having babies of themselves so there's two or three of each key.

I realized then that I wanted more from life and love than what happened that night. I pretty much cut down on my partying, and also realized what a jerk Ronny was. If I was a jerk, that I could fix. If Ronny was a jerk, as he proved not long after, I don't think he was the type to fix anything like that. We moved on, and life continued. I was ready for the next step when Muriel came along.

But I digress. I loved to say that. It always reminded me of Mr. Ferguson. He was so ridiculous that he was likeable.

Unlike men, I didn't complain that I was loose down there when I was touching myself. Well, what choice did I have? When I played with myself, it felt all the more good to be so open like a big hungry mouth all wet inside and waiting.

Years later, when the hippies and the Beatles came around, and I was a married woman, I took yoga from a woman in San Francisco who was blonde but married to a Brahmin from Bombay. She had so much energy, and she sometimes mentioned sex in her drowsy, sunny classroom. The day would come when you could say words like pregnant, breast, lactate, penis, and vagina. The dictionary no longer said playing with yourself was self-pollution. All of us girls in about fifth grade sneaked to the big dictionary in an alcove at St. Mary's Grammar to look forbidden concepts up. It took me a while to figure out self-pollution, which was like "Huh?" So pollen was spread by the birds and the bees (boys when they got big) among all the flowers (us, when we got big). Pollution was the act of a flower being inseminated (another word you didn't use). So self-pollution was when a boy whopped his crank until it squirted. That was self-pollution. Guess what? Webster's didn't even dream that a girl could cream. I'll bet that huge old dictionary at St. Mary's on its wooden podium was from the 1940s or even earlier. If the nuns knew what was in it, they would have taken razors and sliced out all those certain words we budding little ladies were secretly looking up. Talk about furtive. And the conversations we'd have in the far corner of the playground!

So at this yoga class in San Francisco--there were eight or so of us housewives in our sweaty tights, doing slow cartwheels, looking for help outside the gray world in which we'd been raised. She would teach us how to gulp with the muscles our vaginal canals, to hold a man and please him as if with our fingers. Whether I had muscles down there was another question--still unanswered years later--but I tried hard.

It all came down to the fact that I had a loose, wet cunt. *Get over it, Sarah. What is, is.*

She whispered to me after class one day, "You should try letting him put it up your rear end, dear. At least it will feel tight, and he can remember what it feels like to insert in a virgin." But I was no longer an ass virgin, as we know.

Ronny would often eat me as I was getting hot. I'd spread my knees as far apart as I could. He'd push them more apart, hands pressing on the soft white flesh inside my thighs. It made my holes totally open to him. I'd help by holding my pussy lips open for him. It would get loose and wet so he could press his face in it. I was a dirty girl no boy would marry, but I wanted his cock so bad I could taste it--literally. I must have gotten at least five percent of my daily calories from his cum, of which he seemed to have gallons, like he was a fountain, that boy, the worthless shit.

He'd push his tongue deep, so he could taste the inside of my canal. It never lasted long because he'd get so wild he'd pull his wet face up and shove me roughly with his knees as he walked in close, holding his huge cock with both hands, aiming for my ready and open hole. He'd stick his tongue in my mouth, and I could taste my cunt on his teeth. I tasted pretty good, I thought, with a sort of sweet springtime fragrance.

I'd stuff one hand in my cunt desperately to stop him, and guide his gazong into my other hole barely two inches lower. As soon as he was safely in, I'd immediately collapse backward, and be lost in a series of hot, writhing orgasms--like a swirling, red, delicious dream. With my hand stuffed in my pussy, and my other hand circling one slippery finger around my clitoris, I'd get washed by orgasm after orgasm like an ocean tide coming in, wave after foamy wave. It meant having my ass up for him--oval and beautiful. My wrist would get sore from flittering myself, and my pussy would ache for the next hour or two. He'd bang away at my heavily lubricated asshole--you could hear his tight abdomen slapping on my soft woman flesh like a machine--until we both came together in a climax that was like love's agony, what the French called the little death. There was nothing left, at least for a few seconds. Maybe the heart stops beating, and starts again. Ronny would collapse over me, panting hoarsely, spent, with a quarter cup of fresh hot sperm up my ass somewhere. Later, when I used the ladies' room, it would fall out in a dollop and float in circles on the water, against the rusty-ringed porcelain of some dirty diner toilet. I'd sit, hunched forward with my skirt up and my panties down, pressing one finger against the side of my aching little pearl. I'd gush out little squirts of pee, waiting for his wad to drop out of me. We might go to a movie afterward, or sit holding each other in a diner. I wanted it out, or I'd be sitting on that wet goo all evening--a yucky feeling, not sexy at all.

9. Sexy Smiles, Secret Lovers 1893

When I was a kid, on a rainy day, my mother would allow me to climb into the attic and play with her old dolls up there. She'd bring me cookies and milk, and I had a grand old time. Sometimes I'd look through all the old family albums. A lot of them were people I didn't know. They were long gone, and you had no idea what they were smiling about. Sometimes, you'd see two men and a woman lying on the grass looking into the camera. You had to figure it was a sunny day, because they wore short sleeves, even though the photos were all black and white, or sepia.

I particularly liked this one old shabby looking album that must have been put together around 1910. It was the oldest of all the albums. Half the photos were missing--just a shred of glue or a black corner left. These largely dated back to the 1890s, through the turn of the century, maybe until 1910, judging by penciled dates in a long-ago, unknown hand. They were of a branch of our family that my parents didn't know much about.

You could see all these couples as young newly weds in the 1890s surrounded by dirt fields, then as young parents in new cities, and then as aging husband and wife sitting in a Ford Model T or watching a canvas and wood airplane landing on a grassy airstrip.

There were all these lost, long dead cousins and brothers and sisters, uncles and aunts. Some had serious faces. Others looked like they never stopped joking. There were church occasions, school occasions, funerals, birthday parties, and other celebrations of life as you'd expect.

Among them were these two women, from long ago in the 1890s, who looked out into the camera from a world of their own. Their names were lost, and I have no idea if they were distant cousins of the unknown photographer, or a brother, or who knows maybe a third woman who knew the secret of their charming smiles and poignant eyes. I never made the connection then, and only remembered that album after meeting Muriel.

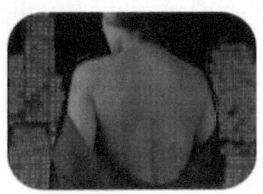

On a trip home, when I stayed in my old room overnight, I found that old album in the attic, probably exactly where I last put it down as a child of ten. I was too sensitive and secretive to ask my mother, so I took it into my room at home and lay in bed with the album. I stared at the pictures with a magnifying glass. It was hard to see under the dark yellow night-table lamp with the frilly glowing shade. The photos were mostly sepia and faded. Some were damaged. Some looked sun-washed from the instant they captured a moment in time. I studied the pictures slowly, one at a time, comparing them, trying to make sense of them.

Among all those long-gone faces and smiles and mysterious looks were two women who were the most secret and intimate of all. It was hidden in plain sight before everyone's eyes. Now, for the first time, it was all so obvious to me--not who they had been, but what they meant to each other. The knowledge hit me silently, sneaked up on me, because what else could it be? The love that dares not speak its name, only back then people hardly imagined it was possible between two white, middle class women of good family and Christian breeding and all that.

I did read somewhere that it didn't shock anyone to see two women in an intense friendship back in Victorian times. People were in denial about what these women did together. It was considered "healthy" for a young woman to practice for marriage with an older, often butch, supposedly sexless woman. They couldn't get each other pregnant, if anyone ever even thought that far. What was the harm? It kept the younger woman away from men and boys, who could do a lot of damage--expose her to sin, ruin her reputation, or get her knocked up outside of wedlock and literally destroy her life and make her a fallen woman in a real sense, shunned by her family and all who knew her. It was all still so real for me, in the 1950s, trying not to get knocked up, but it must have been really terrifying in the 1890s.

So there was S--let's call her (like Sarah), because I never did learn who she was, not even her real name, was she a Dorothy or a Camilla or a Phoebe or a Millicent or what?--a beautiful young woman in her late teens or early twenties. These were all sepia photos and fading, some with spots on them.

Actually, there were only three photos of these two.

Lord knows, I spent hours on that album. I all but fell in love with S myself. I hungered for at least one more photo of her, but three is all I got.

S was a slender young woman of about my age, 20 to 23, wearing a well-made silk blouse with ruffles down the front. All the clothes in these photos were heavily and exquisitely made, a joy to look at. S' hair was done up in the style of her age, bunched over her head, and caught in combs around the back. That left her slender, pale neck beautifully exposed--the only part of her body, except for her hands, to be seen. Her lithe, nubile waist and hips were barely disguised in a plain sack sheath (I would call it), and high-button shoes. The details were exquisite--a broach of ivory roses; a little gold watch pinned to her dress over the slender hip, with a little gold chain running to a pin on her blouse; a large cloth belt buckle, maybe velvet, hard to tell. Whatever you want to say, they made women's clothes extremely well back then.

The older woman--let's call her M, as in Muriel--was stouter, but handsome of face. The clothes were similar, except that M was more buxom. Well, how do you do, how not unlike yours truly Sarah and Muriel.

How I wished Muriel and I could hold hands and travel back in time to meet these two women. What all we could have told each other. Time is a phonograph that plays its beautiful song one time. When it's done, you just hear the little skipping and crackling sound at the end. You can never listen to it again. S and M in their day were such a melody lost in time. The song of me and Muriel was still playing strong as I pored over this album in a gloomy amber bedroom light.

In Photo #1, our young secretly in love couple stand for a studio portrait. S stands in front, showing us her side while she is half turned toward M. S is slender, which we can see from this angle. She turns her delicate, exotic face toward the camera. Compare the two faces. M, the older woman, is solid and proud as she stands behind her girlfriend--her lover. They dare not touch each other, but let's look at their hands. S is holding something in a gloved hand--looks like a prayer book. They were Catholics, but they could have been your garden variety Protestant.

We see the opposite hand of M, who is making a fist at her thigh. For all we know, they were secretly clasping fingers with their hidden hands, while the unknown Mr. Box Camera fussed under his shade cloth.

M looks possessive, like she's daring anyone to come mess with her property. She has a strong, squarish face with regular lines almost like a man. M was the matronly warden, the nun, the no-nonsense barkeep of the candy store. Hardly a nun, from that gleam in her eyes. She must have just licked her lips before pursing them for the shot.

Compared with M, my Muriel had a young pretty face. Muriel's features were narrower, longer, softer. She was sweet and fresh in an athletic way. A younger woman could be girlfriends with her--not like jailer and jail bait.

M looked like she could carry beer kegs around in a tavern. If she was a school marm, then schoolboys beware. I remembered what my father used to say about hunting, if you met up with a black bear: "They can out-run you, out-swim you, out-climb you, out-box you, and out-think you. In the end, they eat you." This woman must have been a black bear, and yet I can imagine how soft and silly and sentimental and gooey she probably was with S when they were alone and intimate. Maybe S was sometimes on top and gave the orders or the spankings or whatever.

Both women wore mannish black neckties that hung down and were tucked into their blouse under the breasts. S was flat as a forest nymph, while M had big boobs like the front of a truck--hello? Could anyone say Sarah and Muriel?

That's what the Victorians liked to see--M taking S under her wing. M was probably a spinster school teacher in public, and a barreling dyke in private. Our tender flower, S, has it all written in her eyes. Her face is slight, startled, enigmatic, doe-like--but her expression has some of that same dare-you hardness, like she's been to Antarctica and back, and fought off wild sea hogs with her canoe paddle. No knuckle biting.

What was it about that expression on S' face? She enchants me. She drew me in. I kept looking at S through my magnifying glass. What was that oddly exotic, strangely magnetic look? I stared at her face until I figured out that it was a combination of fear, guilt, and pleasure. In the first two photos, she looked as if each image caught her off guard. She always looked as if she were startled and terrified to get caught, because she loved having M up that black forbidden skirt. So that was it. She thought it must be so obvious, and yet nobody seemed to get it--but any moment they would, and her life would be over. Once you figured it out, she was so clear to read. Maybe she and M just had sex in a distant bedroom. Maybe their pussies were still vibrating and damp. Darling little S, she looked so shocked, with those big guilty eyes and that mouth slightly open which had maybe an hour earlier had a pink tongue up M's imposing bush. I could imagine how M cried for her, lay back and spread herself, pulled little S' head into her crotch, maybe held herself open while her girl loved her. I smiled at the realization. S enjoyed what she did with M, and loved the things M did to make her hot and wet. I wondered what her voice might have sounded like, a sweet sound, as she cum for M.

Just like with me and Muriel, their whole world made them lead secret lives. And their whole world ignored their secret. It was there for anyone to see if they just peeled their eyes open. Like our world, their world was cruel--and blinded by denial. Luckily.

They would have been run out of town if anyone knew, or confined to insane asylums and slowly murdered with opiates or water torture--luckily they didn't have electroshock therapy, or that operation that became famous in the 1950s--where they cut into your brain with an ice pick and removed the front lobe so you became a vegetable. Theirs was the age when Sigmund Fraud and his contemporaries still thought women couldn't really get hot and come--sexual desire in a woman was some sort of psychosis--so they cut out their clitoris to cure them, in those monstrous hospitals from hell.

These two women might have faced something like that, if 'modern medicine' reached to their empty outpost in post-frontier America. Muriel and I might have faced the ice pick. I'm just saying.

Anyway, darling little S always had that haunted look in her eyes and her slightly open, shocked mouth. Caught! Guilty! Terrified! Loving every second of what her trembling, throbbing desires made her do with that stern-looking partner in sin and crime.

S was a beauty, aside from all that.

After staring hypnotized at her stunning face with a magnifying glass, it dawned on me that one day she would be the heavy standing behind some other young daring and determined doe. There was almost something tragic in her delicate beauty. Her eyes told she and M were sinners and outcasts in a society that didn't even know it was possible for two well-bred mares to drink under the fence in forbidden pastures.

In Photo #2, we see them at a summer picnic. Way in the background, across the whole picture, is a meadow filled with big yellow sunflowers. Around the edges of the sepia picture, we see a man with a straw boater hat (flat on top, black band around) laughing as he waves a beer mug. He has a heavy, nice young blonde on his arm who is dressed from her toes to her ears, but looks like she's enjoying a beer, a romp, and a good joke in the park. In the background are children running, and picnic tables. In the center is a great big tree trunk, spreading in its leafy glory and filling the entire upper part of the picture. It's nice and shady, because S and M are not squinting or anything.

S practically sits in M's lap as they relax smugly against that huge tree, comfortable in their little world together. Same possessive, proud look on M. Same winsome, humorless expression on the enthralling Miss S.

M has harder, gloating eyes like look what I've got my tongue into.

S has this little face that a man (or woman) could lose their self in--exotic, sexy, wild, secret, wounded, dare-you.

In this photo, M sits slightly elevated on top of the tree's enormous roots with her ankle-length dress and undercoats or whatever spread out over grass, sand, dirt, and a million tiny acorns.

Sitting in her lap, leaning back against M's powerful bosom, is a snappy young S wearing a thin black cotton sweater and a thin black necktie. She is a little more cocky in this picture. There is no mistaking the look of pleasure and affection as she leans back against her lover, nor the way her lover captures her by the waist and dares us to take S away from her. S wears a starched white shirt, whose collar rises high up over her exquisite Adam's apple. Behind her, likewise, M wears a mannish necktie and a black sweater or suit jacket.

My god, these two women were dressed like men and behaving like an older man with his younger woman--and a younger woman with her older man. And nobody got it. I got it because I was living it. Muriel came over and seduced me like a huge flirt right under everyone's noses. Even I didn't get it, so silly was I. Things couldn't have changed that much in just sixty years. People turned a blind eye and thought it was good training for S to chum up with M. No matter if they held hands, kissed, mugged, or walked in the park holding hands. Might have been different if they French kissed in public, or if M spend a lot of time fondling S' ass. It was considered 'safe' for the Ms of the world to shelter and nurture the Ss of the world to train the little innocents in how to be a good wife when Mr. Right came along. In the photo, M has one hand around S' waist, while they have their other hands' all fingers entwined. Can anyone say lesbian? Their eyes in this photo were equally defiant. Can you say on a date? Can you say hot and heavy? As S looks frontally into the camera, I can see more clearly her boyish features bordering on--what was that word?--sylph. She is an exquisite creature, maybe a little shocked or resigned at her own secrets and why she can never be like the other people frolicking around them at that picnic. Muriel would fall in love with her head over heels. So would I. I'm sure that battle-axe did. Maybe one day little S would become the M to some younger S, only the culture oblivious to this type of fe-fe marriage vanished by the early 1900s. I looked it up.

In Photo #3, which is the most faded, we see S and M side by side, walking away from us down a driveway (for carriages) so bright-cold-sunny that it fades into white. The camera person has said something, and they both slow and half turn to look toward the camera. Maybe this is a year later. S looks more self-assured with a harder little smile. M has been eating her out, and she knows who she is now. At least, she is not as confused as I was when I first came to Muriel's office.

In S and M's day, it was considered healthy for a young woman to avoid impure contact with men and boys. Better to have M pawing S a little in a supposedly Platonic way, rather than a man. With the man it would be scandal. With a woman like M, it was beyond, well, comprehension and therefore innocent.

The idea was that the older woman could pet the younger woman, or kiss her, or whatever, because it never occurred to anyone that women could have sex with each other. People of the time considered it as training for a young woman in how she should act when she was married. Or, on a darker note, maybe they were cynical in that two-faced Victorian way, and winked an eye shut. They weren't dumb, those people. They were alien from us. We in the 1950s in the puritanical USA were still on the doorstep between that and this.

A young girl--an odalisque, a beautiful caged bird--would learn from the old dowager how to sit in her someday-to-be husband's lap and rest her head back against him, while he showed off like *hey look what I got here*. In fact, nobody could imagine that a woman had sexual feelings. We just undressed in the dark, lay down like good pious wives, and let our legally wedded husband and owner (nobody else!) have his way.

To avoid a confused young woman being assaulted by an unwed man, therefore, it was best to put her under the care of an old milk truck who of course had no sexual interest in men, nor did they have any interest in her, so it seemed perfect for the mentality of the age.

I looked all this stuff up years later. That was why they always had older matrons as chaperones when a male family member wasn't available to babysit in public or on trips to Europe. If a woman claimed to feel things down there, they'd surgically remove her clitoris and pronounce her cured of her morbid psychosis.

In this photo, they are linking arms and wearing full overcoats as they set out on a walk. The gravel around their high-heeled boots glistens and is covered with what looks like dead butterflies or brown leaves, so it is Fall. M is the rock, walking straight upright at a mannish angle with her left hand in her coat pocket and an umbrella visible on her right side being used like a walking stick. S is still slender and girlish. Both women have their hair up, and wear almost matching Russian style fur pillboxes on top. They look elegant and daunting as they glance over their shoulders. Their look is haughty and self-assured, and not entirely friendly. M is steady and upright, making S come to her. S is slightly tilted forward to keep her arm linked through M's, as if she's running one step behind her woman and catching up so she won't be left behind. It's an awkward moment, not at all posed, and a little motion-blurry from their waist areas down. I say waist areas because, in the style of the age, their bulky clothing disguised their figures. It was beautiful, well-tailored, and very stylish clothing--I had an eye for that.

Maybe the camera man was a jerk they knew all too well. Or maybe the camera guy was a nice guy in love with S, but S wasn't interested, and both women were ready to fall on the poor fool with teeth and claws out.

I studied that photo with my magnifying glass. Was no man gonna get between those two. If S looks like a startled sylph in the other two photos, in this one she looks more like a young wife. Maybe neither of these two women ever married men, and thus had no children, so there was nobody by the 1950s to remember who they had been--by the time I lay on my bed at my parents' house, secretly studying their mysteries, their passions, their tragedy, and their happiness. After looking for more clues in all the albums, and finding none, I reluctantly put it away--a sealed enigma for the ages, like one day Muriel and Sarah would be if there was ever a photo of us together--or just our heart behind the radiator under coats of paint.

I thought with a heavy soul about how young that child was, my age, 23, around 1893. She would have been born around 1870. How old would she be in 1953, say? Around 83, if she was still around. M was at least fifteen years older, maybe twenty, and born before the Civil War, so she must be gone by the 1950s. Who were they? What did they do with their lives? I knew enough about life to realize nothing turned out as you expect. The world ias full of surprises. This was one mystery I would never learn more about. They took their secrets with them.

I almost cried a little as I closed that old album. I felt so deeply for them, and hoped they were happy together. I hoped they treated each other kindly, and didn't argue too much.

I hoped M held her and nuzzled her and told her she loved her.

I hope S was faithful to M, and offered her sex and fun and good cheer in return. I bet she had a furry little tuft of a pussy that only M ever got to enjoy, unless there was to be a Mr. Right. Or at least a Mr. So-So. Or even some fucking wife beater who didn't deserve such a gorgeous butterfly, such a wrought and delicate work of art. But we'll never know how it turned out. I never even knew who they were. My mother, when I asked her, just shrugged and shook her head, nor did my father have a clue.

In a fairy tale, I would learn the answer, which was that they lived happily ever after. In real life, I would never know. As I put the album away in the attic, smelling the dust up there, I tried not to think that their moment was so long ago, and so long past, like the dust--so much lost, like the blooms on all those magnificent sunflowers in the field behind them. I hoped it was a fun picnic for everyone, and that they made the most of their day.

10. Sweet Changes

The day Muriel and I became more intimate happened about a week after I started going to Muriel's office on my lunch hours.

I would knock on the door, and I would hear the lock rattle about three minutes later. That was how long it took her to put down her glasses and her pen, push her notes and law books away, and walk around the desk--through her office, into the tiny foyer jammed with supplies and a coat rack, and open the door to let me in.

As time went by, on days when she was really horny or needy, or both, she'd start rattling that lock as soon as she heard my shoes banging on the wooden floor down the hall outside her office. At first, though, everything was still a little awkward.

Until this one day, she would quickly walk away after opening the door, as if she were till a little ashamed or afraid or me or of her own desires. I would enter, and lock the door for us.

She would sit in the chair by the window, waiting for me. She looked businesslike, with her legs crossed. She was a pretty woman for 37 years old, a widow with three young children, and a lot to carry on her shoulders all alone. No matter how she combed or brushed or teased her hair, she had these rings--not little ringlets but big O-shaped and Q-shaped circles of dark blonde hair.

Her hair would hang limp and straight in dry, hot weather if she hadn't worn a hat. On the other hand, it could be a crown of wild curls on a cold, rainy day or a hot, humid day. She had brown, penetrating eyes that scared me a little because she was so damn smart and sharp--and yet at times they had a little bit of a needy look. Her eyes never looked sad, even when she was overwhelmed by court cases or thinking of Joe. Mostly I liked her eyes when they seemed hungry or juicy for me--then they had a spicy way of looking at me. Her lips would get this wry, crooked, shameless look and her hands would get on me. I don't think I ever said no or pushed her away. I liked it a lot when she touched me. I wasn't just horny. I was really alone in the world, and she made me feel pretty and wanted. Strutting in fine clothes was another matter altogether.

I would peel off my gloves and put them, along with my hat and purse, on her desk in the office. I usually wore flat, round saucers with a little net hanging in the front over my eyes. I loved going to movies and wanted to be like those hot women stars. No silly, dipsy-doo Easter bonnets for me.

Behind Muriel was the window, usually a quarter to half open. Its Venetian blinds were usually either totally open to reveal a blue sky with white clouds and old skyscrapers, or closed down to the same level as the slider window was up and open. To her right was the couch where I was expected to lie face down and be quiet.

"Hi, honey," she said that day. She wore light pink lipstick, a light blue eye shadow, and a perfume that reminded me of citrus blossoms. It was the first time she ever called me by an endearment. There was a first time for everything.

I always waited for her to call the shots. I stepped sort of awkwardly toward the couch and then stopped and waited. Part of the jazz was her telling me what to do. And yours truly was a girl who didn't like that from anyone. With Muriel it was special.

She looked up at me from her chair, not quite in a crouch. She sat a little sideways, with her legs crossed and with her knees pointing away from me. She sat with her elbows together over her thighs. Her forearms were crossed, while her hands hung folded over her knees. She wore a peach dress that day with a frilly round collar and medium black buttons coming down the top in front. She wore a wide black belt with a silvery fastener over her belly. The rest of the black buttons came down her hip and thigh on one side to just above the knee. The dress ended in a flared hem just at the top of the calf.

A fan oscillated slowly back and forth. It was sunny, and on the warm side, but not beastly like on a lot of summer days. The air was a bit humid--her big curls moved each time the fan pointed at her.

I didn't know her yet. I grew afraid because of the hard look in her eyes, like I had displeased her. A hard look was like if someone's dark eyes have a little white all around, like when they are angry. I started to apologize and stammer whatever. I kneaded my fingers worriedly, and was overly aware that I had big hands for a girl--light, and delicate, with long fingers, which had squarish plain tips, and wide palms. They were really very delicate hands, girlie hands, but whenever I was in trouble as little girl I would hide them behind my back because boys made fun of me. Boys always regretted many years later that they had liked girls who turned out to be piss pots, and treated badly girls who'd become sex pots.

"Sarah," she said.

I froze inside, like when ice cubes fall inside a soda dispenser.

"You look so beautiful it makes me want to cry."

I didn't know what to say. I was relieved. All the ice went out of me.

"I am so hungry for you."

I think I stood there, still ready to apologize or be yelled at, while at the same time I was shocked and pleased. So those were hungry eyes. I smiled at her and wanted to shoot when I saw the whites of her eyes.

"Turn around slowly for me."

Basking in new confidence, I raised my forearms and turned slowly, which is hard to do gracefully on pumps.

"Be a fashion model."

I put my fists on my hips and turned slowly for her. I must have sighed out the biggest sigh you ever heard. I was so happy she wasn't mad at me.

"Come to me." Her voice sounded full, because her mouth was watering so much. She was drooling for me inside her mouth. She opened her arms for me.

"I'm too heavy for you," I said.

"No, honey," she said in a little groan like she was used to lifting heavy loads, "you are not too heavy for me. You are just right for me." She got a funny light in her eyes and added: "…Like baby bear--you are just right."

She took me on her lap and held me around my thighs, waist, and rear end. Her one hand held my big ass where my cheeks sort of hung over her thigh on that side. I have a narrow ass, but it looks wider when I sit or lie down. I used to wear my older brothers' cast offs around the house, including knee shorts. My mother would tell me she felt like she had another boy. That was before I discovered Look and fashion magazines. I held my own in school, but I put my real effort into all those part-time jobs before I grew up and moved to the city. I always spent my money on clothes, magazines, and makeup. Food and candy I could steal. Rent I had to pay. Fashion was my passion, the game of this dame.

Muriel's other arm crossed over my legs and pulled me toward her as I sat on her lap. Her face was on a level with my boobs, of which I did not have large ones. Why could I not have small hands and large tits? I sometimes thought I was put together wrong because I was the only daughter in a family with two boys and a father who were all garage mechanics. My mother was a quiet, cheerful woman who liked to cook and wash and take care of her men (oh yes, and of her daughter maybe sort of--except that a daughter was expected to help take care of the men and not be taken care of herself, just like mom). Good thing I was easy going, and my parents were really good to me, all in all. My brothers were okay too. Siblings weren't friends--they were just there all the time, part of the wallpaper. I think it all turned out okay, including *moi*. Or *mwah*.

I put my closer arm around Muriel's neck. I didn't know what to do with my other arm, so I touched her cheek with my fingers--a stroking motion. She captured my hand and pressed it against her cheek. She closed her eyes, enjoying my touch.

Impulsively, I leaned down and kissed her forehead.

She raised her mouth to kiss my lips but I laughed awkwardly. "I think I got some red lipstick on your forehead." I dabbed at it with my fingers.

"That's all I need. A woman's big red lipstick kiss on my forehead when I show up in court this afternoon." As she spoke, she held her hand to her forehead in a zero, like one of those shadow puppet hands for a bunny, with a thumb and forefinger for the head, and the other fingers for ears. But she meant a zero. Or maybe it was supposed to be hot lips.

We laughed together, which broke the ice. Normally, she would just wait until I got on the couch face down and then come, sit beside me, and start her long slow ritual of touching and kissing my fully clothed rear end.

Today was all different for some reason. It was nice, now that I understood she wanted to cuddle. I was the biggest old cuddle toy you could ever want, when I was in the right mood. I was rested and peppy that day, but relaxed. "You want to cuddle?" I asked.

"Oh yes," she said fervently. "Would it bother you?" She tightened her grip around me.

I gestured toward the couch. "Why don't we get cozy together?"

"Yes," she said.

"I'm easy." I slid off her lap--not a hard thing, since I was taller than Muriel--and walked to the couch. I kicked off my shoes along the way, as I always did. She followed me but said nothing. No instructions. So I lay down on the couch, face down, but then, before she could sit beside me, I half turned and leaned on one elbow.

I looked up at her and said: "First, I want a hug."

She let out one of those sunny, satisfied hums ("Mmmm.") and came to me with both arms open. We sat together, holding each other and sighing in total happiness for at least five minutes. I could hear the clock ticking. I could feel my heart beating solidly. I could feel her pulse fluttering and her breath coming in quick little gasps. I saw the veins in her neck throbbing rapidly. I felt lost in her. It was wonderful. I'm sure she felt the same thing, because she held me and didn't move.

I made a little conversation. "It's not about the lunch or the dollar."

"I know."

"I just like when you hold me," I said.

"Me too."

"I like it a lot."

"Me too."

She gave me a squeeze and didn't change how her arms were tightly wrapped around my neck, and her face nuzzled by my jaw. "I'm kind of lonely sometimes."

I wanted to cry. "Me too. Very."

"Now you are here with me."

I cleared my throat so I could speak. My voice came out in a silly croak. "I'm here as long as you want me."

She stared to mash me, so excited did she get. I could feel her lips on my throat. Then she stopped and murmured: "That's all you need is a big purple hickey to explain to all those nosy cows in your office. And that dypso fool Ferguson."

I giggled and held her tight, with one girly hand on her back. "We'll keep this our little secret."

"Nobody will ever know but you and I," she agreed.

That day, our age difference stopped mattering. It didn't matter that she was older and had children and was a widow. I was just a 23 year old, flat-chested secretary with a knockout figure, practically still a girl, with very little serious experience other than sex with Ronny in the back of his car while the windows were all steamed up. Later it would turn out I knew a few things she didn't, despite all her education and intelligence, and I had something to teach her about sex. For now, nothing else mattered except that we held each other and weren't alone anymore.

We became girl and girl--woman and woman--friend and friend--soon enough, also lover and lover.

We held each other for a really long time, just existing as one person, breathing together, so totally contented, and not at all alone anymore. That may have been the finest moment of my entire summer, and hers too.

She put her hands on my shoulders and her head against my chest, as if we were slow dancing, just sitting there. I moved my mouth over just a tad and kissed her hand, which was freckled and not quite plump, with a heavy gold wedding band looking too tight on her left hand. I kissed the wedding band, and she turned her hand to caress my cheek. I kissed her palm that held my cheek. Her eyes were half closed. She made that face like a lover, welcoming the other's touch in her deep sleep, and shifting with a pleasured mouth without opening her eyes. She laid her head on my shoulder with her lips near by neck.

During the long silence, while that nearby desk clock ticked loudly-- *click-clock, snick-snock* --I touched her clothing. I didn't rove my hands--I didn't dare, though I wanted to.

I touched her back, her ass, her tits. She let me do anything I wanted. I thought my heart was going to explode in my throat. I moved my hand on her boob and squeezed gently to get a feel of it, now that I knew I could touch her anywhere. She was a full-breasted woman, still very shapely despite her age and kids, but of course you'd expect a little bit stockier and heavier and fuller in places. I wanted to tell her how much I liked her long thighs, but I didn't dare yet.

I rubbed my palms up and down her hard, firm thighs, just like she touched my ass every day. I wanted to tell her how good she felt, but I was still afraid that I'd be too bold either for herself or myself. After all, this was the first time either of us had done anything like this.

She murmured happily in my arms. My fingers grew hot from running over the light woolly material of her dress, touching her and feeling her warmth. I didn't want to let her go. She hung around my shoulders like a sophomore girl at a high school dance with that handsome senior boy she always thought would never ask her for a slow dance. I caught a glimpse of her face--she had her eyes closed and a little smile--my woman was a moonstruck girl.

I almost thought she had fallen asleep with her chin on my shoulder and her face buried in my neck, as if we were slow dancing. Like a boy checking his girl, I pulled my chin back and looked at her. She opened her bright brown eyes, and looked into my eyes. She'd been wide awake the whole time, soaking me in the way a dry sponge drinks in fresh spring water. The sunlight coming in the window seemed dazzling for a moment. Or was it the look she gave me so full and close up--a look of deep affection, of desire--even of love?

11. That Bush in the Mirror

So what was Muriel thinking about what Ronny and I did? Could she picture it? Later, when we got to know each other better--when there wasn't a thing we wouldn't lie close, nose to nose, and tell each other about--I told her every little detail. How did she picture my asshole when Ronny pulled out after coming? I had no idea myself. I'd have to ask Ronny, but I wasn't sure he knew either, since he tended to have his eyes closed and be almost unconscious.

Before Muriel and I became more intimate, I was mortified wondering what she would think when she learned that I have a huge golden bush that only ends halfway between my Venus mound and navel, tapering on each side into to my Y in front, and stretching like an unbroken jungle from one hip bone to the other. I sometimes looked in the mirror while sitting in a chair with my legs up, as a girl of sixteen, and stared at myself wondering what my future Mr. Right would think. Would he like a woman with a beard like that? I suspected not, and felt mortified. And that saggy, loose pussy hole with thick, wrinkled labia, would a man like that?

I thought men would like smooth, girlish pussies that were bright pink, with dainty little hairs if you had to have hairs in the first place. Of course a girl's pussy had to be tight to give him pleasure. It was puzzling how a woman can look so sleek and curvy on the outside, especially when she takes care of herself and takes time for makeup and pretty things--and yet, underneath, she's more like a damp animal that smells and looks funny and furry.

I laughed out loud one time, sitting back in that chair before the mirror, thinking that my pussy looked like a man's bearded face. If it had big teeth it would snarl and look around for somebody to bite. Hi, ho, matey, a pirate's life is the thing for me.

I made barking sounds, like a nut, alone in my room, and fell out of my chair laughing. My mother downstairs banged on the kitchen ceiling with the mop handle, and yelled if I was all right. I opened the door a crack, stood behind it naked, cupping each of my puff pastries in one hand, and yelled that I was fine.

That was the last time I examined my pussy like that--partly because I was sad at how strange it looked, an animal thing out of a jungle, not at all dainty or feminine. But what did I know about being woman, long ago in my bedroom at home?

When I met Muriel, I had maybe slept in that house four nights--I could count on the fingers of one hand--since I left for the city at 18. Rarely, I went home for a visit on some Sunday afternoon. I was always glad to visit, and just as glad to be on the bus heading back into the city.

Thinking of how Muriel must be wondering about Ronny banging my box in back, I had this picture of my asshole pucker dewy with gray cum that smelled of the sea.

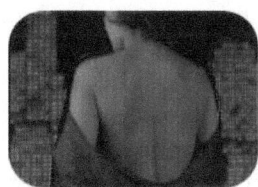

My skin color is a hint darker than Muriel's. Put it this way--if we were naked in a room together, and it was getting darker and darker in there, the first to become invisible would be Mr. Farmer, the tall, tanned, handsome Jamaican delivery man (Charley) who called on our offices twice a day. Muriel and I would linger a while longer, but I'd wink out of sight ten or twenty seconds before Muriel, whose pale skin would still shine until the stars came out to play, like in the song.

It's the Mediterranean-Irish about me. I've looked in the mirror. I used to sit on the bed or on a chair, when I was about 13, and examine myself in the big mirror over my vanity. My heels would dangle against my buttocks, and I'd hold myself this way or that. I'd hold myself open to see how pink (very) I am inside. I could already then look into my pink canal. I was worried about my labia. They were bunchy, but not ridiculously big. Other girls had longer ones--I saw them in the shower and in the locker room. A few of the girls had cunt lips that swung like wrinkled little brown peels between their thighs. I'd see those lips when they put a foot on the bench to towel each leg dry. I would have loved to touch their labia just to see what they felt like. Or even suck them, but it wasn't something you told anyone about in a private, all-white middle class school in the suburbs in the 1950s. I was terrified, as we all were, of nukes and Reds and comic books and above all, sex in all its forms.

Those were the days before people talked about 'the media'. The whole nation was like one giant vagina, from New York to San Francisco, with advertising and news people figuring out new ways to make us cum. All for the money, of course, what else? And we always fell for it.

Take for example this comic book thing, which was such a hysteria for a while back then. The people making all the money-- they spread this dark, horrifying scare that comic books were turning young people into degenerates like those supposed hard-faced women in the prisons with the love that dare not speak its name, or like demons and commies plotting in basements all around America to overthrow our system. You'd think comic books were printed in Moscow, or Hell, or Rome, to poison the innocent minds of American children. I could picture the fine print, hidden somewhere on the last page near the bottom: *Made in Heck*.

That was the fifties. The whole country was full of mothers and fathers, hunched over in their grief, while carrying stacks of comics like it was a funeral--out to the rusty oil drum in the back yard, where they were burned like witches in a pyre.

I never thought enough about any of it to take sides. The only magazine I ever subscribed to in those days was a discreet copy of Mad Magazine that used to arrive in my mailbox in a plain brown wrapper.

There was this really old man who used to live down the hall from me, who used to get a similar brown wrapper on his doorstep with his mail. He lived alone. I never learned his name. I always hurried by his bristly old carpet that said Welcome. One day I noticed mail falling from his slot, and a few pieces on the rug. On the rug among the other things was one of his plain wrappers. I assumed it was a girlie magazine, or maybe one of those science fiction magazines people were ashamed to read in public because you were supposed to not have any imagination or brains.

I overheard a neighbor lady tell another lady the old man was in the hospital and might never come back home. Someone had stepped on his mail and the brown wrapper came loose. There was a man's boot print on it. I saw the same cover of Mad Magazine under the plain brown wrapper, which lay on my kitchen table in my own little one-bedroom (the size of a closet) efficiency. How we misjudge each other when we are taught to be full of bigotry and prejudice, all for nothing. Those of us who got wise to the game can laugh today about things like the old comic book terror.

The 1950s were pretty comical overall, if you weren't listening to old Joe McCarthy on the radio everywhere you went, or angry about how fifth columnists were taking over the government and the schools. That was the atmosphere in which Muriel and I sat holding each other, kissing, just one dead bolt from being hauled away behind those bars where women looked terrified and held their knuckled fist against clenched teeth.

I wished I had taken time to talk with the old man, because I'm sure he was lonely. But he never did come back from the hospital. Soon, a family with three small children moved in. I suppose someone sent his mail back--or forwarded it to heaven, where I hoped he now lived, and had someone to talk to, or at least Mad Magazine to read.

For me, it came back to this--if we all listened to the people who so hated sex and ideas and imagination, pretty soon we'd all be like that librarian, dressed in gray clothing and tall hats--with those little round razor glasses and little yellowish rat teeth, and wrinkled lips that never stopped frowning or hating. We'd become the degenerates we were supposed to be so afraid of. I always wished I were more like Muriel, so I'd know about big ideas and think about them. Now she--there was a gal with imagination and ideas. Although--I supposed it would be fun to own a musket and shoot it off in the park and scare the ducks on the lake, if we had to wear gray hats and be afraid of our own shadows.

What was more natural than a good orgasm? It said so in that Kinsey book.

But I digress, as Mr. Ferguson said when he hollered for someone to take dictation or type a memo about how many pounds of screws are in the holding cubicles of Interplanetary Machine Inc at their East Jibrue truck yard or whatever. I never knew what any of it meant, but in night school I was learning these hieroglyphics so I could speed-write his ravings onto a steno pad and type it up all sunny, drowsy afternoon. Talk about your own typewriter putting you to sleep--by an open window, with sweet breezes floating by me--and there was my curly fur-bush still damp from Muriel's tongue and my own moisture. How I sometimes wished it could be lunch hour all afternoon.

I had this nightmare that, one afternoon after sex with Muriel, I'd go to the malt shop downstairs on my break, and forget to check my office chair. That would be just the day when I'd leave a damp spot on the cloth, and the teenage office boys would sneak in and take turns sniffing where I'd been sitting. It never happened, but I always looked at my chair and felt it whenever I got up to go somewhere, just in case. Of course it that ever happened, which I don't think it did, it would mean I'd have a damp spot on my skirt in back. I could check that by sweeping one palm over my rear-- women could be seen doing this all the time, and nobody ever wondered why. Well, there were various reasons. Either they were feeling if their panty line was in a neat line, or there was a wrinkle across their skirt from sitting too long typing up Mr. Ferguson's babblings, or they had a big moist stain back there from a mixture of their boyfriend's wad (or girlfriend's sex juice) and their own hot damp spot. There was an explanation for all things--often not something you'd find in a dictionary or a school encyclopedia. The gray hats in charge didn't allow the really important things printed or discussed anywhere that kids or people could read about them and learn how to really live in the world, which was why most people remained in the dark all their lives. It was like wearing a sock over their head and wandering around with their arms outstretched, bumping into things.

Talk about the times. I remember a beatnik joke told among red-blooded, patriotic American men in a bar, who hated comic books and commies, and anything else they were told to hate. I had gone to this bar to buy a bus ticket to visit my parents and brothers at home.

This red-blooded American guy is walking down the street one day, and he sees a beatnik. The beatnik is wearing sunglasses and a beret. *Haw haw haw* go all the red-blooded men in this bar, who are listening to this moron's story.

The beatnik is just standing there, not having a job, being a commie, and snapping his fingers in rhythm. *Haw haw haw* go all the red-blooded men in this bar.

The red-blooded real guy stops and says, "Hey asshole, get a job. Why are you snapping your fingers?" *Haw haw haw* go all the red-blooded men in this bar.

The beatnik says: "I'm chasing elephants away." And he keeps snapping his fingers. *Haw haw haw* go all the red-blooded men in this bar.

"What do you mean?" says the red-blooded guy. "I don't see an elephant for five thousand miles around." Bated breath all around...

"See?" says the beatnik. "I'm doing a great job, huh? *Haw haw haw* go all the red-blooded men in this bar as I'm standing there waiting for the bartender to ring up my twenty bucks and print out my ticket on his little machine. I never found out if there's more to this tale for Stupid People.

Then the red-blooded real guy cold-cocks the beatnik and sends him flying back to Moscow with the other commie weirdos and traitors. *Haw haw haw* go all the red-blooded men in this bar. I made that part up. I never heard what came next because I was out of that bar so fast my scarf almost got caught in the door. *Haw haw haw*, went all the red-blooded men in this bar. I could feel their eyes lusting after me, as they laughed after me while I ran out the door. They were being seductive, and it really worked. *Aawk! Ain't. Nix nada nada. Barf. Eega-beega, eega-beega*--drive it from my *mind.* I was glad to get on the bus and leave town--the sooner the better.

Next time, I bought my ticket at a bakery full of women in babushkas, who were chattering Yiddish all in a herd. I was so relieved I almost got myself a babushka to show my support, except a good Catholic girl wears a lace doily thing on her head when she goes to church, after piously going to confession on Saturday evening, and then avoiding mortal sin until receiving Communion the next morning at Mass. Which I probably should do, my mom inside me said. But I didn't want to be guilty of manslaughter if I went to confession and old Father Chalky-Breath had a heart attack when he heard what I had to tell him--about the forsaken prison babes and the love that dare not speak its name, not to mention Ronny's *zazeetch* up my poop shute.

Oh say can you see, can anyone tell me--what makes people hate any one so much, whom they don't even know--whether it's a beatnik, or an elephant, or a forsaken woman? I mean, what harm have any of those three done to them? But my real question is: at the same time, why do they print these cheap magazines with forsaken women in short skirts for men to beat off in garage toilets over, when they'd just as soon lynch them? Do they lynch first and beat their meat later, or is it the other way around? I may not be the brightest penny on the bus, but I'm a genius compared to these red-blooded folks whose thinking is so correct (what little there is).

Okay, yeah, it pissed me off that Muriel and I couldn't go hand in hand down to the park, sit on a bench, feed the pigeons, and moon a little together on a sweet sunny day. We had to hide our little summer love that meant so much to both of us, like it was something insane or dirty. At least those strapped-in, neck-tie babes from the 1890s could grin and look smug while they were hiding their lust in plain sight for everyone to see--and not have a clue what was going on.

12. French Kiss, Tongue Fuck

Next time I saw Muriel, she was still thinking about the fact that I let Ronny take me in the behind. "Aren't you afraid some of the semen will run down and get in anyway?"

"I douche each time, just to be sure. I go through vinegar at several bottles a week. I probably have salad in my pussy." I liked how she said semen. I would probably say jiz. That was the younger generation for you, Jack Kerouac and all. A lot of us thought about being beatniks, even if we didn't dare. You know-- *Snap! Snap! Snap!*--there go the pachyderms, back to Africa.

"I want a closer look at you one day," she said, meaning *sans culottes*. I believe that's French for birthday suit.

I admitted, for the first time, out loud: "I want to see you too." I didn't really know if I did nor not. It was just something to say. But then again, maybe I meant it. Yes, that must be it.

She turned beet red and looked away. "I want to see everything."

"You mean with my clothes off."

"Yes." She was red as a tomato, and looking away.

I rose and started to unbutton my dress, but I got scared and sat back down. "You can touch me," I said. "I won't charge extra." I was actually pretty bold. "Think of it as a free donut--the whole is yours, so eat all you want." I put my fingers over my mouth. Had I said too much?

"The hole is mine?" She laughed.

I relaxed and laughed too. Locker room humor, or garage humor like I learned it around the men at home, is not for ladies' ears.

"My little sweetheart." She always called me little, when the only thing little about me were my tits, and they were too tiny. She leaned close, with her mouth open and her eyes flickering half-closed, and started French kissing me. I was startled at her passion, and started to back away. But then I liked it and wrapped my long arms around her.

My mother used to say I would grow into my paws one day, but I never really did. I've always had wide, squarish hands for a girl, but light and feminine, with long dainty fingers. I was always the kind of girl who had neat little square fingertips and short nails (I played basketball and field hockey) but I liked red or pink nail polish as well. I was a stylish dresser, like a talent I had. I was never a clothes bitch, and I could shoot hoops or score at field hockey, or give Ronny train rides in my caboose, but I was still a girlie girl when it counted.

With those hands, I held Muriel close to me and stroked the back of her head and her shoulder blades as she passionately roamed her tongue around my mouth. On the first contact, as I was startled, I almost opened my mouth to shriek, but just as quickly I liked it and let her stick her tongue all around. My own tongue was kind of shy and crept around hers, demurely rubbing against it, and then lying still to be woman-handled by her tongue. It was one of those moments where I just let her take me, completely. I was her girl. It was so nice. I held her head close to me, with my palm and my pink nails against her hair.

Her tongue got bold and rough, thrusting into my mouth. She went deep, in strokes like her tongue was a dick. She gripped my jaws with her fingertips--I nearly asked her to stop at first--but I couldn't get enough of how she fucked me with her tongue.

Not that I didn't fight back and pull her to me roughly. I tongued back to get more of her. My tongue fighting with her tongue made it all twice as intense. Before I knew it, she was coming. She had pulled up her forest green skirt that was part of her fancy outfit for a courtroom hearing. She pushed aside her sheer panties, and inserted first one, then two, then three fingers into her wet cunt. I could hear sucking sounds as she thrust her body up and down on her fingers. Her dick-tongue descended in and out of my mouth as if it was about to come. Funny, to think of a woman's tongue getting hard and then squirting cum all over the place or down the other woman's throat, choking her (me).

When she did cum, as her body jack-knifed and rippled all over, her tongue thrust into my mouth and throat all the more. She jerked up and down on me, in fits and spasms, letting out groans and yelps. It was really like a man fucking me and coming, the way she pounded her body against mine. Her whole body trembled violently in my arms. I was still just in the petting stage, but she went all the way and blew her wad. She threw one leg loosely half-over my legs to get her pussy closer to mine while she pumped herself with her fingers. Her head was over my face, fucking up and down with that wild, powerful tongue--her hair coming loose and flying, her breath coming in tiny shrieks, her ass in the air while I lay underneath her facing up for a change--until my tongue, flicking around her tongue, grew numb and tired. I lay back and gave, and

she jammed her tongue repeatedly into the back of my mouth. For a
moment I felt as if I were taking Ronnie's slick eel in me as he shot
a load. I gagged and choked, pushing her away. She collapsed at
my side, still holding me, still twitching from that mighty orgasm.
"Oh honey, you don't know how much I needed that. Stroke me,
baby."

"Show me what you want."

She took my hand and guided it to her snatch. "Very lightly.
I'm so sensitive I could scream if I had any breath left. Go on,
baby, I want to feel your little fingers inside me. Don't worry, if
they get wet, I'll lick them clean and dry them on my panties."

I don't have little fingers or little anything--except cotton
candy nipples on my flat chest--but she was cute. I caught a
glimpse down there. Her pussy was lightly haired with fine dark
curls. Her Venus mound was pale and full. It looked very inviting. I
wanted to lick it, but that day wasn't the time yet.

I let her guide my fingers to the hole in the bush where her sex
still poked out like a raw little carrot nib. We kissed languidly while
I walked my fingers around. It was the first time I touched another
woman's genitals. I had plenty of experience touching myself, so it
wasn't a whole big surprise. Especially since I had seen those pages
in the library before Hitlerette came goose-stepping in and chased
me out with all her book slamming and text burning.

I couldn't resist. I must have looked so funny, or my face had a
funny expression because Muriel laughed out loud as I raised my
fingers to my nose to smell her wetness, and then liked my fingers
to see what she tasted like. Her cunt tasted a lot like my own. It was
a clean ocean smell. I knew my own intimately from touching
myself and licking my fingertips to keep them wet; or when Ronnie
had my smell on his hands after finger fucking me in the car, and he
held his fingers up for me to lick myself off of him while I played
with his dick. Sometimes I'd take turns licking his hands and the
little spurts that came out of the hole in his dick when he was really
close to coming.

There, in her office, Muriel's hand lay limply over her hole, as
her fingers loosely guided my wrist and hand. My fingers had a life
of their own. I touched her little lady, which made her squirm.
"Easy, darling. Oh god I'm so sensitive now." She pressed her
thighs together and snuffled behind my ear.

Here was a woman that had three kids and been fucked with a
man's dick right up that wise old cunt more times than I had days in

my adult life. I loved to think about how much experience that pussy of hers had--it had reason to be loose, not like my virgin pipe. Hers was just as wet and pink and full of desire as mine. "Easy, just touch. Lightly. Don't rub. Oh my god. Yes, put your fingers in there. It's so good. Where did you learn to do that, girl?" She crawled up a bit and put her mouth over mine, the way a man gets on a woman, and tongue-kissed me hard like I was her chick. I was hot for her, and pulled her down on me the way I'd pull Ronny down with both arms. I still had my fingers up her hole, but I had my knees apart the way a girl does when she opens her thighs wide for her boy to fuck her. My hand moved like a blur in her open twat. Muriel had her hand in me just as quick, and we quaked and groaned as we came together. She was on top of me like a young buck, the way her full tight ass jerked at me in quick swinging motions as if she was a man fucking me. I wished I had a mirror or a camera to see it from different angles, but I could barely see anything. My eyes were fluttering half closed, and my mouth was open as I cried and shouted and sobbed for her to so totally take me like she was going to drill right through me and end up in China.

13. Kept Woman--Dollar Sex

It all started so quietly. At first, Muriel took me to lunch a few times. We became friends in a kind of strange way, with our age difference, and little in common. We said little, and didn't need to. We both just felt nice being together. Ronny worked across town and never had time to visit me for lunch, so I was all alone. I didn't know he was fucking a nurse uptown while I was playing with Muriel. So maybe it served me right. But it wasn't the same, at least the way I saw it later when I knew the score and thought back on everything.

What could I do? On a sunny day, sit on a park bench with a bag lunch, and finish with an apple or an ice cream? You can only watch pigeons and men's crotches for so long, or stare at women's tits, out of idle curiosity, to see whether they bounce--if at all, given the advanced technology back then for keeping women from jiggling.

They made this bra nicknamed the bomber bra, which had the same kind of ribbing as the nose cones of heavy bombers. We girls were looking at an ad buried in the back of Mr. Ferguson's office newspaper one day, and laughing about it. I guess it meant the red-blooded women of America were going to symbolically atom bomb Russia every time they walked out of the house, or went to that bar to collect their drunken beatnik-bashers off the floor. There should have been War Department posters with pictures of brassieres instead of bombers. Marcie put it best: "That looks soooo uncomfortable. What's the idea? Are we into pain and suffering now? I'll have to call Freddy so he can come over with his whip."

After two visits bringing papers or taking files back to Mr. Ferguson, Muriel asked me to come to her office for peaches and yoghurt one noon. She had me sit by the window and we made small talk. I was fairly street wise and knew something was up. I could feel it coming.

The truth is--if I didn't want it, I wouldn't have gone there. The fact that she paid for my lunch and gave me a little dollar extra (for an egg cream, she'd say) was nice too. I liked the money, but just as much I liked the feeling of being paid.

Maybe people wouldn't understand. It made me feel wanted. It made me feel pretty. It made me feel that someone was willing to give me little presents just to have my company. How's that different from taking flowers or chocolate from a boy?

Dumb as I was, it took me a while to realize she was seducing me. Imagine if she had been a 37 year old man. That wouldn't be so bad if he was nice looking, and treated me well, and had money. Nobody would say anything much. So why not a woman?

I did have a good laugh to myself, in the privacy of my bed in my apartment, when I realized this woman was behaving like a man, seducing me. I fell for it, just like a girl falls for it coming from a clever man. It also occurred to me that I was double-timing Ronny, but with a woman? Did that count? It never occurred to me, to be honest. I was enjoying myself and who'd ever imagine it?

It was my little secret. This older woman was hot for me, and was seducing me. She made me feel like a whore, in a good way. It was all a game, like playing dolls or doctor. The way a woman sometimes likes to feel submissive and owned on a good day. I wanted to surrender sometimes, and be her property. Other time, I felt I owned her.

We took turns, I guess.

The dollar did it.

It was all she could really afford, I knew that. She was so sweet. I understood her end, too. She wanted to take care of me. She wanted to make love to my ass, and hold me like a hamster in her hand, and coo over me, blow in her hands to fluff my fur.

I enjoyed the little fantasy of being her pet. I wanted to be cuddled--because in truth, not that I understood it, being a tough girl as I was, I was pretty damn lonely, and Muriel's love was like sunshine on my bruise.

I had this slick blue-ink pen I liked, and this pad of neat phone notes I never got to use because telephone messages were the receptionist's job. Sometimes I wrote little notes to myself, with my thoughts on them, like *If I get screwed on my lunch hour, am I a lunch whore?* Or *If Muriel eats me at lunch time, am I her luncheon meat?* I'd rip my notes in a million shreds and throw them away so nobody could find them and read them.

Yes, she was getting to be important in my life, but I wouldn't let it take over. I lived alone, far from home, but evenings were all about steno school, or about Ronny and sex and drinking and dancing. I lived my life in slices of time, never thinking much more than an hour ahead, like any other young person. I wasn't going to become one of those babes in the garage toilet, in gray prison uniforms, under the shadows of bars.

On my way home, after it got dark, I'd look up at the Finncroft Tower to see if her window was lit up on the 20th floor.

Sometimes it was one of the bright little rectangles, but she was probably still away at court.

Or it might be dark, meaning she was driving home to be with her children. She sent me away at one, and the nanny away at six, and she'd be with her kids. She lived her life in whatever slices were right for her.

In my heart, I knew I was just one of her slices. I wasn't sure if I wanted it to be more. I didn't want to spoil it, because it was so perfect.

But there was always that deep ache of uncertainty too.

Sometimes, on a cold evening, I'd step out of the Century Building on my way to the bus stop. Halfway down the block, under twinkling stars in the last clear, inky-blue light, I'd stop a minute and put my coat collar up. I'd squint up there at the Finncroft Tower, with the chilly wind blowing around me, and wish.

Pinching my collar with one gloved hand, and holding my purse under my other arm, I'd always sigh, and feel this tug at my heart, looking up at her window.

With leaves blowing around my ankles and my fancy pumps, I'd turn and stride on down to the bus stop with nothing but my thoughts. Some stranger, driving by casually and lost in his own thoughts, might spot the shadow of my perfect ass moving in that twilight of perfume and display window lights, and wonder about me.

Neon and bars might slide by him, smells of steak and cigarettes, making crazy patterns on my steadily moving form. Women would always notice me, either for my figure, or my stylish clothes and my youth.Maybe I seemed like a mystery lady, and that guy would idly lust after my secrets. I would never tell.

I'm sure he'd forget me halfway down the next block and a shade closer to nightfall.

14. Dream of Mario & Muriel

I had a dream of Mario and Muriel one night.

I was asleep, all alone, in the single bed in my little apartment across town, with traffic noise murmuring outside like ocean tides coming and going. All around me, across on my walls and ceiling, street lights and neons shone unmoving, as did the lines of the Venetian blinds, but moving car headlights made roving patterns.

Like a ghost walking in the fog of dreams, I took the narrow little elevator down to the lobby of the Century Building.

I stopped in the chrome and glass diner for a vanilla milk shake. The round scoop of ice cream floating on top reminded me of Muriel's boobs or pale ass. I was wearing my summer dress that men and women could practically see through, the white one with red and yellow flowers. As I sat over my milk shake on the diner bar stool, people walking past stopped to tell me I was sweet. I felt warm inside.

In a rush, I sucked on my straws with mouth puckered and cheeks dimpled. I pushed the heavy glass aside and left a nickel tip. I walked past the gift shop with its greenish plate glass, its knick-nacks and cards. The front entrance had a fine mosaic tile floor and chrome pillars.

I walked out onto the busy sidewalk. It was a hot day, and the sun sparkled on the silica in the concrete. The air smelled of tar and tobacco and coffee and perfume. Men in hats and suits walked by. Women in tight outfits strode by on high heels and under saucer hats. People really dressed nice and had manners in those days, for all that many of them were so neutered. Many of them were as sexed up as I was, but didn't know it. I'm sure I wasn't the only one with a hot little secret making my bush soggy.

I strode across the busy street in my nylons and high heels. I had a matching purse, and velvety gloves that went up a lot past my wrist. I flaunted the bracelet on my wrist, my nice watch, and my fine gold filigree necklace with a rhinestone pendant that glittered in the sun. I wore lush red lipstick and all the things that made me feel pretty.

As I crossed the street, I dodged among huge cars with fins and spaceship lights. The red light lenses on the fins in back stuck out like glowing bomber brassieres. It was there all around us, hidden in plain sight like those two lover-gals of 1893, and you either saw it or you didn't. Those cars were all one big, unspoken wet dream with those matching chrome boobs sticking out in front, and men grinning as they drove them. Girlie sitting happily beside him--she and the car were all part of his huge cock fantasy that he didn't realize he was having. I only realized it myself because being with Muriel made me so sensitive and hazy that sex was like a keen aura all around me, all day long, not just in her office.

I walked into the cool, dark lobby of the Finncroft Tower. It always smelled so nice there, mostly of books and paper, and always the perfume of all those women behaving like passive flowers and waiting for the bee to come sting her. The walls were of wood inlay, the floors tiled. On one wall was an embedded bronze plaque with an image of a Greek goddess holding a leafy branch to cover her loose gown and half-open tit job--*City's First in Architecture 1919 A.D.* like anyone really was going to mistake the Finncroft Building for 1919 B.C. I mean give me a rest. I took out my bubble gum and stuck in a wad on the goddess' crotch. I smacked my lips in my dream, wishing I still had my bubble gum. You do things in a dream that you have no control over, even things you don't want to do.

You haven't lived until you've tasted vanilla milk shake and bubble gum together-- sparkling in a young woman's fresh, saucy mouth.

I took the little wrought iron elevator up to the 20th floor and got out. I walked along the narrow hallways with their milk-glass office doors, all heavy dark oak, with brass knobs. My heels rang on worn wooden floors.

I didn't knock. In a dream, you never knew how you got from one place to another. All I knew was that, when I was inside, I locked the door and bolted it behind me. Then I turned around to see who stood there. I was surprised to see it wasn't Muriel, but a man named Mario who could have passed as her twin.

Shimmering fog...Or was it Muriel who stood waiting for me? If it was Muriel, she was dressed like a man. She wore a dark brown suit with wide lapels, a merlot tie that spread over a starchy white shirt, and baggy trousers whose cuffs curled over brown, laced shoes. Her hair was slicked back and shiny. That made her pretty face look almost masculine, but you would never mistake the soft lines of her jaws and lips, the tall cheeks and forehead, the buffed cheekbones, the full sweet lips, for those of a man. Her eyes sparkled, brown and wicked, but oh so funny. Her mouth was slightly open, and I could see a pink tongue in its shadows, like it was waiting for a milkshake to smother it. Her lips had that saucy, knowing twist like a sexy sneer, but just as much hungry and helpless, and she knew it. I could be a bitch, say no, and have her in tears in a second--but I wasn't that kind of girl. I was easy, like a long drowsy summer afternoon.

*Sleepy fog...*No, his name was Mario. He was full in the shoulders, or was that his boobs--I couldn't tell under the suit. And what was a man doing, wearing slashes of dark red lipstick? He stood with his hands in his pockets, jiggling his body and his coins slightly to assert his authority in the quiet, half-dark room. A light summer breeze ached in the Venetian blinds. I imagined the suit must be hot on him.

He watched me. As he did so, he unbuttoned his fly and slipped the fingers of one hand inside. I imagined he must have felt his cock getting hard. I wondered what it felt like to touch your hard cock if you are a man. I knew what that cock felt like--in my hands, in my mouth, on my tongue, and up my rear--when I touched it as a woman did. But how did it feel if you were the man with the cock? Did a man feel waves of golden hunger ripple all through his body, the way orgasms traveled through a woman?

I held my purse under one arm as I stood before him. I had a sharp young hip cocked up on one side, daring him. I stood under the shade of my rakishly tilted saucer hat, the white one with the black rim all around, and the silky bowtie knot on one side. "What's on the menu for you?"

"Stand there while I play with myself a little bit."

I stood there as told, while he moved his hands around in those baggy pants. They were nice pants, rich material, good cut. "Are we going to have sex?"

"When I say so, yes."

When my ankles grew tired, I stepped out of my shoes. He was a little shorter than me, and now we were almost the same height, only I was still a little taller.

"I like a tall woman," Mario said. Shorter men are always hot for taller women. He had a thick, heavy feminine voice, like a crooner.

I set my purse aside on a steel filing cabinet, on which a gray steel fan oscillated with zigzag blades whirling silently. I plucked my gloves off, one by one. It was hot in that room, and I thought he would never stop looking at me or playing with himself.

I took off my jacket, and fluffed my blouse. It felt good to feel air through there. My armpits were wet with sweat.

"Take off your clothes," Mario said as he removed his jacket. His armpits looked wet also, making his white shirt look blue as starch melted.

"I want to smell you first." I walked up to him on bare feet and leaned my nose close to his armpit. I inhaled the scents of sweat, starch, and manly soap. "You smell nice," I said. He smelled like a bear underneath, warm and rank. It repulsed me, but made me tingle and jingle.

He pushed my shoulder with two fingers. "Go back. Take your clothes off. Do as I say."

His voice was authoritative, and I obeyed. I crossed the dusty, sunny wooden floor in long, deliberately slow strides on stocking feet. I felt my socks scrunch with each turn of the ball of each foot. I could feel his eyes raking me up an down. Let him starve for me, I thought. Let him eat his heart out. Let him feel his crank getting hard and bursting in his hand. If he wants me, I'll be at his feet in a puddle. But he can beg a little bit too. I turned and looked at him as if he were trash.

His gaze never wavered. His hand kept swiveling in his fly.

I unbuttoned my blouse without too much hurry, nor too much delay.

He rhythmically stroked inside his pants now--not turning like he was limp, but stroking like it stood out straight--while I unbuttoned my blouse so it hung loose around me. I unbuttoned my skirt and let it drop to the wooden floor. I kicked it lightly aside.

"The panties," he said, stroking himself gently in machine motions.

I started to take my panties off. I hooked my thumbs in them and turned left and right. I oscillated like the fan, like a stripper, though I've never been inside one of those places where only men go and women like me (as I was at that moment) get paid to entertain them. That gave me an idea. "Am I stripping for you? Are you going to pay me?" I said it in my Jane Russell voice, except she had big boobs.

He took out his wallet and counted out three single dollar bills. He laid them on the edge of the desk in a ray of sunlight. "If they look a little damp," he said, "it's because I'm sweating.'

"From looking at me?"

"It's a hot summer day." He shrugged. "You do make me hot, bitch."

I slowly peeled off my blouse and laid it on the filing cabinet with my purse.

"Bitch," he repeated, stretching it out to sound demeaning.

I peeled off my gloves and put them there. I was his bitch.

He kept stroking himself and watching me. His eyes had a hungry glint. He licked his lips. "That looks like a training bra," he said.

I looked down in shame at the poor little white bra cups. Wasn't it enough that I was his bitch?

"Take it off."

Reluctantly, I reached back and fumbled at the clasps. They came loose. The bra fell to the floor. I crossed my arms and cupped my titties.

"Let me see them."

I shook my head.

"Let me see them." Mario kept making those motions in his pants.

I slowly dropped my hands to my side. There I was again--a tall, gangly girl with long limbs, narrowing boy hips, big hands, and a flat belly rippling with muscles. I wasn't skinny though. My body was padded with little this and that of roundness at all its corners and turns. My curves weren't full, but they were long.

"What size are those breasts?" Mario asked.

"They never get any bigger," I said in shame. "I've been wearing the same bra size since I was a kid in high school."

I raised my hands and placed my thumbs and forefingers at the beginning of the swellings along the lower rims of my titties. "My nipples are pink puffies," I offered, as if that made them more attractive. Actually, I thought they were pretty nice. And they weren't so bad. I looked all this up, like a worry wart. I wasn't what you'd call a full-breasted Tanner V. I was Tanner IV, which is the stage just before it, when the breast becomes a sort of barely noticeable platform (the almost flat chest). The aureole gets wider (that's the pink or brown puddle around the nipple) and the papilla (that's the nipple or mouthpiece) shoots out like a little stem on an apple. And of course I couldn't have normal tits, oh no. I had to have a flat chest, shallow boobs, and instead of regular aureoles and papillas, each of my pancakes had on top a cream puff thing that stuck out like a pink cotton ball. That's when your nipple and aureole are almost the same thing. When I got horny, they looked sort of bluish and swollen. "Would you like to suck on them?"

"What for?" He laughed, still gyrating his hand. "There is no milk in a little titty like that."

"I thought you might enjoy sucking them. You could spit on them."

He laughed, but his eyes had a horny look, and the hand kept moving.

"Wet them with your spit. I'll spit too. We'll both spit until it runs down my belly."

He licked his lips, pondering that idea.

"I'll let you touch my pussy and rub cunt juice on my nipples. You'd like licking that off. You could slurp it. I could masturbate for you and keep dripping more cunt juice on my nipples."

"They look very sweet," he admitted. "I could suck on them gently."

"I would enjoy that."

"Do you play with them?"

I pretended to sound outraged, but weakly. "What do you mean?"

"You do masturbate, don't you?"

"What ever do you mean?"

"Play with yourself. Put your fingers in your pussy and make it wet. Doesn't it feel good? Look, like I'm doing now."

"Oh yes, that feels good. Yes, I play with my nipples while I do that."

"Good. Then do it for me right now."

"But sir--."

"But what?"

"Nothing," I said sullenly. I stepped from one foot to the other and back. Standing there before him, I felt hypnotized by the rhythm of his hand moving in his pants. Slowly, I rubbed my fingers across my nipples. They stiffened, and I felt a shudder throughout my body.

He watched in fascination. So he did find these poor, wretched little things sexy.

I held my left titty in my left hand, the way you hold a peach. With my right hand, I reached across and played with the nipple. I squeezed it gently for him to see. It bounced back and swelled out full. I repeated the process with the other side, reversing holds.

"Play with your cunt," he said.

"No."

"Why not?"

"I don't want you to see."

"See what?"

"What's down there."

"Go on, we've all seen pussies before."

Hesitantly, I hooked my thumbs over the elastic of my panties, and pulled them down. There was a mirror leaning against the wall nearby. I saw everything as my panties slid down. My young limbs were naked. My Irish-Corsican skin glowed like mysterious forest honey with freckles.

"Oh," he said, staring at my crotch. "That is a thick carpet."

Mortified, I almost pulled my panties back up. "Surely you don't want to look at me." What a mess--I had this loose hole, this bristly rug, these wide hands (though they were delicate and girlish), and these flat tits with cotton candy for nipples.

"No no," he said, "please. Continue."

Blushing, I dropped the panties to my ankles and stepped out of them. We both stood staring at my bush--a thick, curly jungle of honey hair. I have a blonde bush like a rug. It's not dainty. It's like a pirate beard.

"Can you find your hole in there when you need to pee?" he asked sarcastically.

"I have a nice hole," I said. "I play with it at night in bed by myself."

"And in the car, when Ronny pokes you up the ass," he said.

"Yes, I stuff my cunt with my hand while he does me. I don't want to get pregnant. I'm scared."

"Does he like it?"

"Oh, yes," I said. "At first he didn't want to, but I told him if he wants to come, that's the only hole he can stick his huge rod in. Or find some other girl."

"But you like his big rod."

"Oh yes, a girl loves a hard rod with a big head on it. It's so ugly that it's beautiful."

"You're not scared?"

"Not anymore, as long as he keeps it out of my pussy."

"I have something here that you'll like."

"I'll bet you do. That's why I like coming over to see you."

"This won't hurt. Are you curious?"

"Oh yes, I'm very curious."

"Are you wet?"

I touched myself with four fingertips. "Yes, I'm dripping wet. I squirted a little pee, but it's mostly pussy juice. Oh please, let me see."

He continued rotating his hand in his fly. "Come closer."

On bare feet, I walked forward. I kept those four fingers on my little lady's bonnet, and my other arm across my small breasts.

"You want to play?"

"Oh yes."

"Get on the floor."

"Like this?" I knelt.

"Lie down so I can see into your bush."

I lay back on my long, agile frame, on the dirty wooden floor, and reached for my ankles with wide, soft girl hands. I lay on my back with my foot soles pointing to the ceiling. It seemed funny, and I giggled.

I glanced over at the mirror. The backs of my thighs rose up, all creamy and sunny. Below, I saw the shadow of my butt hole, and the trees of the jungle coming through the valley from my front, as if they were looking for that hole of mine in back. I was showing him everything. It is the most submissive thing a girl can do, when she really wants the man to take her like a street dog-- when she gives herself to him totally.

He was interested. "Spread."

I held my thighs, propped them on my hands with my elbows on the floor, and let him look at my furry pelt. "Can you see?"

He nodded. "The light is shining through your curly meadow. You have a pretty pussy inside there."

"It's all for you," I said. "All yours."

He sat down on the floor, keeping one hand on his crotch in his pants. He sat a bit sideways, fully dressed in that suit. He held his other palm on the floor, with his legs pointing away, but he twisted his torso toward me. One trousered knee was pulled up close to his chin. His other trousered leg stuck straight away at an angle in the sun beams striking down from the window. His shoe laces were tied in butterfly knots. They hung down in the bright light. His wrist kept turning, and his hand played in his pants.

"Am I pretty?" I asked--meaning between my legs. I could feel a breeze cooling my asshole and blowing over my pussy. It was a dream. We had all the time in the world. The room was like a huge coppery machine all around us, a vast shadowy clockworks that had stopped ticking in this timeless moment.

"You have wrinkled, fleshy lips," he said in a low voice like a sexy woman's. "That's okay. Your pussy is long from top to bottom, and crinkly like the rim of a dark red spice torte."

"I wonder if you'd like to taste it."

"I want to eat it with my eyes first."

"You take a long time looking at things."

"I know how to enjoy the good things in life."

"Teach me."

"Just lie still and obey me."

I pretended to pout. "You treat me like I'm a child."

He shook his head. "No, you are a woman. You are my girlfriend."

I felt a goosh of sweet sex and relief all through my insides, as if someone had opened a bedroom window wide to let in the full sun on a wonderful summer's day. I almost cried, so happy was I. "Oh, thank you. I'll try to be good."

"I'll show you how to be good."

"Please, I'll do anything you say, as long as you're not rough and I don't get pregnant--and nobody must find out what we are doing in this little room."

"Don't worry, we'd both be ruined if anyone caught us together."

"Kind of like playing doctor," I said.

He laughed. "Yeah, right. Two adults playing doctor on their lunch hour. That would make headlines all around town. We'd have to change our names and move to South America."

"Like Juan and Juanita?" I asked, as my fingertip sought my little lady. She was getting swollen and achy, but was still hiding under her hood. When she got really hot, she'd turn purple and stick her head out.

"More like Señor Coffee Bean and his Hot Little Crock." He diddled his cock and balls behind his fly. "Or Cock and Cuntita."

"I'm glad you said I am your girlfriend. Now I don't have to wonder anymore what to call what we are doing."

"There isn't really a name for it, because it's forbidden fruit."

"Mister Banana and his Peach," I offered. "Hey, why am I naked and letting you see all my shameful secrets, and you're still fully dressed and beating your meat looking at me?"

"Because that's how it must be," he said cruelly and matter of factly. "Calling you girlfriend covers all the forbidden possibilities. It's forbidden for you to be my girlfriend, but nobody will know."

"It feels good, so I'll do whatever you want. Even if it's forbidden. And if I want something, will you do it?"

He nodded with reluctant generosity. I could see he was getting a little red around the face, and worked up. His hand never stopped stroking inside his pants. "I'll do what you ask, but you have to do what I say first."

"Oh, you say and I ask?"

"If you're going to be my girl, that's how it has to be."

"You want it that way? It will give you pleasure and make you hard?"

"It will make you eat you and drink you, My Life."

"Did you say My Wife?"

"Yes, My Wife." He stared at my crotch with hungry eyes, while gasping as he stroked his rod. "As long as you give me that."

"It's a deal. Will you lick me?"

"I'm still looking."

"Will you at least sniff me a little? I smell nice."

"Hmm." He leaned forward on his elbow so his face was near my pussy. I could feel his breath on my labia, so close were his lips to mine. He made a satisfied sound. "I hadn't expected you would smell so good."

"How do I smell?"

"Divine, like the sea."

"I wash every day."

"Do you wipe the washcloth in your rear, and other little shady spots?"

"My warm washcloth is a sunny delight. I love rubbing in all of my shady spots that nobody except you must ever be allowed to see."

He nuzzled closer. "Why don't you open the door for me so I can look inside." I could feel his breath going put-put on my pussy lips. I tingled.

I obliged by spreading my lips apart. With my index finger, I checked my little lady. She was hard as a button under her hood, and slick as snot.

Mario took my ass in his palms and put his face on my hole. First he licked my little lady and made me sigh with pleasure. Then he licked my little pee hole that sticks out in the middle like a wrinkly bump with a hole in it, like a man has his head, and the hole in its top.

I shuddered. "I had no idea that feels so nice."

"Maybe later you can pee for me," he said, coming up for air.

"I'll be glad to show you, or pee on your face, or anything you like. If it makes you hot, it makes me horny just to think about. Want me to pee in your mouth?"

He resumed licking my pee hole and the salty little area around it, all full of sensitive nerve endings. "All in due time."

I was in another world. "That feels so nice. I had no idea. Can you feel the hole with the tip of your tongue?"

"Yes," he said, "it's salty where you pee."

"Lick it clean for me."

He licked.

"Stick your tongue in the big hole."

He looked up. "The hole where a man's dick goes?"

"Only after I'm married and ready to have kids."

"My tongue is like a dick, but it won't ruin you."

"Stick it in." I must have sounded dreamy. "I like things that go in my hole but don't scare me or make me knocked up."

I felt his tongue thrusting into my vaginal canal. He had a big tongue, a wide one. It felt nice as it forced its way in. I raised my pussy and pushed against his face to make his tongue reach deeper inside me. I hoped my furry rug wouldn't scare him or suffocate him. A little force from both of us, as he thrust down and I pressed up, and we made it all good.

He pushed my thighs back further. I held my legs toward me with my soft wide girl hands, so that my knees were under my chin, and my butt end rose further up. He licked my asshole. "You like that?"

"Hmm," I said. "I do. I wash every day, just for you, and it's very clean. I make sure it smells nice for Ronny, so he can shove his big fish in there. Is it nice for you too?"

"Hmm," he said as he rimmed my asshole. "I don't smell no stinkin' fish in your pussy. Your pussy smells and tastes like cotton candy and spit. I could lick it all day long." I felt his big tongue pressing my sphincter open as he rimmed me. "I love your beautiful ass above everything else."

"You feel so nice inside me." I pressed my ass up against him so his tongue would be deeper. I held my butt cheeks lightly apart for him so he could get his tongue in me more easily.

He took his tongue out of my anus and substituted two fingers side by side. That felt even better, spreading me as he turned them one way and the other. "I have something to show you."

"Take it out of your pants," I gasped. "I can't wait any longer."

He rose onto his feet and unbuckled his belt. I touched my little lady eagerly while I stared up at his crotch. The trousers fell in a loose pile around his ankles. He did a little dance, stepping out of his shoes and kicking shoes and trousers aside. He peeled off one sock and the other, tossing them aside. His feet were small and pink, like a woman's. All the while, I looked at his baby blue boxer shorts and the bulge in front.

"Are you ready?" he said.

I could only nod while I held my pussy lips apart with one hand, and rapidly stroked myself with my other fingers flat.

"Get up."

I rose, standing nakedly in the middle of the floor. I shielded my puffy nipples with one arm, and put the other soft girl hand over my snatch.

"Let me look at you."

He walked around me, inspecting. As he passed behind me, he slapped one ass cheek so it stung. It was a loud, glancing smack that hurt.

"Ow, you mother fucker."

"That's it, get angry." He smacked me loudly again, and I saw stars.

"My ass cheeks are both burning like they are on fire."

"Good, bitch. I'll put the fire out."

He spit on my ass, about half a dozen times while I waited. He rubbed his mouth snot in with his fingers. He made me bend my head down and spit in his hands. It felt good. He slapped me again. I only stung a little.

"Get down where you were."

I let go of my chest and beaver, and sat down on the floor. I sat with my hands flat on the floor either side for balance, and my legs bent outward with my knees up. It was a submissive, waiting position. I waited eagerly for him, eyeballing his shorts.

He pushed down on his boxers. What emerged was not a man's cock and balls ringed with black pubic hair. Instead, it was a strap-on dildo the color of red liquorice, looking good enough to eat, certainly to suck.

"Oh," I said, "is that cherry flavored?"

"No, silly, you are the cherry. This is the prong that's going to pop your cherry."

"If you can find a cherry, you can pop it."

Somehow, I had known all along. The good thing was it couldn't make me pregnant. My stomach did somersaults in joy and anticipation, because I was about to get a good, thorough, forceful vaginal fuck. Oh god I hadn't realized how much I wanted to get a big rubber rod up my vaginal canal, spreading me in all directions, making me ache yet making it all better at the same time.

He read the hunger and desire in my eyes as he held that red dong.

"Take everything off," I said to him while stroking myself rapidly. I lay back on the wooden floor. Already I could feel the first spasms running through my legs and my torso, as if I had rubber bands in me and somebody was playing music on them. My pussy already felt full in anticipation, and trembled in rapid shudders while I waited to be filled. My athletic, muscular stomach tightened, flat as a drum with ligaments rippling across it as I kept both hands busy below my Venus mound. I gave the orders now. "Come here."

He stepped closer, until he was straddling my face. Looking straight up, I could see that there was an opening in the straps that ran under his crotch. The dildo was attached around the waist and had a buckle on each thigh. He squatted down on me like a woman about to pee. His ass got wide as he squatted over me.

We needed a minute or so to get it right. I raised my mouth, with my tongue sticking out obscenely as far as it would go. He moved his feet and ankles until his bush was directly on my mouth. I lay back and touched the leather straps with my tongue. "Spread," I said. My turn to say. I kept fanning my clit as I stared at his folds and holes behind the leather straps.

Obligingly, he reached down with both hands between his legs and tried to pull the straps apart, but they were jammed in. I freed one hand and slapped his ass. You could hear the crack all over the room. He held himself open with both hands, while I got one finger in there to push one strap aside. Under those straps was a pale, pudgy Venus mound. I saw dark, individual curly hairs. He had a vagina with bigger lips than mine. I poked it with my finger, and it was like checking a turkey to see if it's cooked. His lips parted moistly. The chocolaty-edged labia separated, revealing a pretty pink cunt. I could see it was already glistening with anticipation.

"Yes," he wailed in a soprano voice, "shove your tongue in here."

I used both hands, palming his wide ass, to pull him down closer so the leather rested across my lips. I stuck my tongue through the straps and flicked it back and forth in his hole. He squatted a half inch lower so I could run my tongue around his bud. He groaned like a woman when I forced the tip of my tongue under the edge of the hood and pushed it back so the pulsing little purple boner was exposed and its ultra-sensitive shaft surrendered to my tongue tip. I had found his weakest spot and took advantage of him terribly, flicking my tip back and forth on that tender shaft, coated in juice as it was, while he groaned above me and couldn't get enough of me tormenting him with his own overwhelming pleasure.

I looked up and saw that he'd taken his shirt off. He had big tits like a woman, with prune-colored puddles on their bulging ends. His nipples were erect like chocolate pencil erasers, each with a milk hole in the top. Now, hungrily, he held first one, then the other, to his mouth and sucked on himself. I had meant to guide his hand to my own pussy, but I didn't want to spoil his ecstasy. I would have time to suck on his nipples as long as I wanted later. With my tongue in charge inside his helplessly exposed hole, I could turn my attention to my own soggy, wanting doggie. On the way down, however, my hands strayed all over his beautiful ass. I now understood his endless hunger for my ass. I couldn't hold the broad ovals of his ass close enough or long enough. My palms weren't wide enough, nor my fingers long enough, to hold it all in one wonderful grasp. My own pussy could wait. I used one finger to trace the line from those straps under the dildo, backward to the little slit of his asshole nestled in that shady little valley.

I wondered what his asshole really looked like. So, putting a finger in his pussy and continuing to stroke his button, I slid down about six inches until the ovals of his broad ass shadowed my face.

A shaft of sunlight was spearing in through the window. It bounced off the dusty, raw dark oak floor boards and shone up in to the valley between his holes, and the crack of his ass.

I reached up with my free index finger to touch that little slit that was hidden there, so demure and pert and simple. I played with it, studying it. If he raised one thigh, or squatted so it stretched and spread, it became a wide, puckered hole. If he kept his butt cheeks even, and his legs slightly apart, his asshole looked more like a cute little slit.

I partly pulled him down and partly raised my face up so I could tongue that little slit. It opened easily for me, at least as far as the sphincter band. I heard pleasured new sounds coming from above as my index fingers played with his two most sensitive spots. There were other, inner spots of a different tune, that I would explore later. For now, I had him helpless so he squatted over me like a girl peeing. Groaning loudly, he gripped his tits in both pudgy fists so that it looked as if he were squeezing those wide, gnarly prunes and making them ooze out between his fingers. I couldn't wait to get my mouth on them. Right now, it was important to keep him going on that path. I had him in my hand, and he was helpless. He moaned in dry, bawling and sobbing sounds as I fucked him to orgasm. I could feel ripples traveling through his broad ass. I could see that belly, which was a little loose and floppy from having three children, rippling with cum jolts as the power and the pain ripped through his body. I was electrocuting him with pleasure. I was tormenting him with his own pleasure and desire. He cried out loudly, like a man who was drinking water but unable to quench his passion or thirst.

"Sarah!" he cried out in a lost voice. "Sarah!"

I raised my head like a drowning woman. My lips swam toward his. I rose up and held him in my arms like a child, leaving one hand below to finish the little death. I wrapped one strong thigh around his waist in a judo hold as he quaked and shook and trembled through dry tears--eyes closed, blinded by ecstasy as his tongue quavered and whimpered in his open pink mouth. He palmed my cheek with one helpless, loving hand.

I was his, and he was mine.

"My sweet love," I whispered in his ear, and stroked his curly hair. "I have you, baby. I have you. You can cum in my arms. I'll hold you. I've got you." So on and on I murmured comfort to my lover during the long, shaking orgasm with closed eyes and open mouth. His mouth looked as if he were screaming silently there in my arms while I held him.

During those delirious and delicious minutes he came, again and again, until he fell to one side and lay on the floor--still crying dry sobs. His butt was tilted to one side like a shipwreck, with one thigh tucked underneath and the other thigh exposed to the air along with his round ass crack and his firm butt cheeks and the tender little hairs curled in the folds between his thighs. Seeing his rear end exposed to me, a new passion and urgency took possession of me. I was relentless, like a cow goring a bull. On my knees, I walked forward and shoved against his thighs with my face, seeking the depths of that crack and its holes. I slapped my palms loudly down on his broad oval cheeks, two or three times, each time making him cry out in pain and ecstasy. I had my tongue buried deep in his asshole, obscenely and greedily, when he finally tapped out and said "I can't take any more. Your turn, sweetie."

I was already dripping when he grossly knelt before me like a man. He roughly shoved my ass and my thighs around, getting me in position to please him. It was my turn to be helpless and surrender. "Whatever you want to do, baby," I told him. "I trust you. You'll fuck me good."

"Oh yes," he said, nodding, as he held that red rod glowing in the sunlight shaft, and wiggled himself and it so it protruded into me. I could feel its hard, unyielding head push through my tender vaginal opening. It fell out and bruised my pee hole and little lady, but he leaned over and tenderly kissed my mouth to make it all better. "Baby," he murmured to me, "baby." I pulled him down with both arms and kissed his mouth. Our tongues wriggled together hotly while his rubbery dick filled me up and slid back and forth. I could feel the rocking of his cock, the weight of his heavy hips, the dripping of his own hole, as he pumped and pounded with relentless force. This was one of those dildoes with a prong on the other side that rested squarely in his man-cunt, slithery wet from both of us.

I had hardly ever had a real cock inside me. Rarely did I dildo myself with a banana or a bottle. I usually used a hooked hand to fuck myself when I was hot, whether alone or with Muriel or Ronny.

This was a man pounding me the way it's supposed to be done. If he was a bit soft and round and female, all the better. His lower back had limitless strength in reserve. I could feel the wild strength and determination in the body that had no doubt fucked Joe Gallagher so many times, and brought three robust children into the world. This was not a body to tell no. His full thighs pounded against me the way a storm pounds the loose boats in a stricken harbor. If I was a harbor, he was a storm, and he violated me so thoroughly and completely that I held him tightly and cried out in my own delirium as he forced me and banged me and whaled me until I could feel the relief--the violent spasms in my legs and gut. I cried out in a raw, overwhelmed, hungry voice.

I shouted for him as I beat my palms down on his shoulder blades, while I melted apart for his pounding assault between my thighs.

I shouted for love as I held his curly head in my hands, while he came and came again, and started to sag over me, but still so powerful that it was like getting violently fucked by a man twice his size.

I kept trying to double over upward, as I lay under him, but he laid his heavy chest and those woman tits down on me so we rolled to one side and lay facing each other and all tangled up on the dirty floor. I clung to each tit with my hands, and suckled hungrily on his brown nipples. He'd spit, time and again, to make his nipples foamy wet for me. And still those powerful hips churned and pounded away at me. Again and again I came, and I would have kept coming except my pussy was getting sore. "Stop," I said. "I can't take it any more."

I lay on the floor on my back, exhausted, with one long thigh draped over the other, shielding my candy from further assault.

"My juicy cherry," he said as he snuggled close to me. "I found it. I popped it. It's all mine."

"It's all yours," I said dreamily while brushing my palm lightly with the flow of the hair across his forehead. "All yours."

He managed to wriggle one thick thigh between my longer, thinner thighs. One blunt knee shoved my thighs apart so he could get himself and that red liquorice dick back, close to my slit, which I didn't mind. I could only make lolling and lala sounds and brush my sweaty hair back with my wide girl hands. I have wide hands for a girl. When I was in high school, the captain of the basketball team, a black girl a foot taller than me with wide shoulders and long arms, tried to get me to join the team. They were short one or two girls, but it turned out she was short one freshman to get her fingers in my shorts, so I decided to spend that elective in softball instead. I still wouldn't let her touch me when I was Mario's girlfriend.

Mario crawled close so his torso lay half on me while we were entangled from the thighs down. He had one hand on my bush. "I love those springy curls," he whispered in my ear, so I could smell butter and fruit on his breath from lunch, and hear the spit rattling deep in his throat. "I love thinking about that saddle you ride on, like an animal." He nuzzled my chest. "And these puffy little nipples." He always said 'little' when talking to me or about me. He kept pushing one angel-soft tit down, and the bluish nipple kept popping back up. I could still wear high school bra if need be. "Don't worry," he said, "one day they will swell up and fill with milk. Those cotton candy nipples will harden and become prunes like I have. Hormones will change it all, so let's enjoy those girl tits while you still have them."

Mario played with my small breasts until they got sore, and I turned away from him. I didn't want to slip from his strong, warm embrace. I was still hungry for him, but I was sexed out and couldn't take anymore.

I lay on my side, with my hands under my cheek, and stared at the sunbeam coming in the window, through whirling dust motes, and striking the grain in the floor. Soon, I heard Mario snoring as he lay over my back, arms around me and hands on my breasts, while he spooned my beloved rear end with his crotch. I could feel that red dick loosely stuck somewhere between my thighs and my pussy. I was so worn out that I was soon asleep. Sometimes, in summer, when it's been hot and unbearable for a week, you can hear a refreshing rain coming across the meadows and streets. You can hear the heavy rain drops pounding down as they march toward you. That's how my own snoring sounded. I heard it coming over me before I was asleep.

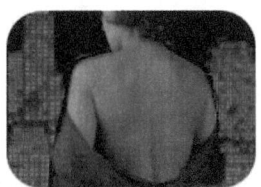

Sometime, as the light faded toward evening, Mario moved my body so he could shove a soft quilt under me. My ribs were sore from the hard floor. When I awoke almost two hours later, my ribs still ached. I sat partially up and looked around. Mario was gone. Instead Muriel had come into the room, and lay sleeping behind me, with her hands holding those oval buttocks of mine that she loved so much, and her cheek pressed against my ass. I looked down along my back and hip at her tenderly. She must have been dreaming about us, because she moved faintly in her sleep. She made a little mewling sound. I think she cried my name in her dream. Her lips puckered up. Maybe, in her dream, she kissed each side of my ass crack. I contorted myself as only a slender young body can, without waking her. I reached my arm out and touched the tip of my finger to her butt pucker. She smiled in her sleep. I pushed the tip in so her sphincter held it prisoner. She moved her head down. Her tongue flickered out and licked my valley. She wrapped her arms around me more tightly, pressed against me, and buried her face in my crotch in back. I lay half awake, looking under a raised arm to watch her angelic face. I put my hand on her head, feeling her hair smooth in my palm, and ever so lightly pressed her face to my rear end. A smile flickered over her features, and she raised one hand to lay its palm over my crotch, covering both holes with her short fingers--with her lips resting on that hand. So we both fell deep asleep. Late that night, in my dream, I took the last bus home across town to my cold and lonely apartment.

I got up in the middle of the night. Padding around the apartment on bare feet, draped only in a blanket, I soon had the heater going and the tea kettle whistling. Be it ever so humble, it was home. I made myself some PBJ crackers to have with my tea, brushed my teeth, sat in the bathroom reading Mad Magazine for a while (no wad to go plop), and was fast asleep as soon as my head landed on the pillow. Or had it all just been a dream? But I was in for a shock the next day at noon.

15. Thrust In Me

I woke up the morning after my dream of Mario and Muriel, feeling deeply refreshed in my soul. I was up early, clear-headed, and eager to see her at noon. I wanted to tell her all about my dream while I held her hands in mine. What a jolting shock I would get today!

There was an ache between my legs, and I walked a bit stiffly. Must have been a good orgasm in my sleep. I made a fist and kissed my knuckles in thanks.

I was ten minutes late for work, but Mr. Ferguson didn't notice. He was pretty good about that. I so often put in overtime at no extra pay.

That noon, I couldn't wait to walk across the street, ride the elevator up to the 20th floor of the Finncroft Tower, and tell Muriel all about my dream. How different it all turned out.

As I raised my hand to knock on the door, I saw that the latch was undone and the door stood a half inch ajar in its frame. I heard voices inside, and leaned my ear close. My first thought was to come back the next day if this was a bad time. I heard Muriel's voice--low, sexy, laughing, the way she got when she was aroused. You could tell that laugh on a woman, especially if you were intimate with her. My heart beat fast, pounding in my throat. I pushed the door open a bit more so I could hear.

A man was speaking in a full, rich voice. I thought I recognized the voice. My heart gave a leap, because there was an intimate sound to their conversation. I thought I heard a sound, like a duck splashing in water. Numb with fear and jealousy, I pushed the door open and stepped inside. I was in the little foyer where Muriel hung her coat and umbrella and stored office supplies. You went through a tiny passage with the toilet on one side and a closet on the other, and you were in her small office. The toilet door was open--I smelled urine and perfume and powder. She kept case files piled to the ceiling in the closet, whose door was always locked.

I stood in the shadows, with blood pounding in my neck, and a feeling I was going to choke. I felt like a ghost, standing in the shadows. Had she left the door open for me? Or just forgotten to close it? I came over every day at this same time, so there could be no mistake. It had to be intentional. There was a man in there, and Muriel was having sex with him. From what she'd told me about her ex-boyfriend, this wasn't Leo. Leo had been a selfish, middle-

aged frump with a bald head, thick glasses, and bushy eyebrows--
all he needed was a tall gray hat and a puritan bib-collar. Like the
old villain in BUtterfield-8, Leo was the kind of miserable prick
who could screw a woman in all sorts of positions that dare not
speak their name, while feeling contempt for her. If he gave her
flowers or chocolates from the discount store, it wasn't a love gift
but a bone tossed to a dog. He could disdain his sex victim as a
ruined slut, yet feel totally self-righteous about himself. He made
no connection between what he did with her, with what she did
with him. I saw his photo on her desk before she shredded it and
threw it out the window like confetti. She'd told me: "Tuition,
that's all. It's the school of hard knocks."

I'd agreed: "They don't teach you this stuff at Harvard, huh?"

But I digress. This was not Leo, so who was that man with
Muriel now, and how could this be? My soul cried: *Why?*

Tiptoeing, I made my way closer until I glimpsed a lozenge of
light--her office, shining with sunlight on a mild summer day. I was
too shocked to say anything, or make a scene, or even run. I was
simply frozen there, like an ice sculpture of a big dolphin I once
saw in the middle of a buffet at a ritzy hotel, where I'd been invited
for a wedding (Mr. Ferguson's niece). Like that frozen mammal, I
stood and watched Muriel and the man for about ten minutes, until I
couldn't take it any longer.

The man was Mr. Farmer, our six foot four package delivery
man. He was actually a nice guy and very popular along his busy
route. He'd bang the door open, backwards, and push in with his
gray-uniformed body of steel, pulling a dolly loaded with boxes and
packages, flats and pouches, and a receipt book for someone to
sign. He'd talk and laugh up a storm, including how his father was
German and he'd married this half Spanish, half Negro woman
from Jamaica. He brought the smell of the street with him, the
diesel of his truck, with those broad shoulders like sails, and take
away with him us girls' perfumes and white smiles and interested
stares.

Even Harriet the Harridan, who supervised us in Mr.
Ferguson's office, once said just after he left: "If I could order him
in a catalog, I'd put on that uniform and pull his dolly up to my
apartment all by myself."

Charley Farmer's graying hair was kinky and cut short. His
skin glowed like meadow honey, that stood in a bottle on a shelf in
sunlight. He had a handsome face with a powerful jaw and these

gray, sympathetic eyes. His body was long and muscular, a lean
build with powerful shoulders, His high buttocks rippled when he
walked--each had a huge dimple in the side, as I now saw through
my tears. He was stark naked as a caramel candy, and gorgeous as a
Greek statue, with a long hose of a cock, whose heavy head was
uncircumcised, like a half-peeled plum.

Muriel laughed at some joke. Speaking of dolphins, she lay on
her desk, stark naked with her heavy tits hanging to the sides and
her wrinkled brown nipples big as ponds, rising erect in hunger for
his mouth. Her full thighs were up, so that her ass lay pale and
squashed like two eggs on the hard wood. Her knees were up, her
forelegs down, as her naked, pretty heels gripped the edge of her
desk. Muriel wasn't as tall as me, but her legs were still kind of
long. She was fuller in the ass, but still young and shapely. Her skin
was smooth and ageless. I thought one day I'd make her lie down
and make love to her behind like she'd been doing to mine. That
was before today.

Mr. Farmer stepped closer to take her in his big hands. As soon
as he touched her buttocks, the laughter went out of her and she got
that dark serious sex look waiting to be taken. She drew in an
excited breath. I looked her body over, including her face--so
pretty, with the first character wrinkles, and her curly brown hair
gathered in a large tortoise shell comb under one ear. I realized,
more than ever, just how lively and sparkly she was. You see these
wonders just when you lose your lover. If you saw just her ass
alone, two pale ovals separated by a curving shadow line, you
wouldn't know her age. It could be a high school girl's ass, a young
ass, and delicately shaded like graying snow. With that ass, she
could have any man--or woman--she wanted. As she showed him
everything, she raised her hands to him invitingly. She had a
hungry expression as she looked down her cheeks, between her tits,
down her belly to him.

Farmer spoke softly in his warm, buttery, booming voice. "I'll
try what you asked, Muriel. We'll go easy. Just remember I'm big."

"I see you're big, honey. I just had most of you in your mouth.
You are a cream pie. When you're done with what I want, I'll let
you fuck me. Would you like that?"

"Lady," said Farmer. "Yes."

"Honey, let's take it one squirt at a time, okay?"

"Yes Ma'am."

"Don't ma'am me."

"Okay, Muriel." Holding his long cock in one hand, he rubbed the palm of his other big hand over her butt cheeks. "You get my Wilson all tuned up, ma'am, and I do mean ma'am."

"I like when you talk to me with sex in your voice. Do you want me, Charley?"

"Oh yes, Muriel." He moved closed and lightly slapped his cock against her thigh so the caramel head of it bounced, which made the tiny bit of uncircumcised foreskin flop. "You like when I talk sexy with you?"

"Oh yes," Muriel said in a breathy voice. "I eat it up."

"You like it when I sex you up?"

"What would your wife say if she knew you are were rubbing your dick on my leg and playing with my ass?"

"I don't even want to think about it, lady. I'd never hear the end of it. I figure you are never going to tell anyone you got serviced by me, and if I told anyone, nobody would believe me."

Muriel rubbed a knee against his erect cock. "We'll never tell a soul."

Traitor! I thought, balling my fists at my side. I was ready to stamp my foot and burst into tears. *I am your girl!*

"Why do you want me up your hiney, Muriel?"

"I have a little playmate who comes up here sometimes. She's a sweet little thing. I have never loved anyone like I love her." She pointed to her pussy. "Come here, Charley, get wet first. But all you get is just a little bit of snatch until you've done your real job today."

As I listened to her, I understood her. Still, it was so painful to see her with another person. It would have been unbearable if it were another young woman. I held my clawed hands to my mouth, and watched through glittering tears. It was the way everything glitters when you drive in the rain and everyone has their lights on, only there was no windshield wiper to clear my hurting vision.

Charley Farmer slid his long cock into her wet, waiting pussy. "You love this little girl a lot?"

"Are you shocked?"

"No, Muriel. You talk a lot. You're gonna make my Wilson go soft."

"Shake it a little in my pussy," she said in a sultry, seductive voice. "It's been a long time since I had a man. Go on, play."

"What is your girl's name?"

"Sarah."

"Oh, you mean the fox over at Ferguson's shop."

Charley rolled his eyes up and thrust so that his Jupiter mound (is that what a man's Venus mound would be?) looked smooth and shiny amid black bristles.

Muriel said in that sexy voice: "She is a real fox. Is that what men call it? My little fox is a smart, adventuresome soul. That sounds so delicious--a fox. My Sarah is a fox. Yes. My little fox has been telling me about her ass adventures, so I just want to see for myself. I've been eyeballing your long, wiry body for some time, Mr. Farmer, and you look like such a sweet, generous man."

"I am here to serve. My mission is to please. I want to leave the world a better place."

"Oh Charley, that's so sweet."

"If I can serve your gorgeous needs, then my job is done--till next time you need Super Charley."

She lay back glowing with pleasure. Her pale legs were spread apart for Charley to take her and use her. She diddled her big nipples, and looked down at him between her boobs as he fucked her in the cunt.

Charley purred in his deep, sexy voice: "You are a fox, Muriel. You are a fox."

Despite my hurt and sense of betrayal, I was getting hot, watching them and listening.

Muriel's intentions were good, but she should have asked me to do it with a strap-on or something. I'd just seen Mario's red root in my dream.

Charley groaned as her pussy pleasured him. He stood on the balls of his pink feet like a dancer. He swayed forward and backward in long, slow strokes. I could hear his abdomen slapping against her soft thighs.

Muriel asked: "How long have you been delivering packages here?"

Farmer shuttled his long cock back and forth through the hairy slit between her uplifted thighs. "Ten years now, I bet, to these office buildings all around here."

"And we never said more than hello to each other before today."

"I had no idea you are such a fox."

"Did you ever think about me, even a little bit?"

"Honestly, Muriel? I thought you were like my wife--a paragon of virtue--like a nun or a school teacher or a nurse. I'd open any door for you, carry any package, bow to you, and feel grateful for a kind word."

"You are so sweet." She shuddered at the first hint of a long train of orgasm spasms. "Oh Charley, slide it in and out. Slide it good."

"I am sliding in and out of your sweet pussy."

"Put your finger in my asshole," she said.

"Does that mean you're ready for that special request you asked about?"

She looked up at him with big, scared eyes. "Warm me up some more."

"I aim to please." He pulled it out, and squatted down so his dong nearly touched the floor. Pushing her legs way up, he maneuvered his dark head into the zone between Muriel's legs. I heard sucking noises, and she closed her eyes in satisfaction.

"Say when, Muriel."

She whispered fervently: "Keep doing that. Tongue my asshole. Make it wet and soft for you. That's how Sarah says it's done. You don't get this at home, do you?"

He came up for air and said: "My wife is a librarian and very proper. No, I don't get enough at home. And I'm a faithful man."

"Ha! You're going to tell me a tall, handsome gentleman like you doesn't get pulled into more offices by horny women having emergencies, like me today?"

"I take it on a case by case basis," he told her tactfully. He looked coy. Poor man, built like Atlas, endowed like a sunny god, what could he say without lying? Tell me about a faithful man. Ha! "With opportunity always comes risk. A proper analysis leads me to the best possible conclusion."

Muriel said: "Do you want to come all over inside my ass, Charley?"

"It can be arranged." He rose and inserted himself in her pussy. "We'll make it good and wet so it won't hurt."

"Thank you," she said in a whisper.

Charley's face was contorted while his cock throbbed near orgasm. It takes men so long to build up to the next one, if they even could handle seconds. A woman in heat just pulses like a garden hose--one orgasm after another, big ones and small ones like mice running down a tunnel.

"Don't forget," she said. She reached down and touched her butt pucker--to show him, to invite him, to tempt him, to tease him.

"Oh god I can't hold out any longer." He rose and, with a resounding slapping noise, cupped her whole wide ass in his hands while his hose waggled over her pale belly. A drop of pearly semen glittered in the high cunt hairs on her lower belly. "Are you ready, Muriel?"

He gently screwed her waiting ass pucker with one big finger.

"Two fingers. Spread me open," she said. She sat up on one elbow, watching him and licking her lips. "Three fingers, Charley. Spit into me. Spit! Get me wet and slippery. Get your tongue in there. Make it all wet and loose."

I waited in the shadows, a tear dribbling down each cheek.

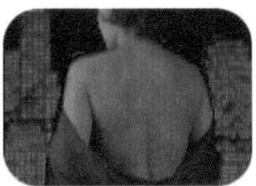

Muriel was a woman. She needed a man. Did I think our little trysts could continue forever? Was I being selfish? Had I fallen in love with her? Did I want her only to myself?

I'd come to think my ass was a sure thing, the way men and women stared after me, and the way Muriel liked to rent a piece of me for lunch plus a dollar. I'd have to pay for my own lunch today, and probably cry a river into it. It wasn't the two bucks for a grilled cheese sandwich with a pickle and lettuce on the side, and a vanilla milk shake. Or the extra buck for an egg cream.

I was in tears because I felt betrayed, and because I didn't feel special anymore. I'd been a kept woman, and now my girl was cheating on me. How easy come, how easy go.

I should have turned on my heel and walked out, never to return. If she called, I should let her feel she might have lost me. I should make the bitch beg. I should wear my schoolgirl uniform and flaunt myself on the street, maybe let her see my white undies and smooth café-au-lait legs, and hurt her by signaling she couldn't have me any more, at least until she begged. I hated myself because the truth was, I'd crawl at her feet to keep her. But she'd pay. I was filled with wild thoughts.

I stayed to look another minute. And another minute. I'd leave soon. But I stayed.

"Let's give it a try," Muriel breathed. "I was hoping Sarah would be here by now to see us and to help me, hold my hand, and reassure me while you shove it in."

They stopped to embrace and kiss. My own tension in the shadows was becoming unbearable. I reached down to comfort my throbbing, puzzled clit that expected Muriel's teeth on it and wondered why no big woman tongue slithered around it in a trail of foams and moans.

Charley gently laid Muriel on her back. She sprawled over her desk so papers and pens and weights fell off while he held up her legs by the ankles. Muriel was totally submissive. It was the sexiest thing a woman could do, to offer herself so totally--to show a man her most intimate parts that she spent every hour of every day shielding from men's eyes. To give herself utterly and totally so he could do as he wanted with her. To spread, to show, to wait for the glory.

Charley's long, wiry body rippled over her like a bridge of honey-colored muscles. He had hard man-tits with tiny blue nipples like ancient coins. His navel was twisted--part innie and part outie-- like after a flying saucer crash. He looked like Tarzan's native twin, glorious. At the moment, his facial expression was becoming extreme: gritted teeth, chuffy lips, and big eyes. Sweat rolled down his temples and glistened in his wiry hair.

"Go on, Charley. I'm dripping wet for you. Get me all wet in back."

Charley used his fingertip to draw her cunt snot down into her asshole so that her pucker glittered wetly.

Muriel spat into her hand repeatedly until there was a pool of mucus, which she rubbed hastily on her butt pucker so that it glistened.

With a cry of release deep from the underworld, Charley lunged forward. His prow poked apart her shiny chocolate and they both cried out loud as his locomotive pushed into her station. All that was missing was a loud steam siren.

Her ass cheeks shook. Her white belly quivered with waves of contractions. Her pudgy fingers slapped the wood on either side of her. She seized her tits in both hands, and wrung them as if to make milk squirt from tortured nipples sticking crooked between her fingers and thumbs.

Charley pounded at her, while holding her vanilla buttocks with spidery chocolate fingers. He raised his head like a wolf and let out a long, throaty wail of relief.

"Charley," she croaked and banged her palms down on the desk again. She was too overcome with sex and hunger to say more. "Take me. Take me."

He cried out: "Lady, I'm givin' it all I got, and I can't take no more." So saying, he grew a foot shorter as his body convulsively corkscrewed. He held on with the long fingers, though, and pounded away until he simply collapsed over her.

That was the moment when I lost my mind. I wasn't mad at her. I just wanted some of that.

In one hot, horny, angry, emotional blur, I tossed my hat and purse aside. Peeling off my gloves like an angel of doom, I strode into that room, making a racket with my heels. My steps made an ominous rumble, like thunder and lightning.

Muriel saw me first. She pulled away from Charley and simply said: "Company." She looked at the ceiling with the stony gaze of someone who has been caught red-handed and has no excuses.

Charley started up in a daze and looked terrified. It was 1950s America--say no more. He froze as if the wages of sin had come to mow his lawn.

"I know you left that door open for me, bitch," I said to Muriel as I walked right up behind Charley and grabbed his beautiful ass. I looked up at him. "Are you doing what you're told?"

"Yes, Ma'am. I'm sorry. I got carried away. She wanted me to fuck her asshole."

"You liked it, didn't you?" I said sternly--then burst into tears.

"Honey," Muriel said to me, "don't cry." She reached over to wipe my cheek. "Now see what I've done. I've made my baby cry. This has all gone terribly wrong."

"You wanted to make me feel bad," I said..

"I'm sorry," Charley boomed. His dick hung limp like a hose. He reached for his shirt with one long arm.

I wiped my tears away with one brush of my forearm. I stepped up close and hugged him to me, with one arm around his waist, and my hands on each of his big hip bones. "You're not done here, Charley. Put that shirt away and grab that dick."

He looked at me sheepishly, a man with a powerful jaw and presidential features. He looked at Muriel full of question marks. He loomed over us two women in that little office. He should have been outside, on top of the roof at that moment, with little airplanes buzzing around him like mosquitoes.

My woman sat up on the edge of the desk with her long, pale legs dangling. "Maybe we can fix this after all." It was her mommy voice. "Honey, take your clothes off like a good girl."

I managed to wiggle out of my skirt, my blouse, my white school-type socks, and my loafers. All I had now were my hair-stuffed panties and flat brassiere.

"Take off your bra," Muriel said. "I want Charley to see your puff titties." She frowned at my reluctant face. "You want him to suck them, don't you? He wants to suck them, don't you, Charley?"

Feeling embarrassed and humiliated about my flatness, I turned so Charley could undo my bra. Charley nodded and undid my bra. I turned to face him and let him feel me.

His hands were very gentle as they pushed on the two flat areas and the pinky-bluish swellings that protruded like cupcakes rising in the oven.

Charley said: "Good things come in small packages." Like a good girl, I stood before him while his hands roved gently over my chest. I kept my hands obediently folded over my welcome mat. He leaned down and tongued my nipples. That made them swell out erect, in their soft, airy way. He sucked on each, while I tingled all over. "Cotton candy," he said. "I'm getting ready to come again."

"Isn't she adorable?" Muriel said.

"An angel," Charley said. He ran his big hands up and down my slender thighs, my strong but narrow hips, my delicate waist, my almost ribby torso. "She's filled in, all the right places, a nice looking young woman--two handfuls and a mouthful."

"An eye full," Muriel agreed as she stroked her wetness with a dreamy look--the way she mooned over my rear every lunch hour. "I adore her perfect fanny so."

They talked about me as if I were an object. I liked it, since I had stayed here on my own. I could leave if I wanted to. I felt safe and sexy and wanted. A girl can play, right?

"Take off your panties, baby," Muriel said to me.

I stripped my pale, sheer panties down my long legs and sat down on the couch. I wasn't sure if they wanted my front or my rear. They could have all of me. I was feeling easy, and wanted them both to take me together. Whatever they wanted was okay with me, as long as Muriel approved and Charley didn't get rough-- and nobody ever found out.

Charley gave my cunt a strum, like a guitar. "That's a rug."

"Go on, baby," Muriel told me. "Turn over like we always do. Let me make myself hot by kissing your bottom. We'll show you, Charley."

"I am eager to learn," he boomed.

I lay on the couch and assumed my position, face down, with my hands under my Venus mound. I had worn myself out with that dream last night, and could use a nap. Their voices became pleasant background music as I retreated into my private garden. The cold couch leather warmed quickly with my body heat. My bare thighs stuck to the leather, making me squirm, which made ripping sounds on the damp leather.

"Watch us," Muriel said. "Sit there for a little bit, Charley." I felt the couch tremor as he sat down, big man that he was. I could feel the faint rhythm as he stroked his cock. A stolen glance under my armpit revealed that he was holding it against his washboard abs with both hands and stroking it. It stretched to his navel, with a head like a smooth, ripe caramel lollypop. The foreskin lay peeled back, revealing a naked plum.

Muriel sighed deeply with pleasure, while rubbing her hands down my rear end. She got into that slow, sexy rhythm that we were both used to. I loved it, and enjoyed knowing a man was watching. He must think he had finally met those forsaken women from the magazines--here in the foyer of heck, practicing their illicit love that could not speak its name.

She whispered in my ear: "That was so amazing. I still want it in front, though."

I remembered that she had said somewhere along the line she'd been fixed, and couldn't have an accident. I was still accident-prone and terrified of the front thing.

"Isn't she beautiful?" Muriel said. She reached for Charley's cock as he sat nearby on the couch. "Come here, Charley."

Charley slid closer. "I've died and gone to heaven."

My woman sounded as if she owned me, and I was glad to hear it. I hoped she wouldn't tell Charley that she gave me a buck or two for sex every day. I was her whore during my lunch hour. Now she was going to show me to him. She was going to offer me to him, like kids sharing a toy. I was the toy, and I liked it. I wanted to be handed around, and touched, and looked at, and fucked.

What was in the air, between me and Muriel, that moment, was that nothing would be the same again after today, and we both realized it had to be.

That was okay now--had to be. It was time to move on, and what a spectacular way to go.

"Charley," Muriel said, "take me." She positioned herself on the desk with her knees apart, and looked at him with hungry, honest eyes. She added in a whisper: "It's been a long time."

"I am here also," I said, not selfishly, but wanting to share myself, deal myself in, to offer more to Muriel than to Charley.

Charley reached one enormous basketball player's hand around and took my ass in it--all of one cheek, and part of the other.

For just a second, I thought about making him stop, because I'd been faithful to Ronny all this time, two years or whatever months I'd been with Ronny, not counting passion with Muriel of course. Without meaning a word, just to put an edge on or maybe to take charge, I pushed Charley's hand away. "I have a boyfriend, Charley. You can look, but not touch."

He took his hand from my cheeks. For a moment, his life again flashed before his eyes. This was the 1950s and he was a mixed-race man. Women can be so confusing to poor men.

I put my hand on his arm. "Don't worry, Charley, we won't say a word if you won't."

His brightening look said he got the joke. "Mum's the word, mum. Mum all the way. Mum, Ma'am." He pinched his lips with thumb and forefinger to seal his promise.

Muriel and I did the same. All three of us pinched our lips shut, then burst out laughing.

Laughter faded when horny, burning, three-way desire rose in that steamy little office.

I gently pushed Charley toward Muriel. He did a little stagger, so he had to steady himself with one hand splayed on the desk. He was close enough for Muriel to grasp his truck with her hand and guide it to her garage. I helped by gently rubbing wet all over her labia, spitting on them, rubbing, and helping him drive inside. He and she emitted simultaneous loud groans of pleasure. I licked them both with my big tongue. They smelled salty and clean, like the disturbed sea on a windy, rainy day. We were swimmers on a fathomless sea, steadily stroking under gray clouds the mirrored the faceless waves; confident of our destination without seeing it--just trusting that all this thrusting was just the right thing.

Charley put both hands on my head as if it were a basketball, and closed his yes. "Oh my my my..." he said. His eyes were a lively, sparkling blue. He had one sparkling, gold-edged tooth among his ivory choppers, and a large pink tongue I fancied might feel good inside of me.

I palmed Muriel's ass with both hands while I licked around their moving parts near my face. I managed to sputter spittily: "You have some 'splaining to do, woman."

"I am guilty on all counts," she said between feeble cries for relief from a pleasure so great it must have nearly seemed painful. "I just wanted to make you happy, baby."

What choice did I have? The summer was almost over. "I'm happy, sweetheart," I allowed.

I got up close to chide Muriel. We two women were nose to nose, face to face. It was a three-way conversation, with Charley's one-eyed glans looking at us like a periscope. "You wanted to know about me and Ronny, so you wanted to sneak a try by yourself. You didn't ask me first."

She cuddled his dick against her cheek. "I left the door open for you, baby. I was waiting for you. Then I got scared that you weren't coming."

"You didn't care that someone else might accidentally walk in?"

She made a guilty face. "I was so horny for you that I didn't care."

"She's got me all horny now, just thinking about you," Charley, while reaching down to tuck her rear firmly into the curve of his waist as he plunged in and out in wetted piston strokes. His eyes narrowed, and his face cocked to one side while his mouth grew slack in the dullness of pleasure.

She told me sincerely: "I was thinking about you. I always think of you." She stroked my hair. "I wanted to be you, baby. I wanted to to feel him in my rear end, and I couldn't wait." She pulled my face tightly against her pale belly with both hands. I licked its pale surface and shadowy navel while it spludded rhythmically under Charley's attentions. "It was exciting to have him do me." She giggled. "I still like the front better."

Charley was inside her, pumping away. His hard hip bones kept bumping my shoulder.

I stood back, and held their asses, one in each of my hands. I also took time to stroke my quivering bud, to get it wet and hard in its tender hiding place.

"Mm-mm," Charley said to no one in particular. His voice boomed low and happy among the cluttered walls with their paintings, stacks of legal folders, and knick-knacks.

His buns were like steel. I had fun petting them and stroking them. He liked that, so I reached between his legs and gently played with his dangling balls.

"Careful, honey," he said in a kind but concerned voice. "I gotta be able to walk when I go. Got deliveries to make, yet."

"O god" said Muriel, while writhing in the path of her oncoming orgasm; and another; and another.

Charley, jazzed up by her hungry and delirious surrender, came again in a shower of moans, while his tall frame contracted and he twitched spastically.

I fanned myself below, with my thighs and knees bowed out while I steadied myself against the desk. I was getting heated up. There would be no stopping now.

Muriel kneaded by small breasts. She played with my nipples, looked at them as if they were pennies in her box, precious treasures she had collected. "Come here, sweet baby," she said to me. She took me in her arms and kissed me deeply in my mouth. As she did so, she had me bent toward her, and now aimed my bottom in the direction of Charley's wet cock.

"Are you ready to do your next task?" Muriel asked, cuddling his erect cock against her face, like a toy, and kissing it repeatedly.

Charley looked ready to push her door open and rejoice. *Hallelujah!* I could see over one shoulder how eagerly he regarded my pale behind while gripping it in strong fingertips.

Muriel stroked me and kissed me, as if I were about to get a scary needle at a school clinic.

"No front," I admonished over my shoulder.

"No front," Charley agreed. He did not sound disappointed as he said: "That nice pucker looks good for what I want to do, my sweet girl." I saw him spit on his hand and felt him roughly moisten my back door. I had both hands over my labia, but let him insert three long fingers to play with me and get his fingers dripping wet. I obliged by raining over his hand--actually, I think I squirted some dribbles of pee, so horny was I.

He abruptly knelt, stopped what he was doing, and stuck his face in my crotch. I cried out feebly as his huge warm tongue thrust inside of me. I squealed a little, because it felt like a crazed mouse, running on the treadmill around and around my clit. I felt my tender clit sucked out into a little worm that nestled in the center of his rotating tongue.

"Where did you learn that?" I whispered hoarsely. "Don't stop."

Frenzied with love and desire, I held Muriel tight, and kissed all over that precious belly. I inhaled her smell and felt her softness. This was a belly that had been fucked and creamed and had borne three children. During all those lunch hours she had taken me for her lover as well. Now she hugged me to her, and I loved her for that belly. I loved her mother belly the way she loved my young ass. I hoped to have a belly like that one day. I wasn't thinking ahead to having some young girl half my age stick her mouth up my pussy and tongue my vagina tunnel. I figured Mr. Right would come along some time soon and make everything okay. I didn't even think about it. I hoped Mr. Right would be the one to nuzzle his cheek against my belly and appreciate it for all its passion and might. But we played the cards we were dealt. I was the queen of hearts dealt to Muriel since fate took her ace of hearts from her--Joe the seed-maker of three children and lover of her womb during those years.

He took me where I had not imagined yet--to a series of shuddering orgasms. I spazzed in Muriel's arms, and she squeezed me tenderly as if protecting me and comforting me. I clung to her because she was the older woman in my life, and I was so alone, and sometimes scared, and cried myself to sleep sometimes at night in my little barren apartment that had no love in it.

While I lay sprawled on my woman's ripe figure, and she petted me eagerly as if I were her little bunny, Charley put his hand repeatedly under my big loose cunt and got enough slimy love sauce to moisten up my dry pucker. He popped into my used car garage, well broken in by Ronny, and resumed his broad, hard strokes. Muriel and I quivered together with each impact. I held onto her big breasts, alternating from one to the other with my free hand. My other hand was stuffed into my vagina like a duck's beak. Muriel rubbed the curves of my back with one hand, and diddled herself with the other so that I could feel her knuckles wiggling like hard little hamster teeth against my Venus mound. I kept one hand stuffed in my vagina.

I felt Charley filling me up. My tender rear fired on all six million nerve endings, or however many, making my whole body tremble as if I had an electric net around me.

Charley knew exactly what to do. He managed to get one long hand into my front. I let him get his fingers past mine--both our hands soaked with goo--while he massaged my clitoris and made me twitch. I rocked. I felt like a fast boat jumping on the waves of a lake. Waves of pleasure fanned out through my body. I trembled all over. Muriel held me tightly, loving me, as if I were going to fall and hurt myself. I buried my face in her tender belly and cried out loud. My mouth made a funny farting noise on her soft, ripply white skin that echoed through her empty womb. She petted me as if I were a small animal. I loved her so. I clung to her while Charley drove into the glory of all that I spread out before him and under him. I reached back and spread my ass cheeks for him. My hands grasped myself with force, making slapping sounds. He pushed all the harder, rocking me and Muriel. I started to come, hard, making hoarse animal noises like a creature running for its life through a farmer's field.

In the midst of my chain of orgasms, Charley's thrusting and banging changed as he experienced a huge, crippling orgasm that brought him -- I thought he was going to die of a heart attack -- collapsing over my back so that the three of us lay like a sandwich on the desk.

Muriel let go of me. She sat back on the desk, leaning back with her palms down, and spread her knees. Instinctively, I began to play with her big nutty brown nipples and French kiss her deeply. She groaned with the luxury of our mingled spit and our cuddling tongues.

Charley was still inside of me, and he wasn't done yet. He renewed his steady pounding rhythm inside of me, while I lay exhausted and trembling on Muriel. His steely thighs slapped against my tight, muscular flesh.

Muriel was so jazzed up by all this that she started to orgasm again. I could feel sobs erupting from her, nose breath hot on my face while she hungrily stabled and chased after my tongue with hers. She wanted to have it all, and I wanted to help her.

Charlie pushed my ass up and away so he could stick his meat down under into her tunnel and give her the heat she desired. I rocked on his lap, my ass and thighs in his big hands as he banged away with his eyes closed, face uplifted, transfigured.

Muriel was the center of our attention. She was the earth mother. It was all about her now. She faced upward, wrapped he legs around my waist, and let us seed her. My ass bounced wide under Charley's face and he bent down to kiss me on my cheeks. I was helpless, pinned between them, along for the ride. I started getting hot again, especially with the hard tight ride of my mid-section which reminded me of going too fast on a rough street in one of those little English sportscars. The thought of that also turned me on. I felt Charley stick his thick thumb down my butt pucker, and his index finger up my twat, as if he were carrying a bowling ball. I knelt on the desk and jumped my ass up and down to get more stroke out of him, even as he rocked Muriel so that the desk creaked rapidly and my woman sobbed with dazed fulfillment.

We settled into a lull, still joined, and enjoying the closeness of our hot, sweaty bodies. We petted each other lightly, and exchanged breathy, languid kisses while the clock ticked as if time did not matter --there was too much of it, spilling over us like the juices that soaked us.

A woman of Muriel's age (still young and pretty, but a little worn in all the right ways that made her even more sexy) has a big ass pucker, just like she has those scrambled egg nipples dark and wrinkly like prunes so kids and men and a girl like me could hang from them and suck ourselves into delirious happiness.

Slowly, we peeled apart, but stayed close in case the need struck us again.

"It's like I never touched your butt hole before," I told her. "I can't get enough." Sliding down a bit, I gave it a kiss, and felt how soft the big, wrinkled brown pucker was. It was soaked and smelled of me and of Charley. I took my time and lovingly rubbed my fingers in little circles so she sighed happily. Then I remembered my dream of the night before, and how I had forced my tongue up into the little slit. If she didn't have one thigh on the desk, stretching her asshole for him, I was right--her asshole would have been a tiny slit, if her cheeks were nicely and evenly side by side, maybe just spread apart a few fingers wide to look at. As it was, it was twisted into more of a dark hole waiting to be played with. "You have a nice asshole," I told her as used two fingertips to smooth the jelly all around her pucker. Then I pushed the jelly into her asshole. I felt her tight, virgin sphincter grip tightly, resist, and then yield to the smoothness of the jelly. "You can't fight this stuff," I said. "See that, Charley?"

"Mm-mm," he said. "I see a nice butt hole."

"I want you to put your finger in there, Charley, and rub until her ass gets loose for you. You can't fuck a woman with a tight ass or it will hurt both of you."

"You are an expert, I take it," Charley said a bit sarcastically.

"Yes, as a matter of fact I am."

"Now I'm intrigued." He reached over and shoved me lightly around. "Show me."

I bent forward for him. He stared at my ass. "You need me to show you?"

"I see what you mean," he told Muriel.

"Isn't she adorable?"

"She is adorable," Charley said.

He rubbed Muriel's pucker with his finger while he licked me. I could feel his big tongue wetting my pucker, licking it like a cookie, sucking on it like candy. I felt his tongue go inside. My pucker had been trained by Ronny, so it loosened up pretty well at the first push. Charley pulled his tongue out and licked my whole ass as if he were cleaning his plate after a good meal. "That is an ass made in heaven," he said to Muriel. "How did you ever find her?"

"That ass is why I first seduced her," Muriel said. "I never flirted with a woman in my entire life before Sarah. I saw her face, and liked it. Her figure is divine--I like watching all those girl athletes on that tiny little television screen, but not to get hot. Just to look. Until I met Sarah at Ferguson's. When Sarah brought my papers over, she was wearing this summer dress that just lifted or swayed in every little breeze. I wasn't thinking when I asked her to put the files by the window. When she stood there, with the sun shining through that loose, white cotton dress, I could see her naked pink limbs and belly right through it. I could see her rear end, even in panties, and that flat bra. Her little ass cheeks were so tight they each had a huge dimple in the side. She had on a tight girdle that held up her nylons. I made her stop wearing those. I could see how pink her skin was--that young, firm, soft skin--and the shadow of her spine down her back, her long thighs and legs. I don't know what came over me, but I knew I had to have her, the minute I saw her at Ferguson's."

"How did you get her to come over?" Charley said as he picked up the lubricating jelly. First, he began liberally applying it to his long cock. Having his hands all over it made his cock hard again. Ronny was well hung, but this man was a horse. Until now, I had been prepared to let him take me. Now I was starting to want him.

"I just flirted with her the way a boy flirts with a girl. Nobody noticed, because nobody expects a woman in her mid-30s to flirt with a woman who is still practically a girl in her young 20s."

"I didn't get it either," I said. "I thought she was just being nice. She brought me an ice cream from the Century Diner downstairs the second day while I sat there typing. I felt I had to thank her. So I offered to come over and visit some time."

"She did," Muriel said. "I was so thrilled. I made tea and we had a pleasant little nothing conversation. Were you looking at me, Sarah?"

"I wouldn't have admitted it before now, but yes. I was looking at you. I thought you were pretty. You have a young, fresh face. That first date when I came over, and we had tea, I didn't want to leave."

"First date, honey? How sweet. Our first day."

"I was glad when you gave me a little peck on the cheek goodbye."

"I was scared to death--not just that I'd be ruined somehow, but that I wouldn't let go of you. When I felt your soft cheek on my lips, I wanted to kiss you back."

I smiled at the memory, while Charley enjoyed playing with both our assholes in his determined, methodical way. He had three fingers in each of our holes by now. *Good work, Charley!*

Muriel continued: "I was so excited and sexed up my fingers were shaking while I served tea. My voice caught in my throat. I was flustered the way a boy stammers and drops things when the girl he likes shows an interest in him."

"I wasn't showing an interest in you."

"You were--you just didn't know it."

While Muriel and I touched each other's butt cheeks and teased each other, Charley continued preparing and loosening our assholes.

"Do her first," I told Charley. It was her show, after all, wasn't it?

"No, no, no," Muriel told him. "I want to see you put it in Sarah."

Charley aimed his cannon at me and stepped close.

Automatically, my hand flew like a cork up my cunt, fingertips together forming a point, as wet as my canal was from desire. "Not my pussy. In back. Go easy."

"I'll be real easy, Sarah. You just tell me if you are uncomfortable."

I winced a little as he started coming in. He was big. He was nice and slow. For a minute I was scared--how far was he going to spread my poor little pucker apart? But he rocked a little in the doorway. I felt him sliding in, a lot like Ronny. I reached down in front to play with my bush, which was wet all over my hand. I licked my fingers to taste myself, and went back for more. Charley slid in and out, filling my rear up so I must have glowed all over with satisfaction. "Mmm," I said as if I were eating a pie.

"Mmm," said Charley, because my ass was his pie. He held me in his big hands while he smoothly came and went, inches at a time, forward and backward. We got a gentle rhythm going--I'd push when he pushed, and then we'd pull apart to come back together-- and my pucker hummed with pleasure. His fucker and my pucker-- what a combo.

"Did you forget about me?" Muriel asked plaintively, still with her ass ready in the air.

Selfishly, because I was halfway up the Matterhorn to a huge orgasm, I didn't want him to stop. "Keep massaging her hole so it loosens up, Charley--you don't want to tear anything."

"I'm working on it full time." He maintained that magnificent rhythm in me. My soft cheeks went *plop-plop-plop*, slapping each time he hit me with his tight abdomen. At the same time, he kept three big fingers in Muriel's asshole. He turned his fingers this way and that, so her asshole became loose and open.

Muriel piped up. "Help me, Sarah, make me hot. I feel like a loaf at a bake sale."

"I'll buy," Charley said kindly as he stroked his dick inside me. I looked over and saw that her pucker was ready.

Muriel said: "Sarah, I want to kiss those nipples. Come here."

The three of us had to do a little re-engineering. To make my small tits hang so they looked like something was there, I got on the couch on my hands and knees. Muriel crawled under me at a cross-angle, so she and I made an X. Her ass hung half off the couch as she braced on strong thighs. That way, she could suck as I hung my puffy nipples over her mouth. It felt exquisite. I felt ripples of new pleasure while Charley banged away behind me. Muriel played with her clit, making wet sounds with her pussy, while Charley kept lubing up her rear end. Furiously, I fanned my clit.

Seeing her playing with my nipples and with herself, and feeling Charley fill me up, I started shaking like an old Model T having a breakdown. Those were long before my time, but my father would have a beer or two while we all ate dinner, and he'd tell funny stories from before the Depression.

As I orgasmed between Muriel and Charley, I felt like I was being pulled apart by the huge waves of pleasure that overwhelmed me--more, and more, and more, while I let out hoarse yells, and finally fell over sideways in a limp pile. Both Charley and Muriel stroked me and comforted me while I trembled and tried to catch my breath. I laughed and pushed my sweaty hair back. I blew with my lips, and drops of sweat flew away. "Oh my god. When was the last time I felt anything like that?"

The clock made slow, steady iron *snick-snock*s that echoed in the little office. Charley Farmer dutifully sat where he'd been told and gyrated his hands around his cock. I started to doze off in mid-diddle while Muriel did her gentle massage and kissed my cheeks, alternating, full of love and passion. She gripped my butt cheeks in her hands, as if she were holding a sacred chalice, and buried her face in my ass crack. Impulsively, I brought my hands around from front, where I had been lightly diddling myself, and put my hands on my buttocks. I gently pulled my cheeks apart for her (and for me). She ran her nose down my crack. Then she moved her chin back up, stuck her tongue against the base of my spine, and slowly ran her tongue down my crack. She savored every millimeter as she ran the tip down my ass crack. I wondered if she could taste the tiny, silvery hairs shimmering in there like the finest down. I was acutely conscious, still holding my cheeks apart for her, when her tongue arrived at my back door. I swear, that girl spent the next ten minutes licking my asshole until it got soggy, or was that Charley's sperm drippings? For all the loving she'd given it, this was the first time she was totally abandoned and crying hungrily while she lapped noisily. She licked every tiny bit of it, each wrinkle in the pucker, and kept dipping her head down to force her tongue through my sphincter and into my anus. I took care every morning to wash myself thoroughly. Anything could happen on my lunch hour. Each day, before I came over, I hid in a bathroom stall in the Century Building, and gave myself an enema. I would then use plenty of tissues and soapy water to clean my rear for Muriel. There's nothing like a young woman with a clean, fragrant ass, and a beautiful older woman in love with that ass.

Muriel said. "You want to take her now, Charley?"

I said nothing, but lay face down on my Venus mound, throbbing with dull, hungry pleasure at being their sex object. It was nice to think how they were fussing over me. I knew, just like Muriel always gave me that dollar, that they would satisfy me totally as they comforted themselves and each other. I was like the table on which they ate their feast together, but I was also their meal and their desert. I was the finest egg cream anyone ever slurped.

I felt a shifting of weights, a rustle of clothing, and then I felt a larger, heavier tongue in my asshole. Charley easily forced my flower to open. Hurting me dully, his strong fingers gently but powerfully spread my cheeks apart so that my pucker was wide open for him. I'm sure I already had a little open hole, the way he held me open. With my hands free, I reached underneath and walked my fingers down my Venus mound, into my thick curly fur, and found my little lady that always loved to be touched and played with. Me and my little lady, we romped together in the tall garden grass, while Charley and Muriel fussed over the back gate.

"Honey," Muriel said urgently in a breathy voice into my ear.

I turned my head toward her, and saw that she had her legs spread and was fanning her pussy blossom.

"Honey," she said, "I want you to show me now."

I only hesitated for a moment, thinking of Ronny. But if Ronny knew all the circumstances, he'd understand. Especially because, next time we did it, I'd be remember Charley's huge fish inside of me, and it would make me extra hot for Ronny. "Sure," I whispered to Muriel.

"You are the best young woman," she said.

The couch creaked as Charley mounted. I wanted his cock in my asshole. I wanted his cock in my vaginal hole, but the mere thought of being ruined made me stuff a hand in there in case he got any ideas. I'd run out and buy another bottle of vinegar on my way back to work, just in case. Mr. Ferguson was going to be out all afternoon, and I would tell Witch Harriet, his chief bookkeeper and mistress of the hen house, that I'd been sick at the park with my mensees. Who cared if the old bag believed me or not, or if I smelled like a salad. My work was excellent, and she had nothing on me.

Charley rubbed a wad of jelly into my asshole. It was nice to feel his big finger penetrate me. I said to him over my shoulder. "Your other hand. Do my vagina at the same time. Don't get your cock near it."

Almost immediately, I felt another large finger slide into my canal. With other fingers on that hand, he diddled my pee hole, my little lady under her hood, and my labia. It was like swimming in the ocean, and having a crab eating your twat. *Eek!* But I enjoyed it. That man knew what he was doing. With the middle finger of his other hand, Charley reamed my ass. He penetrated me slowly and gently, rotating his finger, until my asshole loosened up. He slid his thumb in, while resting his other four fingers on my downy tailbone, and reamed me wider with the ball of his thumb. I touched myself to see how he was doing. I reached both hands around my butt cheeks and felt back there with curious, wriggling fingers. Sure enough, I could slide three fingertips in. "Take me, Charley," I said. "I want your cock inside me."

Even loosened up, it was breathtaking. I felt a brief twinge, like fire. For a second, I was afraid he would rip me with that huge walnut bed post. But he was a kind man who cared about me. He must have heard me yelp or something. He took his dick away and rubbed jelly on it until I could hear his fingers making sticky, ripping sounds. He put another generous plug of jelly on the hole and pushed it in with his thumb. He turned his thumb this away and that, pushing it in so that my hole widened. "Slide it in," I said. "I want you inside me."

I felt it go in, like a train into a tunnel. He filled me up with it. He impaled me on it, and I drowned in a cascade of sensations from nerve endings I never knew I had. The very thought of it made me want to take it in my mouth and gently grind my teeth on it, and suck it on my tongue until his cock was dripping with my spit. I wanted him shoot down my throat so I'd choke while I was cumming myself with my blurry hands and busy fingers down in my dewy bush.

Muriel saw all this and gasped while she fanned herself below. That girl was eager for sex.

"Let me feel your pussy," I said to her. She obediently rose and knelt on the couch near my face, still fanning herself with four wet fingers. I reached over and put four of my fingers up her hole. "We're both nice and loose," I reassured her.

Charley was still too busy with me to service Muriel. He did something I never even thought of. He said to me, nuzzling the back of my neck: "Tight ass, loose cunt. I love it. Here, I want to stuff my balls in there." Sure enough, he reached down between his legs, and pressed his balls into the wetness of my hole. I tried to back my ass up against him closer to take his balls into me, but his huge ram kept moving in and out on jelly tracks. I felt something filling my cunt--probably his soft mouse balls.

"Muriel," he said in a low, urgent voice, and showed her what he wanted. He used one powerful hand to lift my ass up so it pointed in the air, as did my cunt. With his long legs, he hovered over me so that he could press his balls into my hole. "Keep me there, Sarah."

I pressed my flat chest onto the couch, while I reached back and held his balls in me, or half in me, I didn't know how because I was blind and numb and tired. He pulled his cock out, so it lay on top of my ass crack. He had Muriel suck his cock while his balls were inside my cunt.

"Are you ready, Muriel?" he said after a few minutes.

Still sucking him, she nodded.

"You'll like it," I promised her. "Let me put some more jelly in your sweet honey pot."

Muriel swung around and offered me her pale behind, with its two firm egg shapes.

"Bend over, sweetie," I told her.

She brought her hairy hole closer, and I added a generous dose of jelly. Then I offered her to Charley. "Do like you did for me. Go on, take her."

Muriel and I traded places. Now she lay face down--a handsome, shapely woman. She was a bit more full figured than I was, and a little shorter, but shapely and good looking, the kind that still gets plenty of looks on the street.

Charley had a hungry gleam in his eyes. He stuck his thumb in her rear and gently rotated it, while petting her butt cheek with his free hand. Muriel rubbed her pussy from below, and closed her eyes in open-mouthed pleasure. She was already visibly rippling with cum waves.

I put a finger in Charley's rear end, and took his dick in my other hand. I bent down, with my cheek resting against his tight belly, and continued sucking him off to keep it erect.

"Take me," Muriel said in a low, stressed voice. "I'm so ready. Oh Sarah, I'm not scared anymore. Take me, Charley. Fuck me in my ass."

"Whoah," Charley said, "I'm working my way up there."

"It's an emergency," I told Muriel. "He's gotta, or he'll lose it."

"Come on," Muriel said, "take me, Charley." Still lying on her back--just shifting enough to be fully on the couch--she pulled her knees up to her shoulders and showed Charley everything. "Take me, Charley. Everything you see is yours. Do anything you want."

I came around and knelt on the side of the couch away from the wall so I could lick her all over. She reached out to me as if I were a life preserver.

"You look good," Charley said as he slid into her pussy. I helped gently hold it open, and rubbed the labia briskly, while he slid in and out to get wetter for her.

Muriel looked down with hungry eyes while making chuffy lips. "Take my asshole, Charley. I'm ready. Get inside there. Make me come."

I rubbed Muriel's butt pucker with two fingers and tried her-- she was sooo ready. At my touch, her hole simply melted open. I said: "Did you see that, Charley?"

The man gripped his bus and drove it to her back garage.

She grasped my forearm tightly. "I'm doing this because I love you and I trust you," she told me. She was a bit scared, and gritting her teeth.

I grasped his shaft and helped him aim.

Charley slid right through her pucker and entered her tunnel.

Muriel let out a shriek, more of fear than pain. Then she relaxed.

"See?" Charley said. "We buttered you up like a hot piece of toast."

"It's nice," she said.

"You feel full?" I asked.

"Oh yes. There is no way to describe this. I loved watching you get butt fucked by Charley."

I moved closer so that my torso smothered hers. I put my arms around her boobs and squeezed them to me as if I were gathering flowers. I remembered how she tongued my mouth. I French-fucked her with my tongue. She opened her lips and took me with a meek tongue that lay low and let me thrash it with my tongue.

I felt Charley's lubed finger in my pussy, up and down my vaginal canal, and one fingertip on my clit. I reached down and moved his fingertip exactly where I wanted it--touching one side of my swollen clit.

"How does it feel?" I asked Muriel.

Charley's cock was up to its neck in Muriel's ass.

"Ohhh," she wailed. "It feels good. Wow. What a feeling. I feel like a subway tunnel."

"I'm the train," Charley said. To me he said: "I wish I were a giraffe so I could stretch my neck down there and lick you while I do this."

In reply, I inserted two fingers in his tight ass while I continued tongue-fucking Muriel. I wanted her so badly. I felt this warm blast of love for her. I was going to come again. Better yet, she was heaving and rolling her belly muscles, so we ended up coming together while poor Charley hung on--and finally, he too shouted and held himself in both jellied hands while he sprayed all over us, and we both tried to honor his mighty efforts by catching his jizm with our mouths, and then licking him clean. I stuck my head underneath and licked his balls with his own sperm on my tongue, while he and Muriel had a long, leisurely tongue kiss together in a lovers' embrace. If I had had Mario's red strap-on from my dream, I would have butt fucked Charley as well.

I crawled on my hands and knees so our faces, mine and Muriel's, could be close as Charley's express diesel roared into her butt hole. For a moment, her face contorted--more with fear than with pain. She and I held our fists together while Charley trucked her from behind. He laid his palms on the small of her back and slammed her rear end repeatedly so the room filled with splatting sounds.

Muriel uttered a sound, interrupted every time he hit her, like "Ohhh--ohhh--ohhh…" We kept holding hands until her expression changed. She calmed down as she stopped being afraid and started to really like it. She said: "Let me see your ass."

So I let go of her hand. I climbed over her as best I could and straddled her head.

The problem was, she was looking down.

I signaled to Charley, who pulled out and gently moved her legs until she got the idea and spun around. A moment later, Muriel lay on the couch with her legs in the air. She had one hand on her pussy and fanned her clitoris, while Charley slid his ramrod into her ass and machined her in the missionary position, in-out in-out, in-out, with a loud slapping sound each time his hard middle hit her soft thighs and buttocks. That left her pussy cocked up and waiting for her to play in it with both hands and all her greedy fingers.

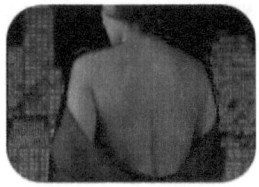

"I think I died and went to heaven," Charley said.

Muriel tugged at me to move a bit, and now my pussy was over her mouth. I felt that same thrusting tongue on my clitoris, licking at my hood, and pinning my little lady to one side in its little wet nakedness. I felt the tip of her tongue exploring my pee hole, tasting my salt. And I felt her tongue in my vaginal canal.

No, I realized then, she had stopped diddling herself. She was in the throes of early major orgasm. There was no going back for her now. Charley slid his boat in and out of her hungry hole, while I could feel her body rocking as he finger-fucked her; one finger, then several, then both thumbs spreading her loose hole open and rubbing her starved clit.

She had both hands free. She couldn't get enough as she played with my butt cheeks with one hand, and ended up putting two fingers up my asshole which was still numb and all jellied up, still in a glow from Charley's bus.

With her other hand, she fisted my pussy. Her hand was small, and there was so much jelly around, that her hand went in easily and filled the front of my vaginal canal. I only had to play with my small breasts and diddle myself as the first of several mighty upheavals rocked me like a boat in a storm.

Muriel and Charley and I orgasmed together.

Charley sort of passed out to one side, but only for a moment's rest.

Muriel and I were just getting started.

Moaning with pleasure, Muriel stared up into my pussy as I straddled her face. "Sarah, my baby, help me. Show me, you young fucking bitch. Get in heat, my sweet honey cunt. Sit on me. Put that hair in my face. Let's go all the way now."

With my bush over her eyes, I brought my ass pucker down until I felt her tongue. I reached behind me and spread my cheeks apart.

"Oh honey, yes," she said. She diddled herself with one hand, while Charley pronged away at her bottom. With her free hand, she fondled my tight butt cheeks. I felt her tongue poke repeatedly up my asshole, parting my sphincter with each thrust. That was the powerful tongue with which she had recently mouth-fucked me. I couldn't resist the flames and spasms flying through my body at the memory. "Eat me," I cried out.

"Are you my girl?"

"Yes," I wailed as I held my butt cheeks apart for her and fanned my own clit.

"Are you my woman?"

"Yes! And you are my lady."

"Are you my glorious cunt hole forever?"

"Yes! You can do anything you want with me. Anything."

"Does your ass love me as much as I love it?"

"Yes! I want to have my mouth on all your holes any time I want."

"Any time you say so; any time you tell me to get down for you."

With the tip of the pinky of my free hand, I carefully sought my little piss spigot. "We forgot one of my holes--the tiniest one." Closing my eyes, and ignoring all else, I followed the delicate touch of my pinkie. I felt the tiny bit of wrinkled skin that stuck out on the upper rim of my vaginal canal, and the hole in it, from which piss gushed when I couldn't hold it any longer. With all the nerve endings there, I began to buck, and groan.

"Honey," she quavered, "if you have to go, we'll clean up afterwards. Don't worry."

"I can hold it," I whispered tensely. "I don't want to piss in your face. I want to come."

I shuddered and lurched as I came again.

She didn't want to stop. She gripped my ass in both hands. She thrust her tongue in and out of my ass, giving my sphincter a dull glowing feeling. "Mmm," said my woman as she savored me, and I savored being spread over her precious face like her whore, totally open and she could do whatever she wanted.

Sometimes when you make love to a person, you want everything they've got. You lay a woman open before you--or better, she spreads her skirt, throws her panties aside, and pushes her knees up and holds her crotch apart so you can see her and drink her and have it all. Sometimes, when you are with a lover, you want to give her all that you have. Same thing. You want to lift your dress and spread your crotch wide open so your cunt is right there--she can choose whether to stick her tongue in one delicious hole or the other--and you just want her to have everything. It makes you so wet to squat helplessly with your softness spread wide. You let her see you and drink you and have you, and wish you had more to stick in her mouth or to show to her hungry eyes.

When it was done, we lay in a quiet heap of naked flesh.

We almost forgot about Charley.

Poor guys. For all their muscles and deep voices, for all their cocks that we compare to trains and busses, they get about half a minute of yelling and pounding and squirting. They get another half minute of realizing it's over. Then they pass out and need to be revived a half hour later for maybe another little go, if they even have that in them. Charley was a bit more of a horse than all that, but not by much.

"I hope nobody heard us," Charley said, as we listened. But the walls only rustled with water running in pipes, and the street noise rose muted to the window. Muriel embraced me. "I had to try it because of you."

"Do you still want me?" I asked. I wasn't done picking through her unfaithfulness. "You smell like pee."

"I love you more than ever," she said, and kissed each of my puffy nipples. "So do you, baby."

Charley slid his trousers on unsteadily. "I still have deliveries to make. Ladies, next time you need help, be sure to call on me."

We lay there on our backs, holding hands. We opened our legs for him, and each of us rubbed his thick hair while he bent close to give each pussy a full minute of his tongue's attention, and a few licks for each of our puckered ass holes.

"You were magnificent," Muriel told him. "Good job, Charley!"

We both kissed him and thanked him as he wobbled out the door in his dark uniform, trying to look innocent.

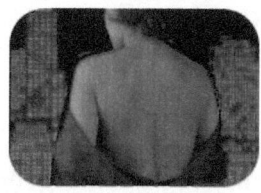

When the door closed, Muriel turned toward me on the couch. We took a moment, with a large towel, to dry it off under us. Her full breasts swung from side to side. Her prune nipples looked engorged.

I pressed her to lay her head in my lap and kiss my bush.

She whispered. "I'm sorry. I meant for it to start out different."

"You're bad," I said sharply, and took her by the hair, but just to force her face down a little farther in to my thick pussy curls.

"I only meant to please you. But I was so curious."

"You don't have to say you're sorry."

She rose up to kiss me sweetly. "You got to pee on my face."

"Next time, baby, you pee on my face. I want to drink you."

She saw the laughter in my blue eyes and tapped the tip of my nose with her pointy finger. "Of course, you ninny."

I kissed her prunes, sucking on each one until it swelled and got hard between my gently biting teeth.

She held me to her and groaned: "Suck me, baby. I love it when you suck me. You know how to chew them just right."

I held each boob with both of my hands and sucked on it as if milk were to gush into my mouth and fill me with sunny bliss--the kind of carnal joy that makes you tremble all over, and makes your guts feel like they are full of warm honey milk.

She reached down and played with my labia. "I love putting my fingers in your slot, down there in those thick curls. One day, you'll be pushing wet bloody screaming babies out there and making new life to give everyone around you joy. Until then, it's just a girl pussy and a boy's sex toy." She stroked my hamster gently.

I said: "Your sex toy--I hope you always get wet thinking of it."

We were so spent, and so beyond any further orgasms. Desire lingered between us. We kept on playing with each other, until she had to walk four blocks to the court house, and I had to hurry across the street and tell Harriet some lie about why I was an hour late on top of my lunch hour. I would tell Harriet as I coughed into the hollow of my fist on the 'a' in agreed: "I *a*te something that *a*greed with me."

I stood and let Muriel dress me, like a child. Muriel fussed so I'd look presentable and not disheveled. She palmed my rear all the way to the door, where we kissed so-long. I hurried out holding my purse and wearing my hat and gloves, as if I'd been for a polite walk in the park. My tits and crotch felt like they were sitting in a hot bath.

The summer still had a fair number of lovely lunch hours to go. There would never again be a man with me and Muriel--not Charley, or anyone else. I never made love to another woman-- never even thought about it. Not before Muriel, not after. I suspect that Muriel didn't either.

We always started and ended with me lying clothed on her couch, and her with a cheek on my butt, and one hand stroking her pillow while she smiled dreamily and the new curtains blew gently in the window. Yes, she finally broke down and bought curtains. She said the room deserved it.

Change is inevitable, from the galaxies in the universe to the little worms in the earth, and our tiny lives somewhere inbetween. Like those two women in 1893, M and S, who loved each other. By the time I found their faded old sepia pictures from the previous century, they were long vanished--and nobody remembered who they had been. I want to think they were happy together during the time they had. Maybe they became a constellation in the heavens. Maybe so did Muriel and I--the Two Lovers.

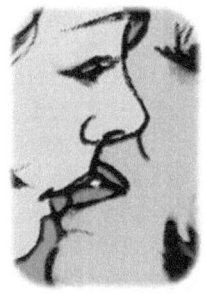

16. All Good Things

Charley Farmer was transferred soon afterwards to a new route uptown, and we never saw him again.

Ronny was fired for drinking on the job and being late. He got a new job out of town that meant we wouldn't be seeing much of each other. He seemed a little cold toward me the last time I saw him. I was afraid it was my guilt showing about Charley and Muriel, but it turned out, as one learns these things quite accidentally, that he'd been seeing a nurse on the side up at the hospital. He blew me off and started going steady with her. I soon learned from my sources (old girlfriends and field hockey team mates--we make quite a network, the hole-in-the-teeth girls) that he got her pregnant and had to marry her. I'll bet he spends the rest of his life remembering our steamy car windows and all together. I'll bet his cock has phantom limb memories and sweet dreams of my young ass--serves him right. I bet he's sorry he never got to put his penis in my vagina. That's how Muriel would say it. He should have stuck around, the fool. But then I wouldn't have met Mr. Right and brought into the world the little Rights.

If he had, with my luck he would have knocked me up and I'd be Mrs. Ronny and the little Ronnys. Whatever I felt for Ronny, it wasn't enough to take me there. I was a nice girl. I wasn't the smartest or the daintiest or the most well-spoken, but I was a sharp looker and a smart dresser. I had (and still have, after three kids) a rear end that men and women both look after as they pass me on the street. I have the legs and all to go with it, even now as I sit in my big house in the suburbs with the window open, and a breeze blowing the curtains, and photographs all around me. It's quiet around the house since the Little Rights grew up and moved out on their own. Mr. Right is asleep upstairs in our bedroom.

Yes, I ended up--a few years and a few boyfriends later--finally meeting Mr. Right. You couldn't ask for a sweller guy. I'm now Mrs. Right, with him and the little Rights who aren't little any more.

All good things must come to an end. But every ending is a new beginning. Every back end has its front end. I've taught Mr. Right a few tricks he didn't know, and I know he'll never two-time me or he'd be a fool. But he's a gem, and we love each other dearly. The Little Rights are all turning out great. We're not rich, but Mr. Right is a steady man with a union job. He's about to retire, so we can travel. We just finished paying off our mortgage in the suburbs. Our first grandchild has arrived. Truly the best we can do is enjoy every minute.

Not long after Muriel got her back door lesson from Charley and me, I noticed a change in her. She met a man, for real, not a two-timing delivery man or another fool like Leo or a dim-witted cock-hound like Ronny, but a doctor with a big house. He was a widower without kids, and needed some nice spirits to jazz up his ivy-covered stack of bricks on the rich side of town. They were perfect for each other. I got out of their way, as Muriel let me go. I never met Dr. Right. I saw them together from a distance, in the park one day, where Ronny and I had sex and lay on the grass drunk one night and tossed our eyeballs on the ground (in English: we puked). They looked so happy with each other in the park, soon to be Dr. and Mrs. (Muriel, Esq.) Right.

I was on my own totally for a while. I was okay being alone after I finally understood Ronny was a jerk and left me. The wonderful game Muriel and I played was a series of perfectly little moments, each time like one of those Christmas globes you shake and the snow flakes twirl around a little cottage inside. We had our last lunch time on that old couch, cried a lot, and said our goodbyes. It was the only moment in my life that my heart was broken and I was full of joy (for her) both at the same time.

"Remember our heart," she said holding my hand.

We held hands and looked into each other's eyes.

"Muriel arrows Sarah," I said.

She said: "Sarah and Muriel heart each other."

"No broken arrows allowed," I said.

It was all over except the heart behind the radiator, which would live for centuries under many new coats of paint as lives and generations would pass by, like clouds rolling past her building. The Century Building was me, and the Finncroft Tower was her--

or, it was us. The Century Building was so-called because it was built in 1900 at the start of a new century with all sorts of hopes for peace and world harmony. My sepia ladies, S and M, were still young and going at it somewhere--maybe. Or maybe S got married to Mr. Sorta, and poor M pined away for the rest of her life. It was just as well that I'd never know. One day in the future, this whole century with its two world wars and all the other horrible stuff will pass away. It will be 2000 and maybe there will be a new building, and new hopes and lives.

Afterward, I could sit in my apartment alone, sipping a beer or a coffee and doing my nails, while I listened to the radio. Or I'd do the crossword puzzle, or play an hour or so of solitaire. Work kept me busy by day, Mr. Ferguson and all--he wasn't so bad at all for an old crank. Harriet had a stroke and retired. She was replaced by Jeannie Rochas, a Puerto Rican lady with five kids at home, a husband on the railroad, and a dimply smile. She was a stickler for the time clock, but that was a small price to pay. Poor Harriet. I don't know what became of her.

Muriel and I would love each other for the rest of our lives-- but we couldn't really stay fallen in love or get married. Time wasn't going to stand still for either of us. I won't know if it was my perfect ass she was in love with so much, or if she was just lonely and in need of some hot sex. She was one of the only practicing women lawyers in the city back then, and a pioneer in many ways the world would never need to know about.

Like I said, after thinking it over carefully the way you're supposed to, I would always come to the same conclusion. If it feels good, and nobody is getting hurt, and nobody will find out--do it. There's nothing wrong with that, no matter what people say. Nobody ever went to hell for having a good time, or for loving someone. Hell is full of prissy, mean little librarians. It's full of gin-soaked preachers with pointy gray puritan hats, who play pocket pool while telling a woman she must mend her ways or be forever damned. They are in hell for all the suffering they caused, and all their dishonesty and brutal, selfish cruelty. Dante wrote about it.

I didn't want Muriel to introduce me to her doctor as her little sister, or her cousin, or her friend from work, much less her toy or her kept girl. One day my girlish figure would sag, and Muriel would stare after the memory with sadness. It was best that we moved on, and let our memory forever stay young. Joe Gallagher would always remain a young, handsome, smiling Irish detective with a beautiful wife and three little girls. It's perfect. Why spoil it?

Mr. Right and I, with the little Rights, were shopping downtown recently. We all had a nice luncheon, in a fine steak house, to celebrate our younger daughter's first baby, Emily--a healthy seven pounds, eleven ounces. By an odd coincidence, Mr. Right and I had three children--one girl and two boys, like my own parents did, and like Muriel and Joe had three girls. When I was 37, I was lucky to have a ripe belly like Muriel had at that age, and a firm figure. I wore a full bra and had big nipples that all three kids and my husband chewed into puddles with prune tips.

The day Emily was celebrated, I left my whole gang under the charge of Mr. Right, my husband of three decades. I wandered off in search of a new watch band. Instead, I found ghosts from long ago.

Without planning it--but do we ever do anything by accident?--I wandered down those old streets, hoping to see a jewelry store. Instead, at a certain intersection, I realized that I stood before a shabby state government office structure named the J. Alfred Prufrock Building or something. The marble header above the faded entrance still read Century Building 1900, as it did long ago in the 1950s, when I was a young woman working for Mr. Ferguson in there, like the man and woman in the office painting at night by Edward Hopper.

The Century Building was over eighty years old by now-- imagine! The diner was long gone, as was the gift shop, replaced by a check cashing place with bars on the windows, winos sleeping outside, and flies buzzing over barf on the floors. The beautiful old mosaic floors were gone, replaced by simple poured concrete finished with brown stain. The chromed pillars in the entrance had been stripped down and covered in torn placards. The thick greenish plate glass in the gift shop had been replaced by plywood that now sagged with age and graffiti. The entrance where I used to strut in and out in my Jane Russell outfits smelled of urine.

I turned and walked down the sidewalk a few hundred feet, wondering why the area looked so much brighter than it used to.

Then I realized that the Finncroft Tower was totally gone-- Muriel's office on the 20th floor and all. The entire building was gone like it never existed, opening up a quarter of a city block. There was only a watery hole in the ground, surrounded by grassy turf, and enshrined inside a high wire fence with warning labels and a big sign: *Shanghai Realty–Lease or Buy. Prime Property. Call Mumbai Investment Corporation for details at our convenient uptown offices.*

I did get a post card from Muriel a few years ago, showing a beach scene in Venice, California. She followed it up with a letter written in skippy ballpoint on onion skin paper. Dr. Right had died of a sudden heart attack at age 70, leaving her widowed again. Her children were all grown up and leading their lives; she didn't say how for better or for worse. She was alone again and was putting up their mansion in some distant part of the Los Angeles sprawl for sale. She wanted to travel a bit in her sunset years, and visit her children and grandchildren. She'd lived with Dr. Right in that house for 30 years and she couldn't bear to be alone with all the memories. I understood what she meant. I wrote her a long letter back, telling her how my life turned out. She never wrote to me again, and I've lost her address. The phone number was disconnected years ago.

I will close this memoir now, and file it away--the only private papers about my life, aside from boxes of yellowing photographs of people with mysterious smiles and eyes, who will be forgotten in a few decades even though I've written their names on the backs.

At least M and S left three faded pictures for posterity to wonder and dream about. I don't have a single photo of Muriel, so there are no images of us together. I'll remember her as she was back then.

One day, when I'm contemplating my last sunset, I may just burn this memoir. But I'm thinking--why? Will it offend anyone? Will I be embarrassed? Will anyone care, when none of us are still around? The world goes on. Someone will build a new skyscraper where the Finncroft Tower used to be. There will be a 20th floor and probably an office at that same spot, with a window looking down on that same street, and if you could lean out and look to the left, you'd see the Century Building--if that is still standing, years from now. Or you read this and yawn and put it away--and someone else will read it a century later. I have time to scribble thoughts like this now. There will always be a 20th floor and a special window if you're invited.

But can you get a decent cup of vanilla ice cream to eat with a wooden stick, and a rare friend of the heart to share it with?

I can see Harriet giving me the evil eye as I come running in from my tryst across the street. I can almost hear Mr. Ferguson's dry voice as he calls me from his office to run in and take dictation. I feel guilty, telling him silently that I can't. I have to go looking for a new watch band because my old one broke.

If you are reading this, it means I didn't throw it away or burn it. It would be a shame to lose the sweet memory of us, as if it had never happened. The only true names in this story, aside from the buildings, are Sarah and Muriel--our first names, to honor what happened between us so long ago.

You'll never know my last name, or the city where this all happened. Good luck trying to find out. If I could meet Muriel just once more, I would tell her I hope her life was a good one, and that mine turned out pretty swell. I never had sex or love again with another woman. Then again, I certainly never found another Muriel. I'm sure she never met another me, which leaves me feeling kinda special--her girl always.

If you are reading this, it means that I've gone to be with my ghosts. You can read my words, but you can't chase me or find me or even know who I was. Be like a kitten, pawing a sunbeam that shines in through an open window onto a wood floor. Have all the fun in a young world, but good luck trying to catch the gorgeous light that's here for an instant, and forever vanished.

I've gone back to the Century Building because it's 1:15 on a summer afternoon, and Mr. Ferguson will be looking for me, belching with his ulcers. He'll be in his rumpled dark suit, just back from an important meeting with horribly dull men just like himself. He's holding a glass of bromide in one hand and a sheaf of papers for dictation in the other hand. I'm coming up the elevator, a pretty young woman with a crisp smile and reckless blue eyes.

It's a sunny day with blue skies. Huge white clouds roll past. A propeller plane with four engines drones by, looking urgent and important as it rushes toward an airport that will no longer exist when you read this.

I'm getting off the elevator on the 18th floor of the Century Building at 1:25 p.m., late from my lunch break as usual. I've been making love and giggling with Muriel. I look a little disheveled, and pat my hair to make my hat sit just right. Men and women turn to stare at my perfect ass in a tight dress. If you were to look closely, you'd see that my face is oddly flushed, and that I have a wonderful glow about me, as if I'd had a nice walk in the park, or something far better--a secret that I can't tell anyone about, maybe not even Mr. Right. He would tell you that I was a very good wife-- asking little, and easy to please, who let him do anything he wanted with me as long as he wasn't rough, and as long as it pleased him. Just as I had my secrets from him, he could never tell anyone what we did in bed or on the floor together. He got to put it in my vagina and any other hole he wanted to, whenever he wanted. I was a good wife to him, and easy going. He was never disappointed in Mr. Right, either.

Nobody but me knows about this erotic memoir. I don't have any photographs to leave of me and my woman, so I think I'll leave these reminiscences to be found one day. That may keep alive the memory of my summer love--Muriel, aged 37, beautiful, struggling, and courageous.

I want to think that our radiator heart, with the arrow and our names--*Muriel* on top, *Sarah* on the bottom--stayed trapped like our love, between layers of paint and decades, and ended up in the dust together in the earth somewhere, in a landfill with the rest of the rubble from the Finncroft Tower for the rest of time.

More Info

What is literotica? We consider it to be erotic (sexually explicit, sensuous, high-quality) fiction of timeless (literate or literary) value. We do not include in this concept the usual formulaic, commercial category 'romance' that is mass-produced, like bland, predictable fast food, by the foreign-owned New York City publishing cartel. Readers deserve far better for their time, money, and trust. Good things come in small packages--and every Literotic Press story is hand crafted for discerning readers on a well-considered theme--quality over quantity.

Literotic Press and Erotic Memoir are imprints of general publisher Clocktower Books.

* * * *

www.literoticpress.com
www.clocktowerbooks.com

* * * *

For another great literotica read, see Literotic Press' **Summer in the Garden of Eros** by Hormonius Young.

Summer in the
Garden of Eros
by
Hormonius Young

Hormonius Young (playful pseudonym of a U.S. businessman who prefers to remain anonymous) was a young man in his early 20s when the true adventures took place on which this novel is based. He had plenty of younger girlfriends. His big complaint was, for whatever strange reason, never meeting a suitable woman of his own age until much later in life. His amatory escapades, during his 20s, included numerous short but wonderful, sensuous flings with slightly older women--in their mid to late 20s. This was not May-December (ick!) but Spring-Summer or May-June (his May to her June). He had a Liberal Arts degree but no job, but he was handsome, long-haired, and a guitar player. He turned out to be a magnet for recently divorced or disappointed young women who sought a toy and some playtime before getting sucked back into life's miseries with the next unlovely husband.

To Hormonius Young, they were intriguing, older, more experienced--unfathomably exotic, therefore, and irresistible. It worked out great for both parties. He got to revel and marvel in her secret garden of endless delights, while she typically also took him out and dressed him, wined him, dined him, and showed him off to her girlfriends while hiding him from her parents and relatives (who were meanwhile babysitting her kid or kids). She, at the same time, could throw it all to the wind and have a crazy, sexy blowout. She could live out her fantasies, swinging with pursed lips at the disco and throbbing to the beat, while rolling her still-tender young body in the heat. He was her willing toy, sensitive to her healing and her needs, while she serviced him with all the imagination of a high-class hooker and a looker. The nearly two dozen episodes--all hetero, with a few MFF tales toward the climax (ahem) of the book--are at once great fun, and also a tender, philosophical introspection on the endless possibilities of youth and the delightful mysteries of an experienced, beautiful young woman's secret garden. It is probably the only book ever written exploring and extolling the joys of spring-summer romance. For those who have lived it, as Hormonius Young did many times in his youth, it is one of life's most exhilarating rides. For men and women who can only wish they had, here is the world's best way ever written to enjoy the experience vicariously.